A SUREFIRE LOVE

A SMALL TOWN CHRISTIAN ROMANCE

THE MANY OAKS ROMANCES

EMILY CONRAD

Copyright © 2024 by Emily Conrad

Published by Hope Anchor, LLC

PO Box 3091, Oshkosh, WI 54903

All rights reserved.

No part of this book may be reproduced in any form or by any electronic or mechanical means, including information storage and retrieval systems, without written permission from the author, except for the use of brief quotations in a book review.

Library of Congress Control Number: 2023924194

This is a work of fiction. Names, characters, places, and incidents are either the products of the series authors' imaginations or are used fictitiously. Any resemblance to actual persons, living or dead, businesses, or actual events is purely coincidental. Any real locations named are used fictitiously.

ISBN 9781957455150 (Paperback Edition)

ISBN 9781957455150 (Ebook Edition)

Edited by Karin Beery, Write Now Editing

Proofread by Judy DeVries, Judicious Revisions

Cover designed by Emily Conrad

Author photograph by Kim Hoffman

Visit the author's website at EmilyConradAuthor.com.

1

*P*ain had cascaded through generations of Astleys. Now at the helm of the family, Blaze *would* stop the flow, even if it required her to face Anson Marsh on his home turf.

The cross protruding into the sky from the church served as a reminder that Blaze ought to feel as welcome here as anyone else—Anson included—but nervous energy flickered in her stomach as she parked. The sprawling building half-encircled the parking lot. Abundant windows, blank and straight-edged, stared out at her.

Blaze pulled her keys from the ignition of her twenty-year-old car and smoothed her hand over the leather steering wheel. Belying her luxury sedan's age, the gleaming black paint and throaty growl normally acted as a portable confidence booster. One that wasn't quite cutting it today.

"You've got this."

Heat licked her cheeks. If she had this—or anything else —under control, she wouldn't have had to set three alarms to ensure she left work when necessary to arrive on time. But for Mercy's sake, she couldn't cower now.

She pushed open her door and stepped into the August heat. Insects hummed in the cornfield next door while vehicles whooshed along the highway.

She fixed her eyes on the cross and forced her feet onward.

As she neared, the glass door reflected her black jumpsuit. Maybe the stylish outfit was too much for Many Oaks, Iowa, where folks were about five years behind on trends. If Anson didn't already know what he was dealing with, the clothes hinted at the truth about her. She was somehow too much and not enough all at once.

The door swung open, and the administrative assistant motioned her into the building. "He's in his office."

"Thanks." Blaze crossed to the carpeted hallway. Her heart kicked faster the closer she came to the door with a placard that read *Anson Marsh, Youth Pastor*.

After a strangled attempt at a deep breath, she tapped on the door. The blond wood swung open, and she found herself eye-level with the hollow at the base of Anson's throat, framed by the collar of his dark blue polo.

Pulse stuttering, she took a half-step back. His jaw and cheekbones cut distinct lines, but full cheeks and a round nose kept him from looking severe. His blue eyes held hers with startled attention, as if she'd surprised him.

Odd, since she'd made an appointment.

A corner of his irritatingly perfect mouth hooked upward, breaking the awkwardness. "Blaze. Right on time."

She straightened her shoulders. "Thanks for seeing me."

"Of course." He abandoned the door and lowered his six-foot-four frame into the leather office chair behind the desk.

A Surefire Love

He hadn't invited her to sit, but she took the seat across from him and twirled a lock of hair around her finger. Anson's attention moved to her hand. She dropped the berry-colored tip of her long dark locks. She might not have chosen a red-tinged balayage if she'd known this meeting loomed in her future.

Anson met her eyes. "You wanted to talk about Rooted?"

"I'd like to help."

His eyebrows notched closer together. "With the middle school youth group?"

She gave a single, firm nod. "As a leader. I heard you were shorthanded, and Mercy is starting middle school this fall."

Anson tapped his thumbs together. "Didn't you get a new job? You sure you want to put more on your plate?"

She smiled as though her promotion at Triumph Automotive was going as smoothly as she'd dreamed it would. "You have your job here, and you coach the basketball team. Those are bigger commitments than my job and youth group once a week."

"Not if you factor in your side gig. And Rooted meets Wednesday nights."

One of the nights Blaze sang with the house band at The Depot. "My boss says family's the priority. We can shift our Wednesday performances to Thursday."

"The whole band can make that change?"

"The Signalmen are supportive." At least she hoped they would be. She'd only consulted Philip, her boss.

Anson frowned, and it couldn't have been because of displeasure about her role with The Signalmen. In a few hours, he'd no doubt occupy his usual Monday-night table at the restaurant and music venue. He must just be disappointed she'd eliminated another obstacle between her schedule and Rooted.

She touched the edge of his desk and forced enthusiasm into her voice. "Hey, with the switch, maybe you can catch even more of our shows."

Color rose on his cheeks. Was he embarrassed to be a fan?

A barb pricked her heart.

"I have leadership board meetings on Thursdays." He leaned his elbow into an armrest. "You're pretty serious about this."

"Of course. Like I said, I heard you were shorthanded." Hopefully he wouldn't ask for details about *how* she'd heard. Eavesdropping, even accidentally, was probably a sin. She reached for a piece of hair and twirled.

"Is this related to what happened during the service project?"

Blaze froze. She had hoped volunteering would solve the problem without having to confront the issue directly.

"The kids were supposed to stay in pairs." Anson spoke evenly. "I sent Mercy and Anna to get a mop from the supply closet, but only Anna came back. She said Mercy had to use the restroom."

Check, check, and check. Blaze's little sister had said the same things. But at some point, his retelling would diverge from Mercy's. Blaze held her breath.

"Because of the buddy rule, I sent a couple of the girls to find her, only Mercy wasn't in the restroom. I found her with some of the high school boys in the gym."

"*With* is a strong word. She was by the bleachers, watching them shoot hoops. She said none of them even noticed her until you started shaming her."

Anson's mouth popped open. "*Shaming* her?"

The word did sound extreme, but the memory of Mercy's tear-stained face pushed Blaze to continue. "She cried for an hour that night."

He lifted his palms. "I asked if she heard the buddy rule."

"In front of the older boys. Then you asked why she left Anna."

"A reasonable question."

"Except, by your own admission, Anna had already informed you it was to use the restroom." Tension arced between her shoulder blades. "Mercy was mortified. She's eleven and sensitive, and the boys laughed at her."

"If they laughed, it was when I pointed out she wasn't in the bathroom." Defensiveness edged his tone.

"So you admit you said something to poke fun at the situation. You made a spectacle of her."

"I stated the truth to address the incongruence, not to make a joke. The buddy rule protects the students, and I wanted her to see that she didn't need to go off on her own. She never even made it to the restroom, so it clearly wasn't an emergency. She had plenty of time to return with Anna, tell a leader, and take a partner with her. The whole thing could've been avoided if she'd followed the rules."

"It also could've been discussed privately and gently."

He settled back in his chair, assessing her. Such broad shoulders ought to be able to bear responsibility, but she knew how this worked. Unless she shifted the blame off of him, he'd never let her onto his team of youth leaders.

Tapping into the same skill that allowed her to control her voice when she sang, she calmed her tone and added sweetness. "You were in a tough spot. There aren't many leaders, so individualized attention must be next to impossible. As a leader, I could take some of these small situations off your hands."

His head tilted ever so slightly. "Meaning you'd prefer to handle Mercy yourself."

Had he always been this direct? Words he'd spat at her years ago echoed through her mind. Yes, he had.

She lifted her chin. "I would."

He nodded once. "Your sister is just one student. Being a youth leader is about a lot more than keeping one kid in line. It's about creating an environment where all the kids can learn about God and grow closer to Him. Leaders need to set a good example and be ready to engage with the students on questions of faith." He lifted an eyebrow.

Inadequacy stirred in her core, but she managed to keep it out of her voice. "And which of those do you think will be a struggle for me?"

A frown played on his too-handsome face. "I just want to make sure you understand what you're volunteering for."

"My faith is important to me, and I wish I'd been exposed to the gospel much sooner. It would be a privilege to offer kids real hope."

"I'm sure you do understand the importance of that, given all you and Mercy have been through. But ..." Anson rubbed his mouth. "Mercy doesn't seem to be coping well."

The statement hit like a physical blow. "What do you mean?"

"I've heard from her Saplings teachers that she was a handful. Talking out of turn, not memorizing her verses, not following instructions. But then"—he shrugged, mouth tipping—"she's had it rough. Your mom was sick for a while before you lost her, wasn't she?"

She clenched her jaw. Mom had been sick as long as

Blaze had known her, but Anson was likely referring to the liver failure that had taken her in the end, not the alcoholism that had haunted Mom as far back as Blaze could remember.

"I'm sorry for your loss." His voice softened. "I can't imagine what it was like for Mercy to lose her Mom while she was so young. Having her half-sister take over as her guardian must've been an adjustment."

As if Blaze hadn't been Mercy's primary caretaker most of her life. As if the fact that they had different fathers made them less connected. The anger boiling in her belly dropped her tone to a warning. "You think she'd have it better with our mom?"

Anson lifted his hands in a gesture of innocence. "No."

What did he know about their lives? She'd been a fool to think she could offer her help and he'd do something as simple as take it.

She jolted to her feet. "For the record, the last four years have been the most stable of our lives." Her voice shook. "Mercy is doing great. It's time to reassess how you've labeled us."

She wouldn't be sending Mercy to Rooted. She might shop for a whole new church. She pivoted to leave.

Anson beat her to the door in three long strides. "I didn't mean to say you weren't doing a good job with her."

"Yet you didn't commend me on doing well either."

"I'm sure you're doing the best you can." Despite his kind tone, he'd again pulled up short of a compliment.

Tears brimmed in her eyes. Her hate for them only spawned more. "I'm sure you are too." She shouldered past him and hurried out.

2

Anson stood in the doorway as Blaze bustled off. Regret gnawed on his stomach. This wasn't the first time he'd sent her away in tears. Apparently, in the last nine years, he hadn't learned as much about navigating difficult conversations as he'd thought. He could chase after her, but he'd likely make everything worse.

Besides, Anson was the only pastor in the building that afternoon, so the man advancing down the hall was probably aiming for his office. The lights in the hall were off, but sunlight from the windows illuminated Eric Newsome's trim build and business-casual clothing.

As Blaze walked past him, Eric turned his head to watch her, highlighting the distinct profile of his weak chin. That the head of the leadership board saw no need to greet her suggested she'd avoided eye contact.

Regret sank its teeth deeper. Anson never should've mentioned Blaze's mom. And voicing doubts about her qualifications to lead? Another error. She'd always thrown him off balance, but that was no excuse.

Eric slowed as he reached him, eyebrows raised.

Anson wasn't about to add gossip to his list of mistakes. "Working out some differences of opinion."

"Ah." He motioned to Anson's office. "How'd your parents' move go?"

"Smoothly. This was something like the sixth time they've moved for a job, so they have it down to a science." He returned to his chair.

Eric shut the door before taking the seat Blaze had vacated. He must not've come for a casual chat. "Good. Glad they're settled." He gave a perfunctory smile. "I'm here to catch you up on the meeting you missed. There's a new initiative I wanted to discuss before you saw it yourself."

"Okay." Anson kept his posture relaxed, even as he went on guard. Nothing significant had been on the agenda. If a new "initiative" had come up at the last minute, they should've notified him or postponed the discussion.

With only a couple of months' experience as head of the board, Eric might not know that protocol. He shifted, widening his elbows. "We've noticed youth group attendance dwindling the last few years."

"We had a couple of big graduating classes. The Henderson triplets were a quarter of Branching Out all on their own." Though in truth, the whole church was down more than a third from its peak of about three hundred attenders ten to fifteen years ago.

"It's not just graduates who leave. The James family and the Oxnards both switched to Grace Evangelical."

"I noticed. I contacted both families about the summer student Bible studies, but they never responded."

"What about fun events? Did you invite them to those?"

"Not specifically. I had already reached out twice to each

family before the first campfire and well before the water park trip. I wasn't going to pressure them."

"I agree. Pressure's not the answer." Eric leaned in like a salesman trying to sell a lemon. "Having fun at all the events instead of just a couple sporadic ones is the key."

"We do." Anson's office was littered with snapshots of grinning students, all taken at various youth group gatherings.

"The dwindling numbers disagree. Something needs to change in a big way to turn this around."

Discomfort tightened around his neck like a choking hand. "There's a natural ebb and flow to the numbers. We're expecting eight to ten students each in Branching Out and Rooted this year, which is only down about two students per youth group from last year."

"And a few more from the year before that. When there are so few students to begin with, that's more than a twenty-percent dip."

"We have large Seedlings and Saplings classes. In a few years, the older groups will be back up."

"Not if the kids aren't having fun." Eric's cajoling tone did little to blunt his cutting point. "They—and their families—will keep jumping ship."

Anson crossed his arms and measured his response. "Did the families who left blame the youth group for their decisions to leave?"

"I have students in the youth ministries too, don't forget."

His eyes widened before he could school his response. "Dylan and Carter have complained?" The boys were two of his most outspoken students. Anson had been pouring into both for years.

"They didn't have to. I've seen the schedules and heard

about how time is spent at youth group. Most of the night is sunk on dry lessons. They're kids. If we want them to attend, it's got to be fun—and not just on special occasions."

Under the desk, Anson clenched his hand. "On a standard night, the lesson is less than a quarter of our time. Add the small group discussion, and it's a third of the night. That's the same format our youth groups have been using since before I was a student here myself."

"That's your answer, then. Times have changed. The old way of doing things doesn't work anymore. Thanks to social media, attention spans are like this." Eric pinched his index finger and thumb within millimeters of each other.

Anson pressed his mouth shut. The "old way" worked. Dylan had prayed with him to turn his life over to Christ on his second night of Rooted three years ago. Carter kept coming to Branching Out every week, despite rejecting the faith. "I'm not sure where this is coming from. Playing more games won't accomplish the church's main mission, which is to share the gospel."

"I disagree. Not with the overall mission, but with how to accomplish it. The happier youth are, the more their entire families will attend. Then they'll hear sermons when they're supposed to. On Sunday mornings."

"In the main service?"

Eric made a casual sweep of his hand. "And in the class you teach after the sermon."

"The families who attend those are already committed. Youth group is a chance to speak into the lives of kids at the edge of the faith community. Some of them are dealing with intense issues. They need interactive lessons specific to their experiences and questions." Conviction powered his voice. These beliefs formed the bedrock of his ministry—his life. "I won't cut back on the gospel to reach an arbitrary numbers goal."

"Attendance is not arbitrary, and the board agrees. The initiative passed."

The statement split the bedrock, leaving Anson on one side, the board on the other, and a churning sea of betrayal in the middle. "What is the initiative, exactly?"

"Each youth group needs to double attendance by the end of the semester."

"Double?" A sucker punch of dismay knocked the word from him. In the five years Anson had worked at Many Oaks Bible Church, they'd never had numbers that high.

"The youth groups at Grace have grown by keeping the kids' interest and providing a safe place for them." Eric spoke with the upbeat tone of an infomercial. "Letting them see the gospel lived out instead of hammering them with it. We believe that with the right leadership, Rooted and Branching Out can also reach more youth than ever. The fields are ripe for harvest."

With the right leadership? Had the board lost faith in Anson? "That harvest is supposed to be souls, not bodies."

Eric shrugged. "One leads to the other. You have until the end of the fall semester."

"Or what?"

"The leadership board will step in to ensure this downtrend doesn't continue."

"Meaning?"

Eric stood. "It's time to get serious about reaching more kids."

Anson rose too. "I'm concerned about reaching the kids we have."

Eric stiffened, his chin all but disappearing into his neck.

"Everyone will benefit if you focus on the part of your job description that requires engaging youth activities."

Anson braced his hands on the desk. "Carter told me point-blank that he doesn't believe he needs a relationship with God." How could that not break his father's heart? It weighed heavy on Anson's. "You, of all people, shouldn't want me to cut back on teaching when one of my biggest prayers for this year is that your son would make a decision for Christ."

"We raised Carter right, and he'll make the right decision, but preaching at him hasn't worked yet. If anything, he's the prime example of why things need to change." His wagging finger was the last thing Anson saw as Eric stormed away.

3

*A*nson slammed on the brakes to avoid hitting a car in The Depot's parking lot. He waved an apology to the other driver. Frustration and regret had him all over the place tonight.

He hadn't realized until their meeting earlier that Blaze noted who attended shows. Considering the teary end of that conversation, he shouldn't be here. But his girlfriend was inside, and she was one of the few people he could tell about his meeting with Eric. Besides, he might get a minute between sets to smooth things over with Blaze.

He pulled into a spot, grabbed his keys, and headed in.

The Depot was owned by Many Oaks' one-and-only claim to fame, celebrity couple Philip and Michaela Miller. After growing up in Many Oaks, Philip made a name for himself with the rock band Awestruck. When he left the music industry, he returned home and transformed the abandoned train station into a restaurant and music venue. His pop star wife toured regularly while Philip played a few times a week with the house band.

Rumor had it, Blaze heard The Signalmen early on and pitched the idea of singing with them. Ever since, the marquee out front advertised Blaze and The Signalmen's bi-weekly performances. She was so dedicated that she'd taken the stage alone once when the flu sidelined the rest of the band.

She'd been mesmerizing.

Yet the woman couldn't get herself to church on time to save her life.

Then again, was Anson's annoyance over her tardiness any better than Eric's emphasis on numbers? Maybe next time it was his turn to preach, he ought to expound on valuing the heart over outcomes. Not that the Lord would want him bashing ideas from the pulpit when he didn't fully understand the board's decision—or its implications.

Responses trump reactions every time, Coach Voss used to say.

The restaurant's dining room occupied the front half of The Depot. Even from there, Blaze's voice beckoned him onward. A bar separated the restaurant from the music hall, and he squeezed between the people clustered around it.

While he waited for a bartender to finish up with other customers, he surveyed the music hall. Waitstaff navigated the tables at the back of the cavernous room. Families finished up late dinners. A handful of others dotted the dance floor. On stage, Blaze belted out a pop cover.

Since their meeting, she'd changed into a cropped tank top that skimmed the high waist of her jeans. Her rings and necklaces glinted under the stage lights. Her thick, wavy hair shimmered with every move.

Why did she claim her potential in some areas—like singing here—while leaving so much on the table in others?

Worship team would be an easy fit for her, but she never stepped forward.

"The usual?" The bartender was already filling a glass with soda.

Anson nodded and turned his attention back to the room. He spotted his girlfriend's sleek brown ponytail over at their usual table. She sat with a few of their friends.

Closer to him, at a bar-height table, perched a young girl with long dark hair and thick glasses. Mercy. She swung her feet as she took a pull of her milkshake. Two women shared her small table.

He'd handled Mercy's little field trip the way he would with any student. He hadn't realized she'd spend an hour crying over it.

"Here you go." The bartender handed Anson his soda.

He paid and made a wide circle around Mercy's table to where Sydney sat with her friends Madison and Honor.

Honor's boyfriend, Jimmy, lifted his nearly-empty whisky tumbler toward Anson. "He's a man," he croaked over Blaze's smooth tones. "He'll understand."

Honor's shoulder lifted as she shifted away from her boyfriend. Sydney flicked a warning glance to Anson.

Another glass sat empty on the table by Jimmy's seat. Anson wouldn't come to The Depot if he begrudged others the occasional drink, but the show had started twenty minutes ago. Jimmy was moving fast.

Anson slid his arm along the back of Sydney's chair as he took his seat. "I doubt I'll agree, but you can try me."

Jimmy scoffed, finished his drink, and stalked off.

"What was that about?" He looked to Honor for an answer, but she dropped her gaze.

Sydney tipped her head closer. "His boss promoted a woman over him. He thinks he's better qualified."

"He does have seniority." Honor pinned her arms to her sides, hands under her thighs, as she peered after her boyfriend.

"And nothing else." Madison glared toward the bar and tsked. "And now he's messing with the Lions."

Anson twisted. Jimmy elbowed his way between two of Anson's former high school basketball teammates. A bus accident their senior year had taken Coach Voss's life and branded everyone on the team in the minds of the community. A decade after they'd hung up the jerseys with the mascot, the people of Many Oaks still called them Lions, especially when they were together like David and Sterling were now.

Sydney elbowed him.

Jimmy wouldn't appreciate Anson interfering, but the night would only grow more uncomfortable the more the guy drank. Anson pushed his seat away from the table. "Be right back."

Nearing the bar, he nodded to his teammates. They shifted to let him join Jimmy, who was shouting greetings to men on the other side of the bar. Jimmy's attention drifted up to the big screen.

"Rough day?" Anson asked.

Jimmy's glassy eyes cut to him. "I thought you didn't understand."

"I heard about the job. I understand disappointment." Even more so after the day he'd had.

"It's discrimination." Jimmy's attention returned to the screen. "Hiring women just because they're nice to look at in meetings."

Anson tensed. The female bartender cocked her head. Jimmy had better watch out unless he wanted spit in his drink.

He prayed for wiser words than he'd spoken to Blaze earlier. "That's where you lose me. Disappointment's one thing. Blame's another. You could trust that management had good reasons."

"And you could get lost." Jimmy pounded his fist on the bar. "How hard is it to pour a whiskey?"

"You sure another one's a good idea?"

Jimmy angled toward him, chest puffed up. "I can tell you what *isn't* a good idea."

Anson kept his arms down and his posture open, hoping if he didn't pose a threat, Jimmy wouldn't get physical. "Everyone back at the table's pretty uncomfortable. Maybe it's time to slow down."

The bartender delivered a short glass of amber liquid. Jimmy swiped it up. "I'll slow down when you mind your own business." He lifted his glass in a mocking toast and swallowed a hearty gulp before he ambled toward the men on the other side of the bar.

Honor might not appreciate this solution, but she deserved a better boyfriend. Maybe a little distance tonight would help her see that.

As Anson stepped from the bar, Mercy glanced at him, then hunched over her milkshake. Regret stepped up like a bouncer intent on preventing him from returning to Sydney. He couldn't pass by as he became the reason faith communities triggered feelings of shame in a student.

As he approached Mercy, voices lifted behind him—one of them Jimmy's. But he was the bartender's problem now.

He recognized one of the women with Mercy. Marissa,

David's little sister, had moved back to town a couple of weeks ago. She must know Blaze if she was babysitting. As he stepped up to the table, she flashed a lackluster smile.

Her companion gave him the once over. "Well, hello."

Marissa chuckled. "Don't get too excited. This is the pastor."

"Oh." The other woman's gaze flicked between him and Mercy. Everybody at the table must know about the service project. They might as well watch him mend fences.

He turned to Mercy with what he hoped was a disarming smile. "I owe you an apology."

She hunched deeper into her seat and froze.

"I'm sorry for embarrassing you."

After a peek at him, Mercy resumed kicking one foot. "It's okay."

"I hope you'll come to Rooted this fall."

Marissa rubbed her back but kept her focus on Anson. "Does that mean you're going to let Blaze help lead?"

The gnawing regret returned. He'd meant to offer Blaze sympathy, not criticize her parenting, if that term even applied when one sister had custody of the other.

The song ended, and Blaze slipped her mic into its stand. "We have an anniversary in the crowd tonight. Candy, Mike tells us your song is 'I Swear.' This one's for you two love birds." She'd spoken like a litigator in his office but now crooned the announcement, smooth and sweet. She stole a sip from her water bottle, then The Signalmen started the classic 90s song.

A gasp yanked Anson's attention from the stage. Marissa lifted her hands as a stain bloomed across her top. Jimmy braced himself using their table, an empty glass in his grasp. He must've stumbled and spilled.

"Sorry, man." A guy from a neighboring table tucked in his chair and headed away.

"Should watch out," Jimmy muttered as he rubbed his face.

"What do you think you're doing?" Marissa's upper lip curled. "Get out of here."

Jimmy pushed away, and Anson steadied the wobbling table. But then Jimmy ran into Mercy's chair. A corner of the seat stabbed Anson's thigh as her hands swung over the table. The milkshake went flying. The stool tilted to an impossible angle, as did Jimmy.

Anson grabbed the chair, but Jimmy caught hold of the seat too. The man's weight wrenched the chair from Anson's grasp.

Mercy went down with a scream.

4

Glass shattered. A young voice cried out. Something in back thudded as loudly as a bass drum.

Blaze's throat closed mid-lyric as every face swiveled toward the back of the event hall. Anson had been pestering Mercy there moments ago, but neither was visible in the clutch of people there now.

"Was that Mercy?" Philip took up station next to her, his bass still in hand.

Hard to say. The two-foot-tall stage wasn't high enough for a clear view. Someone—David?—hefted a stocky man to his feet and escorted him toward the exit. Marissa righted a chair. The chair Mercy had been on?

Philip slipped the mic from her hand. "Go."

She hopped off the stage and threaded through the crowd to the tables at the back. What in the world could've happened?

Some conversations had restarted, but not enough to drown out another cry.

"Mercy?" Anxiety pitched through Blaze's voice. She

bumped past the onlookers and found her sister on the floor, flanked by Anson and Marissa.

Mercy's feet stuck out in front of her, one braced on the ground, the other outstretched. Anson said something and motioned. Mercy's toes wiggled in her sandal.

Blaze knelt beside her sister. Even in the dim light, the flush on her face was obvious. A tear glinted on her cheek. "What happened, sweetie?"

"A drunk man knocked me over." Her lips pulled into a hard frown, and she sniffled. "And now I can't walk."

"I'm so sorry." Blaze wrapped her arm around her sister's shoulders. Her mind spun. Urgent care wouldn't be open this late. Should they go to the emergency room? And what about the guy? She looked to her best friend for advice but noticed Marissa's clinging top instead. "You're soaked."

Marissa huffed. "He spilled in all his stumbling around, but I think it's water."

"Who was it?" Blaze would hunt him down and give him a good scolding. Or better yet, get Philip to ban him.

"Jimmy." Anson said.

"A friend of yours?"

"Not at all." Anson's mouth tightened. "Someone backed their chair into him, and he lost his balance."

"David's showing him out." Marissa's chin lifted, eyes gleaming. Her brother could be intimidating when he wanted to be—which was most of the time.

"It hurts really bad." Mercy whimpered.

"Is it broken?" Blaze eyed the ankle.

"Hard to say," Anson said. "There's nothing visibly out of place, but that doesn't rule out a break. Then again, sometimes sprains hurt just as much. And everyone's pain tolerance is different." He studied Mercy, silently judging.

Tears dripped from Mercy's dark lashes to her reddened cheeks.

"You could ice it tonight," he said. "See how she's feeling in the morning. Take her in if she still can't walk."

Blaze scanned the faces peering down at them. When Many Oaks residents gossiped, they traced family connections. To these people, she wasn't Blaze the singer or Blaze the dealership's new sales manager. She was Blaze—daughter of a drunk and a meth addict. Such a shame, they'd say, shaking their heads. Her grandparents were supposedly good, honest, and hardworking.

Blaze had never known them.

If she made too many mistakes, someone might call child protective services, thinking Blaze was as poor a guardian as her mom had been. Mercy could be taken away. Therefore, mistakes weren't an option.

"We'll go to the emergency room." She threaded her arm around her sister's back.

Anson motioned her to stop. "Let me."

Not a chance. But even skinny Mercy weighed a good ninety pounds. This would take finesse. Blaze pulled the stool closer. "Put your good foot down and grab the chair. I'm here to help, but you'll need to try to stand, okay?"

Mercy clamped her hand around the closest chair leg. Anson braced it, and Marissa stooped to help Blaze. Together, they hefted Mercy to her feet and helped her onto the seat.

Standing again, Blaze spotted Philip talking to a bartender. "Let me get my things, and we'll head out, okay? Wait here."

Mercy nodded.

Blaze patted her knee, then slipped through the crowd to Philip and shared her plan to take Mercy in.

"You need a lift?" he asked.

The fact that he hadn't questioned her decision solidified her ever-shaky confidence. "No. I can drive. It's all right for me to duck out?"

"Of course. Let me know if you need anything."

Blaze collected her purse from the back and rejoined Mercy and her friends at the table. Anson hovered too, but she kept her back to him. "Ready, champ?"

Mercy pushed her hair from the tear tracks on her cheeks. Blaze settled her purse strap higher on her shoulder. She'd need both hands free for this.

"What's the plan?" Anson asked.

She clenched her teeth. "To get her medical attention."

Marissa stepped around the table, hand extended. "Give me your keys. I'll bring the car to the door."

Blaze dug them from her purse. "It's all the way in the back, straight out from the doors."

"Okay." Marissa headed off.

If only Anson would follow. Instead, his eyebrows lifted. "You're going to have her hop all the way outside?"

"I guess that's what people do."

"Not if they don't have to."

"I don't see any wheelchairs laying around."

"I could carry her."

"Seriously?" Accept self-righteous Anson's help? "No. Thanks." Though he at least provided inspiration. Maybe Blaze could carry Mercy piggyback.

Mercy leaned away, suspicion on her face. "*You're* not carrying me."

Fine. Given Blaze's heels, it would've been dangerous

anyway. One Astley sister with an injured foot was already one too many. "Are you game for a three-legged race?"

Mercy shrugged and slipped off the stool. With their arms locked around each other, they made slow progress. They hadn't even made it past the bar and into the dining room before Mercy tipped. Blaze stopped her fall, but Mercy must've put down her injured foot because she cried out in pain.

"Please, Blaze. Let me help," Anson said, close behind. She'd never heard him beg before.

Between the hopping and Mercy's cry, all the customers watched them. They'd only made it fifteen feet before encountering a problem. They were bound to face many more before they reached the vehicle. How much pain would Blaze's stubbornness subject Mercy to? And how little would the town think of her for being too proud to accept help?

"He apologized." Pain etched her little sister's face, but forgiveness softened her eyes. True to her name, Mercy would forgive Blaze for making her pogo out to the car, but she'd also already forgiven Anson.

The man in question rounded Mercy. Hands on his thighs, he dipped his tall frame to her level. "Would it be all right if I carried you?"

Mercy's bottom lip disappeared between her teeth as her brown eyes slid to Blaze.

Still hunched over, Anson fixed his attention on her. "If you agree, I will not take it as a sign that you forgive me for earlier."

"It's okay with me," Mercy whispered.

Anson waited until Blaze sighed and stepped back. Once

she did, he placed one arm behind Mercy's back. "Nice and easy, okay?"

"'Kay." She latched an arm around his neck.

"Here we go." In one smooth movement, he hooked his other arm under her knees and swept her up. With a lift of his chin, he motioned Blaze ahead.

Free of Mercy's weight, she crossed the dining room. She'd never considered The Depot especially big, but this would've been quite a distance to hobble. She pushed open the doors and waited for her entourage to catch up.

She stilled at the unexpectedly sweet sight of Anson with Mercy cradled in his arms. There was something striking about a man using his strength for good. Her and Mercy's fathers hadn't done so for them, yet Anson had pleaded for the opportunity.

He pressed a shoulder against the door, holding it so she could move ahead.

She scurried on. She wasn't going to start admiring him. Except, as they navigated the steps outside, she wondered how she and Mercy would've handled them without him.

Marissa had the car waiting. She left the driver's door open as she circled the vehicle to meet them. "Need anything else?"

Blaze shook her head. "Thank you."

"Anytime. Let me know how it turns out." Marissa rubbed her shoulder, then went back inside.

Next to the rear car door, Anson lowered Mercy to her good foot. After she dropped to the seat and drew the seatbelt across herself, Anson reached for the front door as if to get in the passenger seat.

"Ah ..." Was he planning to ride along? "Thanks for the help."

He halted. "How are you going to get her into the hospital?"

"Don't they usually have wheelchairs by the doors?" She'd seen them there when she'd taken her mom in.

"Oh. Yeah." He shoved his hands in his pockets, and the streetlights in the parking area hit his flexing triceps. He didn't walk away, but he didn't say anything either.

"Thanks again." She took shelter inside the car and closed the door.

Mercy's voice rose from behind her. "That was nice, wasn't it? He picked me up like a sack of potatoes!" She chattered on like she always did when she was nervous, flustered, or excited.

It was a wonder the quirk hadn't kicked in while she'd been in Anson's arms. More than a wonder. A blessing. Blaze couldn't have Anson's head getting any bigger than it already was.

"I heard he was almost famous. Like, because he was so good at basketball. What's DI mean?"

Blaze sighed as she shifted into drive. "Division I."

"So, like, the best college?"

"Something like that."

"Well, one of *those* colleges was going to give him a free ride if he went and played for them, but he turned it down to be a youth pastor and a high school coach because he wanted to be like that other coach who died. That's what the boys were saying in the gym."

Many Oaks had been abuzz with the news when Anson made his famous decision. Of course people still talked about it. Anson's height, athleticism, and dedication to his faith and community made him a local hero who towered miles over her.

Blaze angled her head to spot her little sister in the mirror. "I thought you were in pain."

"Oh, I am. Wow. Have you ever broken a bone? What did it feel like?" She described her pain for a few blocks, then launched into a story about a classmate's broken toe.

If only Blaze could redirect her own mind as swiftly. Instead, as she checked Mercy in at the ER and waited for the verdict, she kept picturing Anson caring for her sister.

By the time they made it home two hours later, Mercy teetering around on crutches with her sprained ankle in a wrap, Blaze had pictured Anson stepping in to help so many times, it was almost a surprise he wasn't there to assist Mercy to her room.

He'd only been doing his part at The Depot. He would've helped any injured student, but only to a point.

Blaze never had anyone to depend on as she navigated the daily challenges of life.

Anson Marsh was the last person who'd ever change that.

5

"I've heard what my dad's up to. I'm going to help you out."

Anson panted, hands on his hips, as he and Carter descended the hill behind the community center. When they reached the bottom, they'd sprint up again. If Carter could talk only seconds after they'd switched to a walk, Anson needed to pick up the pace next time. He sucked in a deep breath. "How so?"

"I'll bring people to Branching Out. Most kids do whatever I say." The boast rang true. A popular athlete going into his senior year, Carter held sway over his classmates.

Anson hadn't been so charismatic. "Why would you do that if you don't see a need for God?"

"It's a good time." Carter smirked. "Mostly."

Despite the tease in the kid's voice, Anson's stomach tightened with disappointment. "You know I'm still going to teach, right?"

"Yeah. It's what you believe. It'd be dishonest not to."

Carter's commitment to honesty was one thing Anson liked about the kid.

Carter slugged his arm and grinned. "Just make sure there's food during the boring parts. Because we like to eat and our parents don't feed us at home. A few times last year, you let us starve."

"Is that why I found a stash of junk food wrappers behind one of the couches last week?"

The student snorted but didn't offer an explanation. He might not know. Anson didn't, and he led all the activities in the youth room.

They reached the bottom of the hill where Carter's younger brother, Dylan, lay on the ground playing on his phone. The other kids who'd played basketball with them in the community center gym had disappeared as soon as Anson suggested hill sprints. Only Carter had accepted the challenge. Since he was Dylan's ride, the incoming freshman was stuck until they finished.

"We're going up backward this time." Carter kicked the backpack his brother was using as a pillow. "Think you can beat me?"

Dylan narrowed his eyes at the incline.

"He is a lot slower backward," Anson said.

Carter scoffed. "Still going to beat you, old man."

He might. Hoping to land a scholarship, Carter had trained intensely over the summer and attended two elite basketball camps. Anson no longer had that much time to work out.

"Come on, Dylan," he said. "Show us what you've got."

The boy lumbered to his feet, and on Anson's signal, they raced. Anson and Carter tied for the lead until Dylan turned and sprinted forward. Carter stuck with the initial challenge, matching Anson step for step. At the top, the race was too close to call. Carter was more concerned with telling Dylan he'd cheated anyway.

Afterward, the boys headed straight to their car. Anson caught his breath on the way back to the community center. Back when basketball was his life, he'd learned to equate tired muscles with progress. His aspirations no longer included going pro, but the heaviness of his arm as he reached for the door still felt like an achievement.

He meant to go change out of his sweaty clothes, but the path to the locker room took him by Sydney's office. As the director of the community center, she often closed her door for meetings, but today it stood open. She sat behind her desk. Her brown eyes glanced up from the computer when he paused at her doorway.

A smile lifted her lips as she rose. "Hero's a nice look on you, Marsh."

The compliment surprised a laugh from him. "Hero?"

Sydney motioned him forward and shut the door behind him, closing them in together. "You would've made a good firefighter, carrying damsels in distress from burning buildings." She traced her fingers down his biceps.

"I see." If only he hadn't been close enough to help because he'd owed Mercy an apology. "There's more to firefighting than that."

"Still." She smoothed her hands over his chest and peered up at him.

His damp shirt stuck to his skin, and her pressing it in felt like cuddling up with a wet blanket. No way he wanted that in the middle of an embrace. He took her hands in his own, but his palms felt slick too. Definitely should've stopped by the locker room first.

"I'm sorry we ended up getting pulled different directions, thanks to the whole Jimmy thing." She squeezed his hands. "Have you heard from Blaze about how Mercy is?"

"I texted this morning, but she hasn't replied. She might be under the impression I don't think she's a good guardian for her sister."

Sydney's mouth dropped open like she wasn't sure whether to laugh or gasp. "Why?"

"Let's just say my meeting with Eric yesterday wasn't the only train wreck. Anyway"—he kissed Sydney's forehead—"how'd it go with Honor? When I got back inside, you looked pretty deep in conversation."

She turned her face down as she stepped back. "Honor felt guilty, and I don't think she believed me when I assured her she wasn't responsible for Jimmy's choices."

"All we can do is try. And pray."

She gave a sympathetic smile. "As if you're any good at not interfering either."

"Fair enough."

"Did Gabby have any good ideas for you about how to deal with Eric?"

To give Sydney and Honor space last night, Anson had found a seat with Gabby Voss, his high school basketball coach's widow. She often served as a sounding board for him, but drama with the leadership board was tricky. Gabby had plans to move away in a couple of months, but for the time being, she was a member of the congregation.

"I didn't bring it up. I don't want to stir anything up if Eric's out of step with the board. Greg will be in the office tomorrow. I'll talk to him then." The senior pastor was a reasonable man with a heart for God. He wouldn't let the church succumb to a comparison trap.

Anson stepped toward the door, then paused. "Speaking of the youth groups, what do you think of Blaze as a leader for Rooted?"

Sydney shrugged. "She's a member, right?"

He nodded. To join, Blaze would've shared her testimony and agreed to the church's statement of beliefs. "Beyond that, she's never been very involved, aside from attending services. Even then, she's always late, and she doodles her way through sermons."

Sydney smiled. "Yours or Pastor Greg's?"

"Both."

"Then it's nothing personal." Her light tone spoke volumes. "Drawing doesn't mean she's not listening, and it's not like she'd be teaching the lessons as a youth leader."

"She might end up in conversations with students, though."

"Rooted leaders don't meet up with students outside of youth group, so you'll be close by if she needs help with something tricky. Besides, you and Nolan could use a female leader on the team. And you're already stretching your ratio. If you do grow the group, more leaders are a must."

Sydney was right. Anson preferred to have one leader for every four students, and the middle school group brought in eight to ten kids every week.

"Plus, around Many Oaks, Blaze is almost as much of a celebrity as Philip or Michaela. The girls will look up to her. Who knows? Having her around might solve your attendance problem without you lifting a finger."

"I don't think she carries that much pull."

Sydney arched an eyebrow. "She gets all of us to The Depot every week." Before Anson acknowledged the validity of the point, her phone rang.

"I'm going to go change. Dinner tonight?"

She extended her hand toward the phone. "I promised some of the Branching Out students a girl's night before the school year starts, remember? Tonight was the one that worked for everyone."

"How about tomorrow?"

She nodded as she picked up the call.

He let himself out. He'd thought Sydney would rule out the idea of Blaze helping as quickly as he had. Instead, she'd given a list of reasons to give it a try. Maybe he'd been too quick to rule her out.

BLAZE'S OFFICE at the dealership was quiet. Too quiet.

She drummed her hands against her thighs. She preferred chatting up clients on the sales floor to running reports in her windowless office. Every day since she'd taken the promotion, she felt like the kid stuck in summer school while the others enjoyed water parks.

To burn off some energy, she hopped out of her seat and shook out her arms.

There. Better. Right? She lowered back into her desk chair, and her gaze wandered yet again to her phone. Responding to Anson's text shouldn't require a day of strategizing. She ought to get it over with. Then she'd have a clear mind to finish her team's commission and bonus report, already a day overdue. If she dragged her feet much longer, checks would be late, and checks could not be late. People depended on her.

But the numbers on her screen blurred together. Anson had never said whether she could help with Rooted. Would her overreaction to Mercy's sprain cause him to turn her down? The numbers wouldn't focus until she had an answer.

She picked up her phone and opened his message.

Hey, Blaze. It's Anson. How's Mercy?

They'd never texted before, hence the introduction. Presumably, he'd looked her up in the church directory. Or on Mercy's emergency contact form, filed away at the church.

He probably saw multiple sprains each season as a coach and responded with far less drama. Then again, carrying Mercy had been his idea.

Blaze typed, *She's on crutches but in good spirits.*

Keeping her on the crutches for the recommended week would be a miracle. Mercy shared Blaze's restlessness.

"Am I interrupting?" Tony's short, heavy-set frame ambled into the office.

She fumbled her phone, and it landed with a clunk beside her keyboard. "Not at all. Mercy sprained her ankle last night. It's a whole thing." She straightened her posture. "What can I do for you?"

"You know why I promoted you?" He dropped into the chair across from her and interlaced his fingers over his belly.

"Because I hold the record for consecutive months as the dealership's top salesperson?"

"Nope. Because of your humility."

"Oh." He had?

He broke into a teasing smile. "Yes, because of your sales record. You were driven and *good* at it."

"Were?"

He exhaled, pity on his face. "No one on your team's risen to your level yet. They need more from you than flyby tips. And your reports are habitually late."

She bit her lip and looked at the spreadsheet on her screen. The one that was due yesterday. "I'm trying. Maybe I could put together a mini-training seminar for my team? And I'll set more reminders."

"I already hear your reminders go off all day. You set them for everything. Including, if I'm not mistaken, to remind you to eat." His bushy eyebrows lifted.

She gulped. The meal reminders had been more necessary when she'd had a job she could lose herself in. "I'll silence them. I didn't realize they were so loud."

"Nah, it's just a little bell. By the third time I hear it, I figure half of the angels have their wings, and you're about to turn something in. Still"—Tony cleared his throat—"not everybody is cut out for administration, and there's no shame in that."

Her shoulder blades hit her seat back. "You want me to step down?"

"I want you in a role where you'll flourish, Blaze. You're possibly the best salesperson to work here since I opened the place thirty years ago, but after this long in business, I've learned to employ people where they're gifted. As a salesperson, you did a fraction of the paperwork and spent most of your time interacting with clients. Reports and meetings aren't for everyone."

"They are for me." She heard the confidence in her tone even as desperation needled her. As a salesperson, her paychecks had varied with commissions. The managerial role meant bigger, more dependable checks that had already made life easier for her and Mercy. "I will do better."

"Finding a rhythm can take a few months, so I'll leave you to it. But *do* find a rhythm. Reports need to be in on time, and sales numbers need to come up. A mini-seminar sounds promising. If you want to brainstorm other ways to accomplish the department's goals, you know where to find me."

"Yes, sir."

His mustache shifted as he tightened his lips. "You don't need to resort to *sir*-ing me. You've got a good head on your shoulders, Blaze. You can make this work. I'm counting on you to do that."

She nodded, barely suppressing another "Yes, sir."

He strolled back out, and Blaze tipped her head down, fingers pressed against her temples. She needed to stop sabotaging herself and start performing. If only willing herself to perform had ever worked.

6

Anson found Greg's office door open. Papers littered his desk, ignored as he typed on his laptop.

Anson stepped in. "You got a minute?"

Greg typed a few more words, then shut the laptop. "Sure. I had a feeling you'd stop by."

Disappointment stretched in Anson's chest as he took a seat across from the senior pastor. If Eric had exaggerated the board's new initiative, Greg ought to be surprised by Anson's visit. Then again, the meeting notes spelled out the ultimatum.

"What's on your mind?"

"Pastors here get a vote on everything but questions about their own employment."

"Well, sure, when they're present."

"I would've been, if I'd known someone put youth group attendance on the agenda."

Greg's salt-and-pepper beard framed a sympathetic smile. "It was a last-minute addition. I suggested we wait for this week's meeting to make any decisions, but Eric made a compelling case. I was overruled."

"What was his case?"

"That sometimes an outside perspective can see what someone closer to a problem cannot." His pause seemed weighty. "For the record, I also voted for a less ambitious goal."

A throb picked up at the base of Anson's skull. "The board didn't think they needed to hear both sides?"

"No one was thinking in terms of sides. Some of the board members are parents, so they have a pulse on the youth group. Attendance is down. That's not up for debate."

"The debate is what our response ought to be."

Greg leaned into an armrest, skewing the cream-and-brown lines on his button-down. "What would you have suggested?"

"Continuing faithfully and trusting God with the numbers."

"I don't know that ignoring the problem is the answer. Goals give us something to aim for."

The throb intensified to constant pain. "Is the answer less teaching and more games? Because that's what Eric asked me to do when he described this plan on Monday."

"You do tend to be on the disciplined side. It might not hurt to lighten up more." Greg sat back and crossed his legs. "This shouldn't require a major change. Doubling only requires each student to bring one friend. The board thought that was reasonable."

"When was the last time every board member brought a guest to church?" Anger crackled in his voice, and he clenched his teeth, trying to get his emotions in check. "They're not practicing what they're putting on me and the students. And what are you going to do when Eric sets his sights on you, saying you need to water down your sermons to increase Sunday morning attendance?"

Greg lifted a hand. "No one is asking you to water down the gospel."

No—Eric wanted him to skip it almost entirely. "It doesn't seem at all divisive that he addressed his concerns about the youth groups the one time the man responsible for the students was absent?"

"Conflict is hard for a lot of people. It could be that he didn't want to offend you and wanted the board's opinion on the matter before pursuing a solution."

"Eric doesn't have a problem with conflict." If he'd wanted to avoid conflict, he wouldn't have paraded into Anson's office with news of the initiative.

Greg stacked the papers on his desk. "All I can say is that he seemed very humble in the way he talked it through with the board. As for the outcome, I suspect that if the board sees positive movement, they'll lay off the whole thing, and the result will be bigger youth groups where you have the privilege of serving more kids."

"The meeting notes—and Eric—say the board will 'take action' if I don't hit the goal. Did anyone discuss what the action will be?"

"I imagine a brainstorming session. But again, I don't see much coming from it. If anyone even remembers to discuss the issue again at the end of the semester."

"So, your advice is to lie low, do what I can, and hope everyone forgets?"

"Sometimes, the best solution is time."

Anson sat silent. Stunned. Disappointed. Anger ratcheted the muscles in his back tighter and tighter. "I would like to add the initiative to this week's agenda."

"To what end?"

"To speak to the board's concerns and have it repealed."

Greg shook his head helplessly. "They won't. A couple of families left for Grace Evangelical, and the congregation that's left is aging. We added to this building in better times, and with membership dwindling, it's a stretch to maintain. Our budget has been tight for years, and we have some big expenses looming. The original portion of the building needs a new roof, for one. If the board sees a way to strengthen our ministries and bring in more people, especially younger people, they're in favor of it."

"Students aren't a gold mine."

"Students have parents. While I agree that this plan won't fix the budget issue, I do believe God will. As He provides, this pressure will fade. But if you dig your heels in and make them firm up their position, it becomes its own issue, something that won't disappear no matter what happens with the finances."

Too tense to stay seated, Anson started pacing. "Kids think they have forever to decide about God. They don't. Sharing the gospel with them is vital."

Greg studied Anson for a few long beats. "The gospel is still paramount. If the board is at one extreme, don't fight back by choosing the other. There's holy ground in the middle where you can weather this storm."

Huddle up like a kid during a tornado drill? Retorts burned in Anson's lungs, but Greg wasn't the problem. Not the whole problem, anyway. He didn't deserve to be berated, and Anson didn't want to damage their relationship by venting more of his frustration.

"Thanks for taking the time to talk with me." He let himself out.

At least they agreed on one thing: this was a storm.

BIRDS TWITTERED overhead as Blaze stepped into the park at the heart of the town square. She checked her phone to make sure she hadn't missed a text saying her pick-up order was ready. Nothing yet. She slid the phone into her pocket again and smiled at her favorite of the Many Oaks oaks.

The park contained all twelve of Iowa's native oak tree varieties. Early officials had marked the biggest of each with a bronze plaque. Nine of those original prized oaks remained standing.

Blaze's favorite was not one of the survivors. With a one-hundred-year lifespan, the chinkapin oak would never measure up to its towering neighbors. She tapped a leaf as she passed under a low branch, then continued down the paved path.

She inhaled the scents of warm earth and greenery. Movement and fresh air renewed something in her that she hadn't known could break until she'd landed her promotion. Spreadsheets had nothing on the rush of matching a client with the perfect car.

As she walked, the trees gave way to the clearing that housed the gazebo. With flowering vines twining through the lattice, the gazebo had drawn Blaze and her friends to stage many a pretend wedding. Boys had always been in short supply, so they'd argued over who got to wrap up in the lace tablecloth and who had to don the black jacket.

If the white paint were refreshed, the gazebo would still

make a great wedding venue, provided the couple could limit the guest list to—she surveyed the area to estimate the size, but her gaze landed on Anson, coming up the path.

He stopped at the edge of the clearing, wary gaze fixed on her like the boys who stumbled across the wedding game and wanted to avoid the theatrics. He hadn't moved to Many Oaks until years after she'd quit that childish game, but she doubted he ever would've taken her hands, looked her in the eyes, and promised to love her forever. She wasn't the kind of girl who won over boys like him, even for five minutes of pretend.

"What brings you here?" she asked.

He motioned toward the gazebo. "Meeting Sydney."

Her phone pinged. Hopefully dinner was ready. "Don't worry. I'm just passing through. As you know, I have other places to be on Wednesday nights." She stepped toward him, meaning to return to the restaurant the way she'd come.

Anson remained in the middle of the walk. "How is Mercy?"

"It's a sprain. The crutches will be short-lived, but in the meantime, they bring some nice perks."

"Such as?"

"Tomorrow's her first day of middle school. She was nervous about finding her way around, but kids on crutches get a helper during hall passing, so she'll have a guide." That fact alone had taken Mercy's anxiety about middle school from a nine down to a five.

"I'm glad it's not serious."

"Me too." She pulled out her phone. "Dinner's ready, so I'll get going."

He didn't step off the path, so she did. Compliments of the hot, dry week, her heels didn't sink into the grass.

"Thanks." Quiet and gritty, his voice halted her.

She glanced over her shoulder at him.

A flash of apology crossed his face. "Thanks for coming directly to me when you had a problem, instead of ... not."

She hadn't *meant* to talk to him about the problem, only about her proposed solution.

His mouth settled into a tight line.

"You seem upset."

The frown deepened. "Not everyone is as forthcoming as you. It's easier to solve problems with direct conversations."

She'd never seen him like this. What was she supposed to do? Try counseling a pastor? She rested a hand on a cocked hip and quirked an eyebrow. "You have problems?"

He laughed once. "I do."

She ordered her curiosity to take a hike and lifted her chin with a teasing smile. "I didn't think those kinds of shenanigans were allowed. You run a tight ship, Marsh."

He shifted as though someone had poked him in the spine, and his line of sight fell to the dusty pavement. "I shouldn't have said what I did the other day. You're doing a great job with Mercy."

"I shouldn't have been so hurt. You don't know us well enough to say one way or the other."

He stole a sidelong glance at her.

The statement wasn't fair. He could observe her and Mercy and guess whether she was a decent guardian. Why hadn't she just taken the compliment?

"You still want to be a leader?"

That was one compliment she wouldn't pass up. "Yes."

He focused on her, forehead creased. "You think Philip can change The Signalmen's schedule by next week?"

She had no idea, but next Wednesday was Rooted's

opening night. Philip could do without her one night if it meant proving her reliability to Anson. "I'll be at youth group."

"Sounds good." He put his head down and continued toward the gazebo.

"See you at the show?" She was pushing her luck, but she'd come this far. "Since Rooted doesn't start up until next week?"

He peered at her over his shoulder, then shook his head. "Probably not."

The likely reason why—Sydney—rounded the gazebo from the direction of the community center. The woman smiled a kind greeting.

"Good night." Blaze took her win and hurried away.

7

Anson had enough problems without stirring up dissension. Why had he been so tempted to complain to Blaze about the church drama at the park?

Four days later, it still bothered him as he vacuumed up popcorn the high schoolers left in their wake after Sunday school. Blaze and Nolan would arrive at any moment for the last-minute leaders' meeting he'd called. While he cleaned, he gave himself a mini-sermon on discretion.

Thank God Blaze had called him by his last name in the park the other day. That reminded him of Sydney, who sometimes called him Mr. Marsh. With Sydney, he could be real. They could discuss church problems. She'd keep it confidential and talk him down when necessary—as she'd done on Wednesday night—without losing her respect for Many Oaks Bible Church.

She'd helped him decide not to confront the board. Instead, he would put in the extra time and effort to meet their goal without sacrificing lesson time. To do that, he'd need help from his leaders. Hence today's meeting, where he'd try to describe the goal without poisoning their respect for the board.

He scanned the room, looking for more popcorn kernels. Cabinets and a countertop ran along the rear wall. Then came a table and metal chairs they rarely used. Anson would replace the workspace with more comfortable seats, but they rarely filled the front half of the room, where a lectern faced two rows of six chairs. A semi-circle of thrifted couches, the most popular seating option, surrounded those.

Blaze appeared in the doorway, angled to talk to someone behind her. She wore a navy-blue dress laced with a dainty floral print. With buttons down the front and puffed sleeves, the feminine style contrasted with her usual choices. For shows, she wore lots of black tops and jeans like what the high schoolers wore. Most Sundays, she opted for sleek professionalism.

Then again, what did he know? Maybe the dress was trendy. It certainly flattered her figure.

His throat tightened. Those were dangerous rails for a train of thought. He turned his back to her and unplugged the vacuum.

"With what?" Her smooth voice asked.

"Worship," Nolan said as he walked in behind her. "I do my best, but we could really use your voice. And if you play guitar or piano ...."

"I'm always happy to sing, but I never learned an instrument."

"Good enough." He plopped onto one of the couches. "You sound a thousand times better than anything I croak out."

Anson wound up the vacuum cord and wheeled it across the hall to the janitorial closet. The space held more than its fair share of supplies, ranging from the standard cleaning products to stray décor. But a sleeping bag? That didn't belong tucked on a shelf. He made a mental note to take it to lost and found, then circled back to the youth room.

His notes waited for him on top of a cardboard box he'd left on a chair in the front row. "Nolan, you heard we added to the team?" He motioned to Blaze.

"It's about time. Now we won't have to grab a Saplings teacher when Carianne disappears into the restroom for half an hour."

Blaze quirked an eyebrow. "Restrooms are a big issue with these kids."

Nolan lifted his hands. "The women's restroom must be a lot nicer than the men's, that's all I'm saying. You ladies have a spa in there?"

Amusement sparkled in Blaze's eyes. "Not last I checked."

"Then I don't know why the girls are always hanging out in there."

Because they'd rather not be at youth group, apparently. Maybe there *was* a problem, and Anson had missed the signs.

"We'll do our best to make sure it's more interesting to stay with the group this year." He inhaled deeply, steeling himself. "We have a goal of doubling attendance before the end of the semester."

Nolan whistled. Blaze's mouth skewed with doubt or concern.

Anson pushed ahead. "As I prayed about this, I realized most of our students have been attending for years. That's made it possible to focus on more nuanced or advanced lessons, but this year, I want to revisit the basics so the kids can concisely explain what they believe and why. They'll need that as they become adults, and in the meantime, they can better engage with friends who need hope. Plus, the lessons will be more accessible when they invite friends without a church background. That's important, because I don't want to grow by poaching students from another youth group. I want to disciple the kids we have and share the Good News with kids who aren't getting it anywhere else."

"Preach." Nolan clapped.

Blaze's expression straightened into a smile.

The approval bolstered him, probably more than it should. "I also want to make it as easy and fun as possible to invite friends to youth group, so I'm working on using social media more effectively. In the meantime, I sent all the middle and high school students home today with an invitation with a QR code that'll take them to an info page on our website."

"High tech," Nolan quipped.

Not really, but updating the website and generating the code was as high-tech as Anson got. They'd need other improvements to attract more students.

He opened the box and lifted out a hooded sweatshirt. The word *Rooted* ran down one arm. The other said *In Christ*. "A couple of years ago, when I ordered *fifteen* of these, the woman on the phone thought I said *fifty*. We didn't catch the mistake until they were printed. I have plenty left to give them as a reward to anyone who brings a friend to Rooted or one of our events." He dropped the zippered hoodie back into the box with the others. "And I heard Blaze agree to sing. Thank you for that." He nodded at her. "What else can we do to make this year our best yet?"

"Snacks?" she asked. "Do you normally have those?"

Carter's speech about food echoed in his mind, and he cringed. "When one of us remembers to pick something up."

"Mercy and I like to bake. Treats can be our contribution."

"Done." He jotted down a note. "I'd also like to arrange more extra activities. Can you two carve out a few hours one Saturday a month?"

"As long as I'm not on duty." Nolan's schedule as a police officer was all over the place. Ensuring he was free every Wednesday evening involved a complex series of trades with his coworkers. Anson couldn't ask him to guarantee another day of the month too.

He looked to Blaze.

"I used to have more gigs, but with the new job, I haven't had time to coordinate that, so, sure. I'm flexible on Saturdays."

"How about the Saturday after Labor Day, eight to two? I know it's short notice. I told Branching Out students about it this morning. With enough leaders, we could open the activity up to Rooted students too."

Both consulted their phones before nodding their agreement.

"Great." Their help would put him one event closer to the attendance goal. "We'll meet here and take a van to Pine Gully Creek for canoeing."

Blaze lifted her hand like a timid student. "How does that work? Do people have to be able to swim to come?"

"Shouldn't be a problem. Pine Gully Creek is shallow and slow, for the most part. We should have enough leaders who can swim to pair with anyone who can't, and the rentals come with life jackets."

She bit her lips together and nodded. Still concerned?

Maybe Mercy couldn't swim, but short of repeating himself, he didn't know how to reassure Blaze. He moved on to planning Wednesday's meeting. Rooted always kicked off with a party, and they needed a strong opening night if they hoped to interest students in anything that came after.

BLAZE PAUSED outside Mercy's bedroom. She'd told her three times to clean up, but each time she checked on her, she found her sister playing with Cinnamon Bun instead of picking up after him.

Now, the rabbit lounged on the floor next to Mercy as she spoke into her phone. "Why not? It's—" She exhaled loudly, waited, then said, "Fine. You don't have to be mean about it."

After a clipped goodbye, she tossed the phone on the floor and scooped up BunBun. According to the dozens of articles Blaze read before agreeing to the pet, bunnies didn't like to be held. BunBun made an exception for Mercy.

Blaze leaned against the doorway. "Who was that?"

"Amelia. I invited her to Rooted, and she said yes, but now she doesn't want to come, and she won't even tell me why."

"Did you fight about something?"

"No." Mercy stroked her lop-eared rabbit's light brown fur. His hair was so fluffy—and prone to shedding—that a puff of it floated into the air. Their robot vacuum was a lifesaver, but it couldn't handle the hay pieces that ended up scattered near the hutch in Mercy's room.

Cleaning was a must, but Blaze knew all about friend trouble and how much it could hurt. "I'm sorry you two are fighting. Maybe you can talk to her more at school tomorrow and find out what happened."

Mercy shrugged. "She says she doesn't want to do anything with someone like me."

"Someone like you?"

"That's what she said." Her chin bunched, and she kept her gaze on her rabbit.

"I don't know what went wrong, but I do know what kind of person you are. You're funny and energetic and caring. She's lucky to have you as a friend, and you're lucky to have her too. You're going to work this out."

Mercy's mouth skewed.

Blaze couldn't blame her for being skeptical. Disagreements with grade school friends hadn't always worked out for Blaze either. She prayed Mercy would have a different result. "I bet you'll be friends again long before Wednesday, but right now, I do need you to clean this room."

Mercy's gaze darted to the corner where she'd abandoned her crutches on Friday. "Maybe my ankle hurts."

Blaze lowered her chin. After the leaders' meeting, she'd found Mercy running around in the gym without a hint of pain. "You can ice and elevate after you finish. Cleaning up will only take a few minutes if you put your mind to it."

"Mom never made me do chores."

"Mom also never got you a bunny. You don't want to live in that mess, do you?" She toed a piece of hay stuck to the carpet.

"I don't mind. I don't even notice."

"I mind." Blaze's phone dinged, but she wasn't about to give her sister an escape by pausing the conversation to check it. "Next time I come check, his litter box and this carpet had better be clean, or I'll give you other chores to do too."

Mercy set the bunny free and stood, but instead of moving to obey, she scowled. "You don't clean our bathroom every day."

"You are as capable of cleaning the bathroom as I am, but BunBun cannot change his litter box. And our bathroom doesn't double as your dining table."

Mercy's mouth scrunched. They'd both been surprised to learn bunnies ate mostly hay—and troubled that their preferred place to do so was in their litter boxes.

Blaze's phone sounded again. Trusting she'd made her point, she stepped away and slipped the device from her pocket. "When you're done cleaning, come show me your homework."

The afterthought went unanswered, and Blaze let it go. For now.

She unlocked her phone.

Anson had texted her and Nolan. *Thanks for the ideas today. Glad to have you on the team.*

Interesting. She hadn't expected him to play cheerleader.

The other message came from Nolan. After the names of four worship songs to brush up on for Rooted, he'd added, *This is gonna be awesome!*

Blaze snorted. She and Nolan had been in the same class at Many Oaks High, a year behind Anson. They hadn't interacted much, but apparently that hadn't been because of any judgment on Nolan's side. Or if it had been, he'd outgrown it.

I'll be ready. She added a thumbs up for good measure and sent the message before heading to the kitchen to heat dinner.

The texts and Rooted commitments on her calendar

made her feel a little less like an outsider. She should've volunteered to serve years ago. Instead, she'd assumed no one at church would trust the girl who'd once burned down a building. Assumed her own childhood difficulties with friendships would follow her into adulthood.

If there was hope for her yet, there was also hope for Mercy's friendships, but her little sister wouldn't be encouraged to hear that improvements might take another fifteen years. Anyway, Anson had dragged his feet before letting Blaze lead. This might be tenuous cooperation, not full-fledged acceptance. One mistake and Mercy might not be the only one in need of a pep talk.

8

Blaze caught a glimpse of her sister in the rearview mirror. "I'm sorry Amelia didn't come around, but we're going to have fun tonight."

"None of my friends are coming." With her head turned toward her window, only a thick shock of dark hair and the rim of her glasses were visible.

"If it makes you feel any better, I won't know many people either."

"Yeah, but you're a grown-up."

"I still feel more comfortable when I have friends, especially when I start something new." She'd come to Christ as an adult, and something told her that youth group would be different than the Bible studies she'd attended. Considering her inexperience, it was no wonder Anson had hesitated to let her join the team.

"Can I bring my book in?" Mercy had never cared much for reading, but she was ahead of the assigned chapters in *A Wrinkle in Time*. "Ms. Johanssen says books can keep us company when we're bored or alone. She says reading is really good for us."

"I'm sure it is, but you won't be bored tonight. Or alone." Chuckling, Blaze turned into the church parking lot. "You know what we're supposed to do during hard times?"

"Pray." Mercy's voice held a store of skepticism.

Blaze didn't bother trying to coax more enthusiasm as she watched for kids and a parking spot. "Lord, I pray you'd connect us with the right people so we can all show each other a little glimpse of your love." She navigated into a spot and parked. "Thank you for the gift of community. Amen."

The church glowed in the late-day sun. Children ran for the main doors, adults trailing behind. Beside the building, Anson was hanging a volleyball net. A circle of chairs and a snack table waited nearby.

Blaze grabbed her purse and a bag filled with snacks. "If nothing else, we have the best peanut butter cookies this side of the Mississippi. We're bound to make friends."

Mercy slinked from the backseat.

Blaze stopped at the table. Bottles of soda and juice and bags of potato chips weighed down a vinyl tablecloth. "Do you want me to open any of this?" she asked.

Anson turned from the net, one hand holding it in place. "We'll play the game first, so better keep it covered for now."

She added her bag of treats—the cookies she and Mercy had made, plus pretzels and gummy bears—to the collection. With a deep breath, she straightened her shoulders and gave Mercy a peppy smile. "Let's go make some friends."

Mercy trudged inside. Laughing and raised voices spilled from the youth room and into the hallway. Mercy, one step ahead, passed the threshold first. An inflatable ball drilled her in the ear. She squawked and shielded her head as the ball bounced away.

"Sorry." The boy didn't even look at Mercy as he retrieved the ball.

When he launched it again, Nolan intercepted it. "Let's save it for outside." He nodded to Blaze, clamped the ball between both hands, and returned his attention to the two kids he was talking with.

About ten students laughed, played, and chatted. Mercy bit her bottom lip and her eyes darted around the space.

Blaze rested a hand on her shoulder. "We're meeting here quick, then we'll all go outside and play some games. Let's find a seat for a few minutes." She guided her through the fray to a couch, only then noticing a blond girl with flushed cheeks. She picked her nails as her eyes mimicked Mercy's half-panicked, half-envious scan of the room.

Compassion and hope welled up, and Blaze nudged Mercy toward the girl. "Let's sit over there."

Mercy plodded over and plopped onto the far side of the couch.

Blaze took the seat between the girls and angled toward the blond. "I'm Blaze, and this is my sister Mercy. What's your name?"

She swallowed. "Hadley."

"Are you here with anyone?"

She shook her head. "My mom wanted to go to an exercise class but didn't want to leave me home alone. But I'm twelve. I would've been okay."

Blaze put together the age, name, and the apparently single mom to place Hadley. "Is your mom Ashley West?"

Hadley nodded, her ponytail bouncing. "You know her?"

"Sure. She was ahead of me in high school. She was

nice." Ashley had started off popular, but when word of her pregnancy broke, she'd been ostracized. She and Blaze hadn't exactly become friends, but they'd had each other's backs a few times.

It would be Blaze's pleasure to look out for Ashley's daughter. In fact, this was an answer to the prayer she'd offered in the car. God didn't usually move in her life in such obvious ways. Her request must've lined up with what He wanted for once. Perhaps Blaze was learning. She sat up straighter. "What do you like to do for fun, Hadley?"

BLAZE LOOKED SO amazed she'd caught the ball that Anson didn't have the heart to tell her she'd stepped out of bounds. The kids weren't so merciful. Even her own teammates cried, "You're out!"

"What?" Her mouth dropped open, and she looked down at her feet. Her shoulders slouched, but she surrendered the ball to another player.

On the sideline, she fell into conversation with Hadley, one of the new students. By the looks of their hand motions, they were talking strategy, even though they'd only have a few more minutes to use it since parents were due any moment.

The first minivan pulled up. A woman got out and waved at her son. Anson headed over to her to give his spiel about the canoe trip.

When he returned courtside with a signed permission slip, Hadley was jabbering while Blaze's face remained the picture of patience. Impressive.

Over the next ten minutes, the rest of the parents came.

As he gave his canoe pitch one last time, Blaze packed up the snacks. He collected the last slip, then jogged back and snatched a peanut butter cookie as she dropped the lid on the container.

She pulled back with surprise. "Big fan?"

He swallowed his bite and held up the remaining half of the cookie. "Yeah. Whoever made these outdid themselves."

"We did." Mercy appeared at her side with a hand raised proudly.

Blaze chuckled and set the lid aside. "You can take them. We left a few at home."

"You said you liked baking. I didn't know you were a master chef."

Her hands fluttered until she clasped them together.

Had the compliment been too much?

A sweet smile lifted her lips. "I'm a master internet searcher. After that, all I do is follow the recipe." She clipped the last bag of chips shut and stashed it in a bulging grocery bag. "Where do you want this?"

Mercy snuck a cookie and slipped away.

Anson decided not to out her. "In the youth room. The kids can eat it on Sunday."

"Okay." Blaze scanned the lawn. "Need anything else from me?"

Besides the snack table, which he and Nolan would carry in, the only thing left out was the net. Nolan had that under control, so Anson passed her a permission slip and pen. "Just your signature. I know you'll be along, but we still need one for Mercy."

After Blaze signed, he helped Nolan with the net, and the sisters left. Only the container of cookies remained on the table. Anson set them aside, and he and Nolan took opposite ends of the table to carry it in.

"Fourteen kids were here." Nolan paused as he turned the table to navigate a doorway. "Close to that goal of doubling already."

"There's always more the first night." The trick would be getting the kids to come back with friends. He hoped his devotional about the first disciples telling others about Jesus would inspire the kids. They'd also used small group time to pray for friends who might need the hope and community youth group offered.

All that, and the part that had made the kids light up? His promise of a Rooted hoodie for anyone who brought a friend. Then again, could he blame the kids for valuing the wrong things when the leadership board was doing the same?

With the table back in place, Nolan dusted his hands. "Numbers aren't everything."

They certainly weren't supposed to be.

9

Though written in cursive, the letters clearly spelled the name Jennifer. Anson squinted. Still Jennifer. He'd watched Blaze sign this permission slip. Why had she used someone else's name?

When his office door swung open, he peeled his gaze from the paper to make eye contact with Sydney. Her brown hair lay loose and naturally straight to her collarbones instead of in its usual ponytail. She'd completed the look with a blue tank top, denim shorts, and flip-flops.

"Who is Jennifer Astley?" he asked.

She tucked her fingers into her pockets. "That would be Blaze."

"But ..." This was going to sound foolish, but he was also certain. "Her name is Blaze. We went to high school together. She's always been Blaze."

"Mercy's been enrolled in after-school and summer care at the community center. Blaze always signs official paperwork for her with her legal name. Jennifer."

He blinked at the page. "Is Mercy's real name Mercy?"

Sydney lifted one slender shoulder. "Must be. It's what she wrote on the form, right?"

He double-checked. "Yeah." He knew two Jennys, a Jen, and a Jennifer, but only one Blaze. The originality suited her: edgy, bright, and entrancing. "I've known her for over a decade, and I'm just now learning her name?"

Sydney crossed her arms. "Were you ever close?"

"No, but I met her on her first day of high school. She tested ahead in math, so she was in my geometry class. Without hesitation, she said her name was Blaze."

"My understanding is it's a nickname, but if you want the story behind it, you'd better ask her. I've heard outlandish theories."

The stories he'd heard as a high schooler clicked into place, and he couldn't believe he hadn't connected them to Blaze's name. The one agreed-upon fact was that the Astleys' garage had burned down. Theories varied regarding who'd started it, why, and where Blaze had disappeared to for a while afterward. Some said she'd run away, some insisted she'd been sent to a youth correction program.

Sydney gave an uncertain smile. "Ready?"

The question—and the hesitant way she posed it—doused his curiosity. Why did he care how well he knew Blaze? Sydney was his priority. Had been for the last year. They had the same goals and a real future—not to mention plans for the evening.

For Labor Day, the town square had been closed to traffic to make way for food trucks, a petting zoo, and carnival games. Outside his office window, a high layer of clouds filtered the sunlight without threatening rain. The forecast predicted a high in the low eighties, just about perfect weather for the festivities.

He checked his watch. "How long do you think the food truck lines will be?"

"Many Oaks is up to almost eleven thousand people." Humor glittered in her eyes.

"And we'll end up behind all of them?" He chuckled at the exaggeration, placed the slip on the stack with the others, and scooped up the box of unclaimed lost and found items. "Then I guess I'll donate all this tomorrow."

Sydney touched the edge of the box as she peeked inside. "Some of that's nice stuff. That brand of water bottle is going viral. At the community center, someone would've claimed it whether it was theirs or not."

He pressed the box between the wall and his body, freeing up one hand to lock the office. That done, they continued toward the lobby. "The sleeping bag got claimed, but almost nothing else. There are clothes in here, serving platters, books, a ball of yarn, a lamp."

She opened the door, and as he passed through, she trailed her fingers down his arm. "At least it speaks well of the church that people aren't claiming stuff that isn't theirs."

"And now someone at the thrift store will find a viral water bottle." He balanced the box on one hand just long enough to secure the building. As he turned toward his SUV, his knuckles hit Sydney's hand. The box tipped, rattling the contents before he caught it.

"Sorry." She stuffed her fingers into her pockets.

He winced. "I didn't mean to push you away. This box is awkward, but ...." He adjusted the box on his hip so he could take her hand, but when he reached over, the load nearly slipped.

"Don't worry about it." She kept her eyes ahead, lips pinched.

Apologizing again probably wouldn't help. Anyway, what did she expect with his hands full?

They reached his SUV, and he stowed the box in the back as she climbed in the front passenger seat.

He slid in behind the wheel. "Did you get much done at the community center today? You were working on the mentoring program, right?"

She shrugged and clicked her seatbelt. "I went through all the applications, and I think I have the pairings figured out—for the kids we have mentors for. We could use about a dozen more adults."

"I could take on a student or two."

"Where would you find an extra hour or two each week?" She spoke with tired amusement. "We already both worked on Labor Day."

He steered onto the street. "I'll find a way if it helps you."

"Help isn't really what I need from you." Now she just sounded tired.

"I know. You're plenty capable all on your own." He smiled at her, but she stared out the windshield and tapped her fingers against the armrest.

She'd wanted to get the mentoring program off the ground since she accepted her role at the community center. The lack of volunteers must really be grating on her. "I know some high schoolers who would make good mentors," he said.

She sighed. "I don't need help, remember?"

"Right. Sorry." He clenched his hand around the steering wheel. "What do you need?"

Nothing but the hum of road noise answered.

He glanced over. "I can listen. Tell me about it."

She breathed out a quiet laugh. "There isn't much more to tell."

Over the next two blocks, regret accumulated. They weren't on the same page today, and he didn't know how to fix it.

"I'm excited about it and invested in it." The quiet weight of her voice drew his attention from the road in time to see her mouth lift ruefully. "But sometimes I wonder if I'm the only one."

That echoed how he felt with the board. He reached across the center console and opened his hand to her. She laced their fingers together and squeezed.

He squeezed back. "You're not alone. All those students signed up, and there may not be as many adults as you want, but the people who volunteered are invested."

Her grip loosened until her hand slid from his. "Right."

A red light gave him another opportunity to look over, but she turned her face away.

He tried changing gears. "I think I saw on the flyer that the gyro truck you like is going to be at the park tonight."

They discussed dinner options until they parked and fell in with the crowd headed for the square. The closer they got, the louder and busier the sidewalks became. Sydney slipped one hand around his elbow and wrapped her other hand around his.

At church, they rarely touched because the youth group kids weren't allowed to. Walking like this when church members and students were undoubtedly in the crowd felt conspicuous. But if connection was what she needed, that was what he'd give. He pulled his arm from her hands and wrapped it around her, drawing her to his side.

She grinned up at him. He must've finally gotten it right.

~

THE SAVORY SCENTS of roasted meat and warm bread promised dinner would be delicious—once Blaze finally reached the front of the line. As she waited, she kept a wary eye on Mercy and her friends. Since Mercy had hung out at Amelia's and Sarah's houses all summer, Blaze offered to keep tabs on them tonight. Amelia's mom had assumed the offer extended to her one-year-old, and Blaze hadn't had the heart to correct her.

She rocked the stroller back and forth, grateful for the cloud cover that kept the sun from beating down on her. Across the street and down a couple of vendors, Mercy and Amelia hadn't spoken to each other yet. At least, not as far as Blaze had seen. The trio of girls reached the front of the line, and Amelia ordered. Then Amelia said something to Sarah, who checked her pockets. Apparently coming up empty, she turned to Mercy.

Mercy opened her little purse. Blaze laughed when the first thing she pulled out was *A Wrinkle in Time*. Next, she wiggled a wad of cash free. All those ones made her look like quite the high roller as she peeled off a few bills and passed them to Amelia, who put them toward her order.

"Attagirl," Blaze murmured as she mindlessly followed the line forward.

Melinda started fussing, so Blaze hefted the munchkin from the stroller. Didn't smell like it was time for a diaper change, and Melinda ate before Blaze took over twenty minutes ago, so she settled the baby on her hip. The change of scenery seemed to work.

When she looked at her sister again, Mercy and Amelia stood to one side, talking, while Sarah ordered. No more tension. Another answered prayer. Blaze needed to remember to talk to the Lord more often, like about how poorly work was going.

Melinda yanked her hair. Blaze stifled a cry and untangled the pudgy hand from her locks. "Sweetie, ladies don't treat each other like that."

A chuckle rose from behind her.

She offered the woman a sheepish smile. "Twenty minutes, and I'm already trying to reason with a one-year-old. I don't know how moms do it."

"I think you might have an idea. You're Blaze Astley? Mercy's guardian?"

Blaze pulled her hair over her shoulder away from Melinda's prying fingers. Most people weren't so formal about her connection to Mercy. They either assumed Blaze was her mom or they knew her life's story and called them sisters. "I am. But I'm sorry, I don't know you."

The stout brunette extended her hand. "I'm Alicia Johanssen, Mercy's English teacher."

Blaze shifted Melinda to free up her right hand, but Ms. Johanssen saw the struggle and waved it off.

"Mercy has been talking about you," Blaze said. "I don't think I've ever heard her excited about reading, but you seem to have done it. Hopefully the enthusiasm sticks until she finishes the assignment." Blaze had never made it through an assigned book until *Pride and Prejudice*. The love of classic romances had stuck, but movie adaptations were more her speed.

"With frequent check-ins, we'll try to all stay on track to finish." Ms. Johanssen massaged her thumb against her palm. "I wasn't going to mention this until I got to know

Mercy better, but maybe it's a sign that we ran into each other. Has she mentioned anything else about class?"

Blaze's mouth went dry, and she shook her head.

"She started talking when she was supposed to be filling out a worksheet. When I said something, she looked like she might cry. Then she was too down and distracted to participate at all. I happen to know her fifth grade teacher, and I was in the office when she called you to bring her clarinet. The secretary said she's already forgotten her lunch a couple of times too."

Three times. And the school year had barely begun. She'd also forgotten her gym clothes once. If Blaze were more on top of things, they'd have this figured out already, but she had a hard enough time finding her own things every morning, let alone Mercy's. She bounced Melinda. She'd rather change a diaper than continue this conversation.

Across the square, three strangers stood in line at the nacho truck, but no Mercy. Panic zipped Blaze's attention from one place to another until she spotted the trio at a picnic table.

"Does she forget things a lot?" Ms. Johanssen asked. "Have a hard time staying on task?"

Blaze's defensiveness came out in a loud sigh. "Kids forget things. Everyone does. And school wasn't my favorite either." That was one reason she skipped college and entered the workforce.

"Trouble making friends?"

Blaze motioned to the girls.

"Okay." Ms. Johanssen stepped back. "I don't want to speak out of turn."

Blaze's pride smoldered. Yet Mercy loved Ms. Johanssen,

despite being corrected by her. That said something. "We've come this far. What are you thinking?"

"Mercy is a great kid. If you ever notice her struggling in some of those areas more than other kids are, the school could help you investigate ADHD."

The letters, familiar yet unexpected, knocked a breath from her. "Is that the one where boys are hyperactive? Mercy's not like that at all. When she cares about something, she can get so focused she loses all sense of time." Blaze had experienced the same during busy sales days or when researching an interesting topic. She'd lost hours to songwriting and videos about rabbit care. If only more practical matters drew them in that way, they could avoid conversations like this one.

"Hyperactive boys are the stereotype, but just as many girls have ADHD. It goes undiagnosed more often because most females have a type that's less outwardly disruptive." She spoke with her hands more as she continued. "They forget important things—like lunch—often. They might be chatty, but they lose focus when others talk so they might not know the answers in class and miss social cues. That can cause disconnects with peers."

Blaze shot another look at her sister. Was their normal really so ... abnormal?

Ms. Johanssen touched her forearm, drawing her attention back. "Those struggles can lead kids to feel like they don't measure up or fit in, which can contribute to anxiety or depression. I'm not saying I see all this in Mercy, but the forgetfulness, sensitivity to correction, even the chattiness ...."

Sensitive. How many times had Blaze described Mercy that way? What if it stemmed from something more complex than a personality quirk? And much of what Ms. Johanssen said applied not only to Mercy, but also to Blaze.

Not measuring up? Check.

The ability to focus on some things and not others? Check and check.

She raked her fingers through her hair. "So I've passed on one too many bad habits, huh?"

"Oh, no. Parenting doesn't cause it. Mainly, it's genetics."

A ball tightened in Blaze's chest. Was ADHD yet another curse from their parents? Their grandparents? Would she and Mercy ever be free of the negative impacts of their family line?

"Next!" The man in the food truck window shouted.

Grateful for the excuse to end the conversation, Blaze promised the teacher she'd look into it, then moved forward to place her order. Afterward, she avoided being pulled back into the conversation by busying herself with Melinda.

"Jennifer?"

She ignored the man's voice as she lowered the girl back into the stroller and secured the safety belt.

"Jennifer." The voice drew closer.

She turned and found herself face-to-face with Anson.

He studied her with his eyebrows drawn. "Your name is Jennifer?"

"Oh." She looked down at Melinda. How many awkward conversations was she going to have before dinner? "Only when it needs to be."

"How did I not know this?" His sneaker scuffed against the pavement. "We went to high school together. None of the teachers called you Jennifer."

"We only had one class together." Besides, in little Many

Oaks, most of the teachers had known her nickname before she entered their classrooms.

"Chicken pita!"

"That's my order." Blaze pushed the stroller a step away, but Anson touched her arm. A shiver jolted her shoulder.

He lifted his hand, then stuffed it in his pocket. "How did a girl named Jennifer end up being Blaze?" Curiosity softened the steel blue of his eyes.

Why was he asking like this was a revelation? They'd met the first morning of her freshmen year. When a cute guy treated her kindly, she hoped high school would be a fresh start with different friends, better opportunities, and fewer obstacles. But when she'd said hello the second day, his lips barely twitched in a greeting. She'd assumed his friends had warned him off by filling him in on her history. All these years later, she could still taste the shame and disappointment.

"I'm sure you've heard. I really need to get going." She stepped up to the window and claimed her food. She rested the pita on the stroller's visor and fit her soda in a holder on the back.

Anson's voice rumbled beside her. "You want me to rely on rumors?"

A scoff caught in her throat. "They've gotten you this far."

He winced. "You're right. I never should've listened to the stories. I'm sorry."

She tangled her fingers in the ends of her hair, too shocked to reply.

Sydney bumped through the crowd and took Anson's hand as she joined them. "Hey, Blaze. Who's this?" She wiggled her fingers toward the stroller.

"Melinda. Amelia's sister. I'm on kid duty for the night, so

I should get going." She steered the stroller around the couple, but she couldn't help a look back.

Anson was watching her. She gave a little smile meant to say she forgave him. Still, she didn't regret guarding her story. An apology didn't prove she could trust him with the truth.

10

If the canoe launch was one of the last things Blaze saw before she died, at least the area was pretty. The creek glistened, and tall grasses and trees rustled in the breeze.

"Who knows how to swim?" Anson asked.

Blaze rolled her lips inward as her fingers latched onto the straps of her life jacket. Not only could she not raise her hand, but nightmares about drowning and slimy sea creatures had deprived her of so much sleep the night before that she felt a little like she was floating. Would that translate to floating if she capsized? Unlikely. The life jacket had better work.

Around her, the students raised their hands to indicate they could swim. Other than Blaze, the only hold outs were Mercy and the high schoolers who'd paid extra to rent kayaks.

Anson's eyes tracked the kayakers as they unloaded their boats and carried them to the launch. "And who knows how to steer a canoe?"

Again, Blaze kept both hands lowered.

With a clunk, Carter situated his kayak's nose in the water.

"Hey, guys, hold up until we're all ready to go," Anson said.

"We won't go far." Carter slid his paddle into the seat and nestled a fully loaded backpack into the cargo space behind the small backrest.

His four friends lined up behind him.

Meanwhile, one of the guides from the outfitter took up station beside Anson, waiting his turn to address the group. Two other guides continued lining up the canoes.

Carter hopped into his kayak. Anson excused himself from the group and went over to deal with him.

The guide, a teenager in board shorts and a T-shirt, focused on the leaders. "There's not much to know today. Follow the black-and-white arrows on the trees when you come to a fork, but when in doubt, keep going downstream. Just past the pick-up point, there's a bridge that's too low to pass under, so you can't miss it. The picnic area is also pretty obvious—it has picnic tables."

A few people chuckled.

Blaze fought with the mental picture of being brushed out of her canoe by a low bridge. Her banana-and-coffee breakfast churned in her stomach.

"Just before the picnic area is the one tricky spot on the route, the S-curve. There, it gets narrower and twists. To keep it exciting, there are two trees that decided to come down, like, in the curvy part. Just stick to the middle and you'll be fine. 'Kay?"

Most definitely not.

"Thanks so much." Ray, one of the Branching Out leaders, shook the guide's hand.

Why were they even called guides? They weren't joining the group on the stream. The vans that carried the group and all the canoes and kayaks to the launch rumbled to life, and the last guide scrambled inside with a jaunty wave. Moments later, she was officially stranded—no way forward but the boats.

She trailed the others toward the water. Carter and his friends were already out of sight. Sydney and some high school students launched next. Anson stood at the water's edge, getting kids settled into canoes and assigning leaders to pairings.

The group dwindled, and the knots in Blaze's stomach cinched tighter and tighter.

"I want to ride with Amelia *and* Hadley." Mercy's voice sounded distant, as if Blaze's head was under a pillow.

"Sorry, but you girls are going to have to split up." Anson dragged another canoe into place. "Only three people can ride in a canoe. Since you can't swim, Mercy, you'll have to stay with Blaze."

Mercy's laugh obliterated the imaginary pillow, and her next statement blared like a tornado siren. "Blaze can't swim or steer either." The girl hooked her thumbs in the straps of her life jacket and stuck one knobby knee to the side as she shifted her weight. "She's afraid of water."

Anson's gaze swung to Blaze. Hadn't he noticed her clinging to her life jacket for dear sanity when he'd polled the group? He rested his hands on his hips, near where his white T-shirt met his green swimming trunks. *Afraid?* He mouthed the question, as though subtlety were still an option.

She struggled to keep her chin up as memories of her nightmares made her shift her feet. In some of the dreams, seaweed encased her ankles and pulled her under. In others, fish attacked. Logically, neither thing would happen. Emotionally, she wasn't ready to risk it. She tugged her life vest tighter. Underneath, the waterproof pouch holding her phone bit into her collarbone.

Anson scanned the dwindling crowd at the canoe launch. Ray was about to push away from the sandy bank with two Branching Out students until Anson motioned him to stop. "Can you hang back?"

Anson, Ray, and Nolan talked among themselves, then Ray paddled away with the last two boys.

Hadley clung to Mercy. "Please, Pastor Anson? Let us stay together."

Mercy grabbed Amelia's hand. "I'll sit on the floor. I don't need a seat."

At least Mercy wasn't turning her back on the friend she'd invited.

Anson and Nolan exchanged a look.

Nolan nodded. "Mercy's the only one of them that can't swim, and they're all in life jackets."

"All right," Anson said. "But you three are going to have to listen to everything he tells you, okay?"

The girls cheered, but Blaze's stomach plummeted. This arrangement left Anson to ride alone with Blaze. As Nolan and the girls loaded up, she fiddled with the nylon strap on her life jacket. Kids under the age of thirteen were required to wear them. Blaze was the only non-Rooted paddler who hadn't stowed hers under her seat.

Anson hauled the last canoe as close to the water as he could with the girls still getting situated.

Blaze peered down at the metal seats. "I thought it wasn't important to know how to swim for this."

"A few places are too deep to stand. Besides, someone in each canoe has to know how to steer."

"It can't be that tricky."

"Better safe than sorry." He packed the remaining gear into the last canoe while Blaze eyed the road out. Hiking back to the outfitter's lodge would take a while, but she'd rather hike than drown. Why had she committed to this?

A squeal from Mercy drew Blaze's attention.

Nolan laughed as he wiggled in his seat, rocking the boat. "You don't like turbulence?"

Amelia gripped both sides, and Mercy and Hadley launched shrill objections. But their smiles told another story. If that had been her, Blaze would've insisted on a different escort.

"Okay, okay." Nolan quit rocking the boat and pushed them into the stream. "Smooth sailing from here, then."

Soon, they slid around a bend and out of sight.

The remaining canoe scraped as Anson dragged it into the water. His T-shirt pulled taut across his back and shoulders as he waded knee-deep, leaving only the point of the canoe on dry land. He dipped his chin, indicating the seat closest to him. "I'll keep it steady for you."

She pointed to the closer bench. "Why can't I sit on this side?"

"Because then you'd have to steer."

"Maybe I want to steer." She'd seen how far Mercy's boat tipped. She'd rather not traipse the length of the canoe.

He straightened, the canoe bobbing against his legs. "You don't know how."

"I'm sure you'll teach me."

His eyes narrowed. "You're afraid of water."

"So?"

"If you're afraid, you should want to be in the best possible hands."

His hands? Her breath fluttered with ... must be fear, because it certainly wasn't attraction. "Maybe I'd feel better if I were in control."

"Even if you don't know what you're doing?" The skepticism in his voice contrasted with the peaceful bird calls and trickling water.

She nodded once, more definitively than she felt.

Anson scoffed, but amusement lit his eyes. "That's a surefire way to fail."

He wasn't wrong. "Well, my name *is* Blaze. Surefire failure is kind of my thing."

His eyebrows lowered toward a scowl.

Better move things along before he dug into that. She stabbed her hands onto her hips. "This isn't just some point of male pride, is it? You're actually good at this?"

He laid a hand over his heart. "I, Anson Marsh, solemnly swear to protect you from the raging torrent that is Pine Gully Creek." The water sloshed as if to demand more respect. "Have I mentioned the person in back has to work harder? And in the front, you can enjoy the scenery instead of staring at the back of my head all day."

Did that mean he would be staring at the back of *her* head all day? She chewed her lip and eyed the canoe. He'd better pay more attention to the water than her head.

Anson waved her forward. "Come on, or we'll never catch up to the group." He bent, grasping the bow of the canoe. "It's going to wobble, but I won't let it tip."

If he did, she was out of here. The sand sucked at her

slides as she stepped into the cool water. When she lifted her foot to get in the boat, the flap of her sandal flung water across Anson's seat. She sucked in a breath and waited for a reprimand.

Instead, he nodded like he'd expected it and motioned her forward. "It's most stable when you keep a low center of gravity."

She crouched so her hands hovered above either side of the canoe and crept ahead. Anson maintained his hold on the bow. As she stepped over her seat and into the nose of the boat, her shin brushed his thumb.

He released his hold suddenly, and the boat rocked. She plopped onto the bench. Was there ... a problem?

He sloshed to the shore. A moment later, he returned with a paddle. "Hold it like this. And paddle like this." He reached the paddle forward, then drew it back. "Keep your body upright in your seat and reach with your arms, then twist your core. Nothing crazy or we'll capsize."

"You promised we wouldn't."

"No." His voice rumbled low. "I promised to protect you from the river. That includes if we capsize, but I can't protect you from yourself. If you do gymnastics up here, you'll tip us."

"Gymnastics? You're seriously overestimating my athleticism."

He eyed her. Usually, she didn't mind having some curves, but the life jacket wasn't doing her any favors. Neither were her pasty legs. Not that it mattered what Anson thought. He had a girlfriend who'd looked tanned and toned in her athletic shorts and tank top.

Shaking his head, he handed over the paddle. A moment later, the boat tipped treacherously as he hopped in. She squawked, but he didn't apologize. With one last scrape of sand against the hull, the canoe glided into the stream.

She stuck her paddle in the water and attempted her first stroke. Awkward. She tried the other side. Also uncomfortable. She switched back, so her dominant hand was closest to the blade and tried to find a rhythm. Not easy when her arms tired quickly and she had to keep switching sides.

Anson didn't correct her as they navigated the center of the waterway, so she must be doing something right. Like leaves falling from a tree, her fears dropped one by one and the gentle creek carried them away.

"We make a good team," she said.

He didn't answer.

"Right?" She twisted to see him.

He nodded once. "We get by."

Her nightmares had been unfounded. Gliding down the stream was a kind of peaceful way to see Creation from a new perspective. She dipped her paddle back into the creek and hummed a worship song.

BLAZE HAD the voice of an angel.

The thought wasn't theologically sound. Nonetheless, it circled through Anson's brain.

Blaze didn't perform Christian music with The Signalmen. Today, though, perched in the bow of the canoe, she sang his favorite worship song. The quiet tones resonated, true and clear. Forget that he didn't have anything special for a voice. He could hardly breathe for how badly he wanted to sing along.

He also longed to ask about her nickname. Maybe she'd

tell the story if he offered to share a secret of his own. She'd probably scoff, disbelieving he had any. Boy, would she be surprised.

He longed for that too—to share the shocking parts of his story.

But they were in sight of Nolan, Mercy, and her friends now. The conversation he wanted required privacy.

Besides, baring his soul to Blaze would be unfaithful to Sydney. He already felt guilty. When her leg brushed his thumb earlier, the flare had shot through every cell in his body. Blaze lived up to her nickname—proximity to her was like standing next to a wildfire. The flames had died immediately, but it was all wrong.

His relationship with Sydney was more like a campfire. Enjoyable and useful. Healthy. He had no business wandering off toward a wildfire. At the picnic spot, he would assign Blaze to another leader and focus on the students.

For the thousandth time, Blaze switched her paddle from one side of the canoe to the other. For the thousandth time, he adjusted his stroke to keep them on course. They'd come to the deeper, narrower part of the creek. He couldn't see the bottom. Based on how eagerly the nose of the canoe veered as they rounded a curve, the current pulled harder here too.

"What do you know about ADHD?"

Even her speaking voice had a soothing quality to it. He forced himself to concentrate on the content of the question instead of the melody. "Some basics. Kids with it can't sit still or pay attention."

"Turns out, it's more complex than that. Have you ever heard of rejection sensitive dysphoria?"

"Should I have?"

"RSD is common among people with ADHD, which isn't

just a kid thing, by the way. RSD is when someone is extremely sensitive to correction or rejection. Small things have a huge emotional impact."

She must have Mercy in mind. Ahead of them, the girl pointed at some dead trees that nearly blocked the stream as it turned. While talking to Carter, he'd missed the outfitter's routine speech about the S-curve, but he'd heard it on other trips. Soon, they'd reach the beach. In the meantime, he'd do his best to navigate a conversation that was at least as tricky as this section of the creek. "I don't think sensitivity is the determining factor in diagnosis. I can always tell if Tate hasn't had his meds because he can't stop moving. He literally bounces off the walls."

"Boys are different," Blaze said. "Girls are more likely to have the inattentive type, which can come across as chatty, distracted, forgetful, or even depressed."

"Mercy's depressed?"

"No ..." Blaze drew out the word. "But she is chatty, distracted, and forgetful. Three out of four is a lot. One of her teachers suggested it. ADHD would explain some things, like how hard it is to get her to do her homework and chores and her friendship troubles."

Speaking of chatty. Thankfully, she forgot to paddle while talking. Following Nolan's approach, Anson guided the canoe toward the right bank to avoid the first tree. Getting around the second would require a quick left.

Mercy's teacher must've had reasons to mention ADHD, but it wasn't the only possibility. "At age eleven, those are all pretty common problems to have."

Blaze glanced back, a frown tipping the corner of her mouth.

"I'm not saying it's impossible. I don't know her like you do."

The current flowed through the branches of the second tree and vied to take them with. He dragged his paddle to veer left. She returned to paddling—switching sides again. He compensated by lowering his paddle farther into the water.

The navigable waterway between the branches was only a few feet across. Hadley called out complaints when Nolan cut a little close to the tip of the second tree.

Blaze's silence didn't seem good. "Why do you want it to be ADHD?" he asked.

"You know what I said about being a surefire failure?" She rested her paddle across the bow and swatted at an insect. "That was ... It's just that things are hard for both of us in some of the same ways. I don't think it's a lack of effort. I'd like some explanation besides that we're not cut out for li —" She shrieked and bolted to her feet.

Her paddle flew into the stream. The canoe lurched. He leaned the opposite way but couldn't right it. With a cry, she splashed into the creek shoulder first. A second later, cold liquid engulfed him. He fought to the surface. He had a promise to keep.

11

Blaze sputtered, suspended in the murky water. The life vest kept her head above the surface, but panic seeped into her lungs.

The current nudged her toward the branches of one of the dead trees. She kicked, desperate to go the other way. Didn't work. Her foot struck something hard. Then pain stabbed her other knee. Underwater branches?

A soft object slid against her thigh, and she screamed. Jerking away, she jabbed the sole of her foot into something pointy.

This was a nightmare come true. She had to get out. *Now.* Panting, she flailed her arms, but there was nothing to grab onto. *God, please.*

She kicked again and hit something solid but not painful. The object pressed against her back. Something had wrapped around her. She swatted to push it off.

"Easy. You're okay." Anson's breath warmed her wet ear.

He was holding her. Solid, calm, and ready to make good on his vow.

Her lungs sucked in their first full breath since she'd hit the water. "Thank God."

His free arm stirred a wave. He kicked—somehow without hitting her—and his body tipped back, bringing her along. Two powerful strokes later, her feet cleared the branches. He shifted, facing her backward as the current bumped their upside-down canoe against the fallen tree.

If not for Anson, she'd be stuck there too, probably trying to figure out how to climb to shore without impaling herself on the tree. She wrapped her hands around his arm. Between her fingers, hair bleached blond by the sun glimmered. His wet skin covered firm muscles. How difficult was it to haul another person through the water?

His body shifted again, and her leg dragged against the bottom. Before she got her bearings, he propped her into a seated position on the sand, water lapping around her arms.

Anson kept a hand on her shoulder as he crouched in front of her, panting. Rivulets ran from his hair down his cheeks. His shirt was plastered to a masculine chest that did indeed look like it belonged to someone who could drag a drowning person from a river. "Can you stand up?"

An involuntary shiver coursed through her. The wasp stings that had caused her to jump throbbed, as did the bottom of her foot. Nothing hurt so badly as to prevent her from rising. She just ... needed a minute.

Vegetation crowded the bank, and brown water stirred around her legs. What had brushed past her before Anson caught up? Seaweed? A catfish? Despite the unknown, she knew one fact with certainty: She'd felt completely safe in Anson's arms.

Cheering registered—the kids, at the edge of the sandy

beach. Everyone had seen her tip the canoe. Humiliation heated her cheeks like a sunburn.

"Everyone okay?" Nolan splashed toward them, Mercy close behind.

"Yeah." Blaze rubbed the tender sole of her foot. The skin didn't feel broken. Fading adrenaline left her feeling weak, but she was okay. Physically. Her emotions might as well be white-water rafting. As if simultaneous relief and embarrassment weren't disorienting enough, something more than gratitude toward Anson swirled in her core.

As Nolan and Mercy neared, Anson stood and extended his hand toward her without making eye contact.

She accepted the offer, but he still didn't look at her. As soon as she balanced on her shaky legs, he stepped away and wiped his hand on his dripping shorts. As if Blaze were dirtier than the grit in the water.

He had a right to be annoyed.

"You did warn me about gymnastics in the canoe." She smiled apologetically, but he didn't look.

"You missed your calling." Nolan clapped Anson's shoulder.

Mercy threw an arm around Blaze's waist and rested her head against the life jacket in a side hug. "I was so scared."

Finally, Anson glanced at her out of the corner of his eye. "What happened?"

"A wasp. I think it got me more than once." She tipped her leg. Like something out of a sci-fi movie, the blood vessels in a four-inch circle had reddened on her thigh. The area itched and stung.

"Are you allergic?" Anson checked over his shoulder, toward the overturned canoe. The first aid kit had been inside. Was anything in it still useable?

"I've never had an allergic reaction to a sting, so I think I'm okay there."

Mercy burrowed closer. "I thought you were going to die."

Blaze squeezed her. "The life jacket did its job, and I was with a good swimmer." She risked meeting Anson's blue eyes—a sincere expression of gratitude required it. "Thank you."

He exhaled visibly. Under the clinging shirt, that didn't take much.

When a subject interested her, Blaze became obsessive. She'd spent hours reading up on ADHD, for example. Now, she felt the force of that attention tipping toward Anson.

She could not allow him to become her next obsession.

He motioned them toward the beach. Arm still around Mercy, Blaze obeyed. Judging by the splashing behind her, the men followed.

"Since you're soaked anyway, want to swim out and get the canoe?" Nolan asked. "Between the two of us, we could handle it."

"I'd rather use the kayaks."

"If only they were here."

Blaze scanned the little beach. A couple of students tossed a football in waist-deep water. Others milled around the beached canoes and the picnic tables. Not one kayak in sight.

"Where are they?" Frustration deepened Anson's voice.

"Dunno. It seems they didn't stop."

"Have you tried their cell phones?" Anson asked.

"Not yet."

"Could you? Mine's in my backpack."

"Which is where?" Nolan drew the question out.

Blaze held her breath. She'd feel terrible if Anson lost or wrecked his phone because of her.

"Clipped to the back handle of the canoe. It's in a sealed plastic bag."

Nolan sucked in a breath. "We ought to get that sooner than later."

"If Carter isn't here in ten minutes, we'll swim. We'll have to watch the branches, though. One of them got me pretty good."

Blaze glanced back to say she'd hit one too. The words drowned in her mouth when she spotted a trickle of blood running from the side of Anson's knee and disappearing into the stream. She hadn't hit anything that hard, but she hadn't been kicking hard enough to move two bodies either. "I'm really sorry."

Anson shook his head. "Forget it."

Could she? He was upset with her. Or perhaps he was just in pain.

Sydney met her at the edge of the beach with an open towel. The kindness jabbed her harder than the underwater tree had. Not only had she dumped someone else's boyfriend in the river, she had the nerve to feel attracted to him.

Unacceptable. She would not crush on someone else's boyfriend.

ANSON REREAD CARTER'S TEXT. *Relax. We didn't stop at the picnic spot. See you at the end.*

Well, the group was at the end, and Carter wasn't. Neither were any of his friends. As the first set of students, leaders, and their canoes loaded up for the outfitter's lodge, Anson texted again. *Where are you?*

Right behind you.

Behind? He took the path from the lot to the creek. Tall grass encroached on the walkway and dragged against his gouged knee. A low bridge spanned the water to his right. To his left, the stream glistened around a bend.

A hand smoothed across his back, and Sydney stopped beside him. "What did he say?"

"They got behind us somewhere." Anson clenched his jaw. "The only way I can imagine that is if they went on shore, kayaks and all, somewhere other than the picnic spot."

"You'll get to the bottom of it." Sydney rubbed his back, and guilt filled him. He never should've gotten in a canoe with Blaze. As she'd gained her bearings on shore, the trust in her eyes sent satisfaction swinging through him like a wrecking ball headed for his relationship with Sydney.

He refused to be controlled by emotions, no matter how powerful. Sydney deserved better from him, and she'd get it. His interactions with Blaze would be strictly business. If she needed individual help, he'd delegate. Attending her shows once a week wouldn't do either.

"There." Sydney pointed. The nose of a kayak came around the bend.

Carter grinned. "Hello!"

His friends, as they came into view, shifted in their kayaks and avoided eye contact. Sydney squeezed Anson's arm then headed back to the group, giving him space to deal with the students.

Carter ran his kayak into the ground at Anson's feet. The boy stepped into the stream and wobbled.

Anson grabbed the kayak handle and pulled the boat onto the dirt trail. "How did you get behind us?"

Carter leaned on his paddle as he straightened his T-shirt. "Isn't exploring the point of trips like these?" He found his footing and collected his backpack from the kayak. It clanked as he slung it over his shoulder. He stepped around the kayak and into the tall grass, using the paddle like a walking stick as he started for the van. When he passed Anson, the smell of sweat and alcohol wafted off him. Carter's stumble and the noise in the backpack assumed new meaning.

Anson's grip on the kayak tightened into a fist. "What's in your bag, Carter?"

"Nothing." He hiked it higher on his shoulder.

Anson abandoned the kayak and followed Carter to the parking lot. "I can smell it on your breath. Show me what's in the bag."

Dylan ran across the lot toward them. Anson raised a hand to stop him, but the boy ignored the signal.

"You can't make me," Carter said.

"The truth is, I don't—"

Dylan yanked the bag off his brother's shoulder.

Carter yelled, and Dylan darted off.

"—have to." Anson muttered the last two words. Smelling alcohol on a student's breath was enough proof to require Anson to take action.

Dylan swerved around Sydney before ducking behind the van. Carter bowled into her. The pair tumbled to the ground. Carter climbed to his feet as Sydney checked her hands.

Anson jogged over to help her up. "Are you okay?"

"Yeah." She frowned at Carter.

An object arced over the van and landed with a clank. A second UFO flew after it. Silver and the size of hockey pucks —crushed aluminum cans.

"That's enough, Dylan," Anson said.

One last projectile tumbled to the ground and skidded to a stop between Anson and Carter. Anson didn't need to straighten the can to recognize the beer logo. Carter shifted unsteadily. His friends came up the path, carrying the kayaks. A guide met them and grabbed Carter's kayak. They followed him to the trailer.

Dylan trotted back, holding the backpack like the spoils of war. "They were drinking! I knew something was up!"

Anson motioned to the vehicle. "Wait in the van, Dylan."

Sydney touched Anson's arm in a silent show of support, then accompanied Dylan into the van. Once the doors were shut, Anson walked several yards away. Carter followed without prompting.

His friends tried to get in the van, but Sydney met them at the door and sent them back. They plodded over and stopped behind Carter. Anson recognized one of the boys from basketball tryouts. The girl had attended Branching Out with Carter last Sunday. Anson hadn't met the last two boys—identical twins—until they showed up with permission slips.

"Who wants to tell me what happened?" Anson asked.

Carter kicked the dirt.

Twin One smirked. "If I tell you, will you put in a good word for me with Blaze?"

Dumbfounded, Anson grunted.

The kid pressed a palm to his chest. "I'm eighteen."

The girl smacked him. "He's not going to set you up with his girlfriend."

"Blaze is not my girlfriend."

"Really? Well, you're super cute together." She lifted her phone. "My friend posted a video of your amazing rescue."

There was a video? Worry wound through his chest, but no video could've captured the rush he'd gotten from helping Blaze. He shouldn't be letting the kids sidetrack him. "If you don't want to take this opportunity to tell your side of the story, that's fine. I'll—"

"At least we were going to recycle and not litter." Twin Two grinned.

"Is this a game to you?" That was a reaction, not a measured response.

"What are you going to do?" Carter lifted his chin. "Tell us we can't come back? Without us, you'll never hit your goal."

Anger hardened in Anson's throat. He thought Carter respected him more than that. Maybe it was the alcohol talking. Maybe desperation. Maybe both.

"I'm calling all of your parents."

Carter stepped closer, shoulders back and arms tense. "My dad will never believe you."

"He won't have much of a choice. And you know what else this means, right?"

"You're going to lose your job?"

Anson's frustration mounted. "I am going to talk to your parents"—he scanned the group so they'd know no one was getting off the hook—"and report this to the administration."

Carter's eyebrows drew together. "What administration?"

"The school's. I'm not just your youth pastor. I'm also your basketball coach. The penalty for drinking is a six-week suspension from practice and games."

One of the twins stepped back, mouth gaping and eyes wide. He must be an athlete too.

Carter sputtered. "It's not even basketball season."

"Doesn't have to be. If you're not participating in any extracurriculars now, the suspension kicks in the next time you go out for one."

"But I'm your best player. I'm a senior. I'm up for scholarships!"

"Then don't rack up any other alcohol violations. Scholarship committees don't tend to favor them."

"My dad isn't going to let you do this." Carter's voice cracked.

"It's not up to him. The administration will hold a hearing where you can explain yourself before they decide the outcome." What happened on the church level was another question. The board, including Eric Newsome, would want a say. "Get in the van."

He waited until the students had complied, then he collected the cans from the ground and returned them to the backpack. This wasn't the Carter he'd built a relationship with all these years. This was someone else entirely. Someone far too similar to Anson's brother.

12

The next morning, Anson stared down at the familiar pattern on the plastic container that waited outside his office. Reluctantly, he picked it up from the floor, then let himself inside his office. He popped the lid, and the aroma of peanut butter confirmed Blaze had left the cookies. But why?

They were already as close as he was willing to get—closer, even. He hadn't crossed a line, but accepting spontaneous gifts inched closer to the boundary. He'd make the gift less personal by sharing it with the youth.

He plucked the card from inside the container. *Thanks for the assist yesterday. Blaze*

A simple thank-you, not some loaded effort to deepen a relationship. His relief washed out in a quick exhale.

"No student should've been left unsupervised, especially not long enough to throw a party in the woods."

At the voice behind him, Anson's chest bound up again. Eric had taken yesterday's news of Carter's misbehavior quietly. Anson had hoped that meant Eric would endorse the consequences and levy some of his own. Apparently not.

He prayed for wisdom as he set the cookies on the desk and turned to face his accuser. "Carter disobeyed my instructions to stay in sight of the lead canoe."

Eric stood in the doorway. "Kids will be kids. You should've anticipated that."

"The permission slip specifies that students are responsible for following directions, respecting leaders, and obeying all applicable laws. Carter violated all three."

Eric's face reddened. "If anyone else had done this, you wouldn't be banning them from everything. This stinks of a personal vendetta."

Anson crossed his arms and half-sat on the edge of his desk. "The consequences are the same for all the students involved. They're all sitting out for the next special event unless a parent attends with them, and I emailed the school about the situation."

"It was not a school issue. It was a church event. A poorly run one at that."

"There was nothing wrong with how we ran the event. We had plenty of leaders—"

Eric sliced his hands through the air. "You had *distractions*, not leaders. One was your girlfriend. Another was so unqualified, she had to be fished from the river. It's a wonder nothing worse happened."

Anson let the space of three breaths pass. With each inhale, his knee-jerk defensiveness ebbed until he could issue a productive reply. "Everyone on that trip will confirm Sydney was not a distraction. As for Blaze, she came to relate with the kids, which she did. If your son had stayed with us and acted in the spirit of the event like she did, we wouldn't be having this conversation."

"You don't like the mandate to increase youth group attendance. You're retaliating through my son."

"I assure you, that is not the case." Interesting that he brought up grudges, though, as Eric seemed to have one of his own.

A vein protruded from Eric's neck. "No one in the history of this church has reported to the school administration. The church is independent and its own authority."

"God is the authority, and His concerns for justice go beyond what we do in this building. Carter and his friends set a bad example to the other students on the trip. And it wouldn't be fair to my other athletes to turn a blind eye to an alcohol violation committed right in front of me. Teenage drinking has serious consequences, the least problematic of which are the ones issued by churches and schools."

"Meaning what?"

"Kids die." He felt sick just saying it.

Eric recoiled, then scoffed. "Kids act out. It's up to the adults to respond well. Your actions only make it more likely that he'll hide his behavior in the future."

"He was already trying to hide it."

At Anson's quiet response, Eric backed toward the exit, but then paused. "With this attitude, I won't have to worry about you much longer. You'll never get the numbers, and that's all the cause I need. And what will the school say when their star athlete doesn't come back this year?"

Anson imagined they'd say good riddance. The principal wouldn't give in to Eric's bullying. Before his last conversation with Greg, Anson had had as much confidence in the church. Now, he could only pray for the strength to stand or fall by his convictions.

Forgetting something?

Blaze frowned at Marissa's text. She left work a couple of hours ago, had dinner with Mercy, and … she jerked away from her computer. The Depot. How could she have forgotten her Monday night performance? Singing was the highlight of her week.

"Mercy! Are you ready?" Without saving the document she'd been filling out, she abandoned the desk in the living room and ran to the mud room. She snatched her purse from a hook. "We need to be there!"

A muffled reply sounded from the lower level.

Blaze jammed her feet into her shoes. She'd contacted the school's recommended behavioral health department and set Mercy's intake interview for Wednesday. They'd promptly sent a twenty-one-page new patient form. Blaze hadn't realized she'd have that much paperwork to do in the next two days—or that she'd get so engrossed.

"Mercy?"

The girl clopped into the room, her blue purse in hand, a book under her arm, and shoes half on her feet. With a couple of shuffles, the backs popped up over her heels. "Ready."

The girl knew the drill. They'd rushed out the door this way a million times.

Thirteen minutes later, Blaze waited in the wings as Philip finished a song. Her boss usually preferred to stay in the background, but he had a more-than-passable singing voice. The crowd's applause signaled their agreement.

He spotted her and leaned close to the mic once more. "And now, the singer I know you've all been waiting for. Give it up for Blaze Astley!" He waved his farewell and retreated to his usual spot as cheers—more enthusiastic than Blaze expected—welcomed her.

She closed her fingers around the mic. "Thank you. You're very kind."

She strained against the stage lights to identify her outspoken fans. Over at her usual table, Sydney clapped along with the crowd. A couple of women sat with her. No Anson.

A swell of disappointment, followed by guilt, hardened her diaphragm. She forced a deep breath as the band started a song. She couldn't pine after someone else's man. Especially someone as kind and thoughtful as Sydney.

Two model citizens, when Anson and Sydney got married and had kids, they'd be the poster family for the American dream.

On her cue, Blaze came in. She'd sung the song dozens of times, so after a few bars, her thoughts returned to Anson.

Maybe she didn't have feelings for him. Maybe what she really wanted was the kind of life he modeled. She wanted to be dependable, do more in the community, stay on top of things, and not have to scramble every day of her life. She wanted a life not defined by a generational curse.

Sydney fit that description as well as Anson did. Maybe if Blaze befriended her, some of Sydney's good traits would rub off, and Blaze's foolish heart would drop this interest in Anson.

Between sets, Blaze first stopped to say good night to

Mercy. Marissa always took her home about halfway through the show so she could get to bed at a reasonable time. As they left, Blaze approached Sydney's table.

Blaze recognized the women on either side of Sydney from around town—Madison and Honor. Based on how often she saw them together at Monday shows, the three must be close.

Sydney smiled at her. "You sound great up there. How're you doing?"

"My muscles ache more today than yesterday, if that's possible." Blaze rolled her shoulder. "How about you?"

"Oh, I'm good." Sydney motioned to an empty chair. "Take a load off. You amaze me every week, standing all night in heels."

"I guess we all have our talents." Blaze took the seat beside Honor. "So. Girls' night?"

"It wasn't planned that way." Sydney sipped her soda.

"I'm newly single." Honor's blue eyes seemed to hold determination.

"And better for it," Madison said.

"Yeah. I don't know why I ...." Honor shook her head, and her blond hair swung. "Sometimes only hindsight shows you how far off course you let things go."

Sydney rubbed Honor's back, her silence packed with compassion. After a couple of seconds, she refocused on Blaze. "And Anson's at the gym, blowing off steam. There was drama with some of the kids from the canoe trip."

Blaze nodded. She heard about the drinking, but not what had been done about it.

Madison leaned closer to Sydney. "Unless he wants you to think he's at the gym. Maybe he's off making elaborate anniversary plans."

"Anniversary?" Blaze tried to remember when she'd first seen Sydney and Anson together but came up blank. "Congratulations. How long?"

"A year since our first date. We came here, actually. To one of your shows."

Madison laughed. "As if that counts. You both came here regularly before you started dating."

Sydney cracked a smile. "But that night, we held hands."

Madison snorted. "Which is as steamy as you two get."

Honor grinned. "Will that change after he proposes, or are you saving kissing along with everything else for after the vows?"

"Stop it." Sydney pressed the back of her hand to her cheek. "We kiss."

Madison crossed her arms with a smug smile. "Not that I've seen."

Not that Blaze had seen either. Maybe that was why she kept having to remind herself Anson was off the market.

Sydney opened her mouth, but then bit her bottom lip.

Blaze had to help her out. She'd never forget the searing shame of being caught making out with her boyfriend outside the high school. Maybe Anson and Sydney were on to something. "Discretion is underrated," Blaze said.

Honor grunted. "And you know what? Maybe kissing's *over*rated."

Madison gasped and pressed a hand to her chest. "Jimmy did a number on you. There's nothing quite like a good kiss. Right?" She nudged Sydney with her elbow.

Sydney pursed her smiling lips and shook her head, refusing to comment.

Madison braced a hand on the table. "When a kiss is all fireworks and thrills and ... and safety. Does that sound weird? Because I think that's key. Safety in the midst of all the exhilaration. *That's* when you've got a keeper."

Sydney chuckled, and Blaze knew she ought to laugh, but her lungs refused to cooperate. The last time she'd felt safe, she'd been in Anson's arms. But she was simply grateful she hadn't drowned. That was all she felt. Gratitude.

Time to stop obsessing about it. She smiled at Madison. "You're quite the romantic."

Smirking, Madison eyed Sydney, who sat a little too still with two fingers resting on her lips.

"If you *are* waiting for the proposal," Honor said, "then I bet Thursday's the day."

Sydney lowered her hand. "He has a meeting on Thursday. We're getting dinner on Saturday, but he hasn't said anything about special plans."

"That's even more of a sign." Madison stabbed the table with her index finger. "A guy like Anson doesn't forget an anniversary. I bet he hasn't said anything because he wants you to think he forgot so the proposal is more of a surprise."

"You're crazy." Sydney laughed, but as Madison focused on other topics, Sydney's expression sobered, and she withdrew from the conversation.

Blaze wanted to ask why she'd turned so thoughtful, but they weren't that good of friends. She checked the time, then rose to get back on stage. "I'm sure you two will have a wonderful anniversary. Congrats."

13

"Can't avoid me forever, Carter." Anson clapped his hands and held them up, requesting the basketball.

Carter and Dylan had skipped Branching Out on Sunday after Eric's visit to his office. However, Anson knew Carter's passion for basketball would bring him to the community center's courts eventually, so Anson stopped by daily. Finally, on Saturday morning, one week after the canoe trip, Anson's repeated trips to check for him paid off.

Carter turned his back to Anson and lined up a shot. "I'm all set for the basketball season." The ball swished through the hoop. "Or I will be, before November."

Anson rebounded the ball and dribbled out past the three-point line. "What does that mean?"

"I joined the crew for the fall theater production with Dylan. Six weeks of working on the set will replace the suspension." Carter guarded him lazily.

Anson scored. "School administration approved that?"

Carter claimed the ball. "Yeah."

Anson followed him to the three-point line. Carter's plan would be time-consuming, but less punishing for him than a basketball suspension.

"Are you mad?" Carter dribbled once.

"Nope. Not about the compromise, anyway."

"Then what are you upset about?"

"That you were drinking at all."

"You never drank in high school?" Carter attempted a misdirection.

If Anson hadn't taught him the move in the first place, it might have worked. "Nope."

"Not even once?" Carter took his shot.

Anson tipped it away from the basket. "Nope. Own it before it owns you."

"Let me guess. Another Coach Voss quote?"

"Yup."

"Nothing owns me."

"Being benched could've been detrimental to scholarship offers. Letting alcohol affect your dreams gives it an awful lot of control." When Carter had made the varsity team as a freshman, his dad started boasting that Carter would play for a Division I team. Anson warned them of the steep odds, but it'd still been hard to watch time pass without an offer. At this point, if Carter wanted to play college ball, they needed to focus on a broader range of basketball programs.

"We've got some promising leads."

Promising to Eric, maybe. Anson held the ball outside the three-point line, suspending the game. "If you keep drinking, you're going to run into this problem again, only the consequences will be harsher. Then you'll have fewer options. If something goes wrong, it could impact the rest of your life, not just a basketball season."

Carter motioned him to get going.

Anson spun around him for a layup. They focused on the game until Anson gained a six-point lead. "What's the draw?"

Carter dribbled near the free-throw line. "Playing."

"Not that. What's the draw of drinking?"

Carter took the shot. Missed.

Anson rebounded. "Behavior like yours suggests you wanted to get caught. Is something going on that you need help with?"

His cheeks were splotchy from the workout, so it was hard to tell if he flushed at the question. "No."

"Then help me understand where you're coming from."

Carter shook his head.

Anson made another drive for the net. Carter moved in to steal the ball and rammed his elbow into Anson's cheek. Pain fired from the point of contact. He raised his arms, stopping the game as he blinked to clear his vision. He ran his tongue over the inside of his cheek and tasted blood.

Carter cringed. "Sorry."

"You were meant for more than this, Carter."

"Like what?"

"Kids follow your lead. That charisma is a gift from God. He had a reason for giving it to you, and it wasn't so you'd host parties on youth group trips."

"You're gonna say it's for youth group?"

"Maybe. But I also hope you'll lead the team to state this year."

Carter scoffed. "Is this about God or not? Because no way He cares about basketball."

"'So, whether you eat or drink, or whatever you do, do all to the glory of God.'" Anson paused to let the Bible verse sink in. "If we can eat or drink for His glory, we can play basketball for it. Sports teach us discipline, teamwork, and our own limitations. If we let God work with us through that process, powerful things happen."

"Like we win state?"

"Like whether we win or not, we can be fulfilled. God does that—not championships, not scholarships, and definitely not underage drinking."

Carter turned his face away.

Anson shot up a prayer for wisdom. "You're not invincible. Alcohol can make mundane circumstances dangerous. Take the canoe trip. What if you'd fallen in the water? I know from experience that it's disorienting to be dumped into the water, and swimming fully clothed in a current is challenging enough. You stumbled as you walked, and you weren't wearing your life vest."

"I would've been fine."

"That's what people tell themselves, but trust me. They're not always fine." When Anson had told Gury to be careful, he'd laughed. That was Anson's last memory of him.

Carter should know.

Anson hated reliving the story, hated his part in it. If logic wasn't enough to reach Carter, why would sharing about Gury change anything?

Carter studied him for a long moment. The overhead fans hummed. Laughing kids ran past the door. The prompt to share about Gury might've come from God. Anson's mouth went dry.

Carter rolled his eyes. "That's why you're worried about

me. You think I'm going to die, and you don't think I'm going to heaven."

Anson steadied himself with a slow breath. "I wouldn't want to walk through life or death without Jesus. I don't wish that on you either."

Carter shrugged, then his mouth tightened. "Sorry about your face."

Anson chuckled. "Looks that bad?"

"Nah. A little red."

Anson touched the tender spot. Warm, but superficial. It probably wouldn't even bruise, though he'd be biting the raised spot inside his cheek for a week. "I'll survive. Just promise to think about what I said."

Another shrug.

Pushing harder would get nowhere. Anson retrieved the ball from where it'd settled against the wall, restarted the game, and left the rest to the Lord.

"REMEMBER, it's possible—likely, even—that we'll have to try more than one medication and dosage before we find the right fit. Be sure to reach out if any side effects become too problematic." The doctor, a smartly dressed woman in her fifties, spared Mercy a sympathetic smile before passing Blaze yet another print-off. "Do you have any questions before you go?"

Blaze shook her head. After the initial behavioral health appointment and a round of assessments, they'd come in for this follow-up. Now, Mercy had her diagnosis. ADHD. Blaze had been so focused on getting them this far, she'd failed to read up on treatments. She would have to study the papers before she knew what questions to ask.

She put her arm around Mercy as they shuffled out of the clinic. Well, Blaze shuffled. Mercy bounced.

"As soon as the drugs work, I'm going to be normal like everybody else?"

Blaze's lungs deflated. "You think you're different?"

"Well, yeah. I can't ever remember stuff. Nobody else knows all the office ladies like I do because I'm always in there calling you. And sometimes people aren't real nice about it, like I'm doing it on purpose or something. But I'm not. I'm just different, and now I don't have to be, right?"

Blaze rubbed the center of her chest, but the ache didn't ease. "I didn't realize you felt that way."

"Don't you?" Mercy broke away from her and skipped sideways. "You forget stuff too. It's, like, our family thing. Mom used to forget a lot too."

The ache anchored in her heart. Mom had forgotten things, sure, but addiction was the most obvious cause of her problems.

Mercy tugged Blaze's hand. "When can I start?"

"The medicine?"

She nodded.

Blaze swallowed. Alcohol and drugs had done such damage to their family. Now medication to alter Mercy's mental state was the prescribed answer? She'd steered the doctor away from stimulants, but the thought of putting Mercy on any medication constricted her ribs.

Would lifestyle changes alone be enough? The pamphlets outlined dozens of strategies for coping with ADHD. If only the changes weren't so severe. Like, how in the world would they avoid all food dyes? Many Oaks didn't have a natural foods grocery store.

Help me know what to do, Lord.

The only next step that came to mind was to keep their Wednesday night commitment. "Right now, we need to get home and eat so we can get to Rooted." Blaze unlocked the car, and they piled in. "Remember, the doctor said it's going to take time for the changes we make to make a difference."

"So the sooner I start the drugs, the better." Mercy's seatbelt clicked.

"Let's call it medication, okay?"

"Okay. So, tonight?"

If only distractedness would kick in now. Blaze steered out of the lot. "I need time to research treatments and pray about what we should do. Medicine is only one option. And you heard the doctor. The prescription can have side effects. Things might get worse before they get better. If we start with other changes first, your symptoms might get better without the rough adjustment period."

"Like what changes?"

"Getting rid of food dye. Less sugar. Eating more home-cooked meals." Blaze's body rested heavily in the seat. As much as she enjoyed puttering around the kitchen, she didn't want the pressure of cooking as soon as she got home from work every day.

"Can we start that tonight? I want to be normal."

The sentiment echoed in Blaze's spirit. She'd already called her primary doctor's office for a referral to work toward her own diagnosis and treatment. According to the receptionist, her doctor could handle it, so Blaze scheduled an appointment. At least one step had been easy. "I need more time to think about medication, but we can start looking at nutrition labels."

The concession created a monster.

While Blaze heated their dinner, Mercy compared ingredient lists to one of the pamphlets and purged the pantry. By the time their chicken, pasta, and frozen vegetables were ready to eat, a pile of their favorite foods waited on the floor.

"There." Mercy fluffed open a garbage bag.

Blaze motioned her to stop and picked up a box of cereal. "What are you going to eat for breakfast if we throw this out?"

"I dunno. Toast?" Mercy eyed the dinner plate Blaze had filled for her. "None of that has dyes in it, right?"

"As far as I know." But considering the pile on the floor, she'd probably have to change her answer if she checked the label on the honey mustard dipping sauce. Thankfully, Mercy's mission hadn't reached the fridge where they stored it. Yet.

She took the garbage bag from her sister and set it aside so they could eat. During the meal, her attention kept wandering back to the pile. Some of her own favorites lay there. Plus, this food was expensive.

But to help herself and Mercy, she ought to get on board while her sister was still so excited about the bandwagon.

After dinner, she and Mercy sorted through the food on the floor. They would donate the unopened items to a food pantry. They carried the rest—minus some chocolate, a bag of chips, and a box of Blaze's favorite soda—to the trash can outside before heading to the church.

By the time they entered the youth room, Anson was already running through opening announcements for the ten students who'd come. Maybe they needed to offer more enticing food to increase attendance. Pizza? Although that was probably a processed food that could worsen Mercy's ADHD.

And perhaps Blaze's. If she had it.

The kids sprang up and dashed toward the hall, and she realized announcements had ended. Nolan went with the students.

Anson pulled an inflatable ball from the bottom shelf of the supply cabinet. Passing the ball from one hand to the other, he turned from the cabinet and froze upon seeing her lingering. "There a problem?"

So many problems. She could use an outside perspective, especially from someone with experience with kids, but he'd hardly said two words to her since the canoe trip, and he'd skipped both Monday shows since. Seemed a little extreme to avoid her for being clumsy. She shrugged and stepped into the hall.

But wasn't giving advice part of what pastors did? Anson cared about the students. He'd probably break his silence to help Mercy.

Blaze started for the gym at a slow pace, forcing him to catch up. Once he was beside her, she said, "Mercy was diagnosed with ADHD. Do you think putting her on medication right away is a bad idea?"

Anson's brow furrowed. "Medication isn't a choice to be made lightly."

"Exactly. It's just, she's struggling in a lot of ways. I don't know. All the implications and options and revelations are overwhelming. This whole time, I suspected we were the problem. Apparently, she did too. I never knew she thought that about herself. Now that I know it's a disorder, I don't know if I should be relieved or depressed. Especially since I think I might have it too."

He blew out a breath. "If those are the options, pick relieved."

Maybe that was wise.

Anson jogged ahead then, leaving her to walk alone past the sanctuary, offices, and kitchen. She scoffed. What was that? Two platitudes and then he bolted? His absence at her shows and his reluctance to talk to her couldn't be coincidence. Something had gone wrong.

If they were going to serve the youth together, she'd have to find out what.

14

Anson never had occasion to avoid one of his leaders before. Good thing, since youth group left him a sitting duck. Or, at the moment, a kneeling one. He reached under the couch to collect another remnant of the kids' unauthorized jellybean war.

The students had picked up the majority before heading out. Because of an early shift, Nolan had jumped ship when the students left.

Blaze, however, lingered. "Hey, girls, can you check the gym for my phone?" There was a theatrical flair to Blaze's voice as she addressed Hadley and Mercy.

Suspicious.

Likely happy to escape cleanup duty, the girls' incessant chatter faded as they trotted off.

Blaze didn't waste time once they were gone. "You can't be this mad over the canoe thing, can you?"

Since she was so determined to be unavoidable, he sat up.

Her hands rested on her hips. She wore a graphite, long-sleeved top that looked softer than anything he'd ever owned. "You're avoiding me," she said.

Not well enough. He lowered his head and stuck his arm back under the couch. "I'm focusing on my responsibilities." Including his responsibility to Sydney. His fingers touched a wrapper—one that didn't deflate under his touch. He dragged the item out. A granola bar, still sealed. With another sweep of his arm, he brought out a stash of candy, granola bars, an apple, a sports drink, and a soda. Nothing had been opened. Had someone stashed this on purpose?

"You never said thank you for the cookies." Hurt wove through her tone.

"Thank you. They were unnecessary but good. The students said so too." He scanned for other stray items. Something as large as a couch cushion blocked the light near his feet.

"The students said they were unnecessary?"

She had a point. He could keep his distance and still be polite. He abandoned his treasure hunt to smile at her. "Good—we all thought they were good."

"*You were stung by a wasp, Blaze.*" She'd lowered the pitch of her voice. Was that supposed to be him? "*What happened was completely understandable. And by the way, ADHD makes a lot of sense. I'm glad you're pursuing the help you and Mercy need to thrive.*"

He rubbed his forehead. Sure, he could've said those things. Part of him had wanted to, even. But how close was too close? She was a wildfire, after all. "Sounds like you don't need me for anything."

Blaze huffed. "One of Sydney's friends made you out to

be this insightful, evolved man, but you're like all the rest, aren't you?"

A pit of discomfort opened in his gut. "Why were you talking to Sydney's friends about me?"

She sighed and straightened the chairs. "They were at The Depot wondering what you would do for your anniversary."

"Anniversary?"

Her hands froze as she turned wide eyes toward him. "You didn't forget, did you?"

He and Sydney had been dating since last September. Just over a year ago. He schooled his features and took the deepest breath he could without giving away his panic. How had he forgotten? If Blaze was to be believed, no one else had.

"One of them thought you'd propose. I guess Sydney was wise not to buy it."

Propose? Shock rocked him forward. He covered by reaching under the couch for the final item. Given his intentions of eventually marrying Sydney, the idea should've occurred to him. He wasn't about to dissect why it hadn't with Blaze, of all people. He tugged at the large object by his feet.

An all-too-familiar wad of fabric slid out from under the couch.

"Is that a sleeping bag?" She left the last chair askew as she approached him. "What is all that?"

An excellent question. The only church activities that required a sleeping bag were retreats and summer camp, neither of which were any time soon.

"Has someone been sleeping here?" Blaze's question echoed his own suspicions.

"Or hanging out. I found a bunch of empty wrappers a few weeks ago. I've been locking the room ever since. This sleeping bag was in the closet across the hall. I put it in lost-and-found. Someone claimed it almost immediately."

"One of the kids brought it back here and hid it?"

He scrubbed a hand through his hair and surveyed the room from where he knelt beside the couch. Disappointment and worry tightened his back. "I don't know. I never leave this room open and unattended for more than ten or fifteen minutes."

She crossed her arms. "That would be enough time."

"To hide it. Not use it." He lifted the sleeping bag. Looked clean. Didn't stink.

"Which is good, because some of the Branching Out students are couples, aren't they?"

He groaned and dropped the bag. No student would go that far at church, right?

She squatted nearby and picked up a candy bar and the apple. "What do we do about it?"

He braced his arm against the couch and ran possibilities. "There's an extra key in the spare key lock box, so I'll start there. If that's a dead end, I'll ask the students. And the leadership board. They have keys to the lock box, so indirectly they—or someone with their key—could access the youth room." He rose to stand beside her. "Have any students expressed problems that might lead them to look for a place to hide out? Maybe Hadley?"

"Hadley?" Her eyes narrowed. "Why her?"

"She loves attention." Lately, she'd been calling Anson Dad. It started when he instructed some students not to run in the hall.

"Okay, Dad," an eighth grader had said.

Over the next half hour, a few of the others copied the boy. When Anson didn't react, everyone except Hadley dropped it. Two weeks later, she still crooned it at him once or twice each Wednesday night.

Blaze frowned as she set the food down.

"She's not acting out in dangerous ways," he said. "I'm glad she's coming to Rooted. But she goes out of her way to be the center of attention. Sometimes that's a sign of a problem. I don't know if it's a sign of *this* problem." He nudged the sleeping bag with his foot. "But we have to consider it."

Blaze scratched her temple. "I hate to think of any kid feeling like they need a backup plan like this, let alone one of the younger students."

"Me too. But we owe it to the kids to get to the bottom of this, and that means considering the possibilities."

Blaze stared blankly toward the stash. "None of the girls have said anything in small group that leads me to believe they're unhappy or unsafe at home. Have the boys?"

He shook his head.

"What about Carter?" Her brown eyes warmed with concern. "Drinking on a youth group trip is a much bigger warning sign than Hadley's seventh-grade humor."

"According to Eric, the drinking is just a sign of bad leadership."

Her eyes and mouth opened like a fish. "What?"

He clenched his jaw. "Forget I said that."

She side-eyed him like he'd asked her to forget witnessing a murder.

He probably ought to give some context. "Eric's behind the initiative to double the youth group. We've been butting heads. That's all. Our differences aside, I talked to Carter on

Saturday and he came back to youth group. He hasn't let on to anything. Plus, he'd stockpile a lot more food. He eats more than I do. And how would he get in here?"

"How would Hadley? Or any of them?"

They had more questions than answers, and posing them to each other wouldn't get them anywhere.

Mercy appeared in the doorway. She'd earned a Rooted hoodie for bringing Amelia on the canoe trip, and she yanked the zipper up and down, up and down. "Looked everywhere. Couldn't find it."

Hadley edged in behind her, nodding empathetically.

"Hm." Blaze crossed to the purse she'd left on the couch and produced her phone. "Sure enough, it's right here."

Mercy snickered. "At least it was easy to find this time. Remember when you left your keys in the bag of lettuce in the fridge?"

"I do." She moved toward the door. "We should get going. We need to get Hadley home, and Anson has places to go."

Right. The missed anniversary.

As soon as they left, he took a plastic bag from the cabinet and piled the snacks inside. Then, he wrote a note on a slip of paper—*I'm here to help. Call me*—and dropped it inside. He stuffed the whole collection back under the couch.

That done, he drew out his phone, but guilt and embarrassment stopped him from using it to contact Sydney. He should've remembered. He should be excited to propose too. Instead, picking a ring, talking to her parents, choosing a place, and figuring out the right heartfelt words felt like a chore.

That was stress talking. Once things settled down with

the leadership board and they discovered the truth behind the sleeping bag, he could refocus on Sydney. If he wanted proposing to still be an option when the dust settled, he needed to treat her with more care in the meantime, starting with apologizing in person.

15

*A*nson stood on Sydney's front step with the most expensive flower arrangement available at the grocery store. She would probably say he shouldn't have bought them, but she'd dip her face to smell the flowers as she spoke. He pressed the doorbell. Around him, crickets hummed and distant traffic swished like one long sigh. Another calm night in Many Oaks.

The door opened. Sydney, dressed in leggings and a tank top, leaned against the frame. Head tilted, she eyed the flowers. "What's this about?"

"I'm sorry."

"Ah." She stepped back to allow him in.

He'd imagined she'd immediately let him off the hook. She hadn't even accepted the flowers.

Regret pooled in his lungs. "Why didn't you say something?"

"We didn't even get together the day of, and I thought I was okay with that, but a call or something would've been nice. Then, on Saturday when I did see you, you were pretty discouraged after talking to Carter." She perched on a stool at her kitchen island and pulled one foot up under herself, a steaming mug of tea beside her. "I asked if you wanted to talk, but you said you'd rather watch a movie."

"I would've gotten out of my head if I'd realized I was missing our anniversary."

She shrugged one shoulder. "If it had been important to you—"

"I didn't forget because you're not important to me. I forgot because I'm an idiot. I got caught up with work. Carter and Eric...." He shook his head.

Her mouth thinned into a line. "I think it's more than that."

It was. Carter reminded Anson too strongly of Guriel. But if he explained, the conversation would go in that direction when he and Sydney needed to discuss their relationship. "I hate failing. I knew doubling the youth group was a stretch, but I thought I'd be closer than I am. Now, there's Carter, and on top of it, I've failed you." Shame heated his face and arms, right down to his fingertips.

She wrapped her hands around the mug. "Tell me about our relationship. How do you see us?"

At least she was still willing to talk. He placed the arrangement in the center of the island. "As the perfect match."

Her eyebrows hiked.

"I'm serious." He took the stool beside hers. "We complement each other. Our faith and values align. I trust you completely. I respect you and what you're about." The words came easily. Perhaps he should've bought a ring. "We make perfect sense."

She fiddled with the paper tag hanging from her tea bag. "Logically, maybe."

The words lodged center mass. "Maybe?"

She turned her glassy eyes away. "Logic gave us this year together, but a relationship has to make sense in other ways too. My friends remembered our anniversary over a week ago." Sydney chuckled. "Madison is more of a romantic than I realized, but even if it's not fireworks and thrills every time, it'd be nice to have romance sometimes."

"Don't we?" He eyed the flowers. "What do you want from us that's missing?"

"Passion."

His spine straightened. She'd come up with that pretty quickly.

"My friends questioned whether we even kiss. I know you're a pastor and we have to set a good example for the kids and the congregation, but even when we don't have an audience, you're hardly affectionate."

He looked down at his clasped hands resting on his leg. Only inches separated them, yet he hadn't reached out. Hadn't thought to.

"I'm not just talking about our physical relationship. Even after a year of dating, I hardly know you better than your students do. It's like you've let the job dictate all of who you are, and I don't get anyone but Pastor Marsh."

"No one else in Many Oaks knows about Guriel."

The corner of her mouth turned up ruefully. "You only told me because I stumbled across a picture and asked the right questions, but you never got into the details. Same with the bus accident. That night must've been horrific, but you act unaffected."

"Of course it affects me." Even her reminders of the

tragedies turned his throat raw, and the words burned like bleach in a wound. "It's why I do what I do."

"Right. You want to imitate your old coach. You want to help kids before they end up like your brother. That's what you focus on—the actions and reactions. You pretend that all those losses did was motivate you, not inflict any scars or doubts."

"You want me to be scarred?" He lifted his hands. Scoffed. "And I should doubt what? God?"

"I want you to be human with me. But ..." She dipped her chin, eyes sad. "But I can't hold that against you, because I ... I think I've been one-dimensional with you too. I know what you expect from me—and what people at church expect—so I stifle things about myself."

"Like what?"

"My spontaneity."

Anson shook his head. "Why would spontaneity be a problem?"

"Because you like routine. Even if you didn't, the church calendar dictates how you spend several nights a week, and soon, you'll be juggling basketball again too. If we manage to schedule a date, you know everyone in town. Unless we leave Many Oaks, every date is a group event. I get the whole role model thing, but people have opinions about everything, and keeping them happy is exhausting." She sipped her tea and blinked slowly as she put it back on the counter. "The whole lifestyle is exhausting."

Anson crossed his arms as they tightened with offense. Where was this coming from? And what was he supposed to do about it? Change jobs? "I've been a pastor and coach as long as you've known me. My lifestyle shouldn't surprise you."

"You're right." She ran her fingers into her pulled-back hair, mussing her ponytail. "I did know, and for the love of my life, I wouldn't mind the sacrifices."

And there it was. A truth as powerful as it was ugly.

He swallowed hard. "But I'm not the love of your life."

Her exhale stuttered, but she held his gaze. "Am I the love of yours?"

He'd wanted her to be.

"Come on, Anson." Her tone softened. "I think if you take a step back and honestly look at what happened, you'll see you chose me with your head, not your heart."

Sharp words formed barbs in his throat. "I don't even know what that means."

"When your *heart* chooses, you will."

In a flash, he was back at the canoe. His hand tingled where Blaze's leg bumped his thumb. Her voice filled his ears. He fought the river's current to get to her. Relief and pride flooded him when she relaxed into his arms.

Had that been his heart choosing?

Didn't matter. He couldn't build a life on emotions. As a pastor, he'd witnessed too many people follow their hearts into trouble. God gave him a mind, and with that, he knew he and Sydney were better suited for life together.

But she wanted more.

She walked to the door and opened it, then looked at where Anson still sat at the island. Shocked, he followed. He paused by the threshold and considered trying to change her mind, but she'd said this wasn't love.

Maybe it wasn't.

"Goodbye, Sydney." He stepped into the night.

BLAZE STOOD at the counter between the kitchen and dining room as she reviewed Mercy's school assignments as her sister scrounged up an after-school snack. Sandwiched between other papers, the plastic report cover for her Argentina paper stood out. The project impacted a big portion of Mercy's grade, and she'd spent weeks working on it. Blaze pulled the report from the backpack.

The social studies teacher had inserted a grading sheet over Mercy's hand-drawn illustration of the country. Penned in red, the word *Incomplete* topped the paper. Blaze's shoulders dropped. She'd questioned Mercy about whether the project was done. Mercy had insisted it was and, for proof, had pointed to the assignment's checklist. Every item had been marked off, but now that she looked more closely, some of the items weren't even listed in the table of contents, let alone in the report itself.

"You swore this was done." Blaze lifted the teacher's notes. "But you skipped two of the required sections. What happened?"

Mercy dumped sweet potato chips into a small bowl without answering. Since Mercy's diagnosis two weeks ago, the cold shoulder had been getting worse and worse the longer Blaze resisted putting her on medication.

"You need to talk to me about this, or I'm going to have to respond as if you purposely lied. Is that what happened?"

Mercy's chin jutted forward. "I forgot."

"The list was there to remind you. Why did you check them off if they weren't done?"

"I thought they were." She pivoted away and rattled around in the fridge.

Blaze lowered the grading sheet to the counter. She believed Mercy could've been distracted from finishing the report. That happened to Blaze at work all the time. But when reminded of her work, Blaze always knew what she had and hadn't finished. Yet when asked, Mercy had sworn the work was done. Could she have forgotten, or had she lied?

Mercy dropped a piece of string cheese on the counter. "It's your fault, you know."

"Excuse me?"

"It's been forever, and you still won't put me on medication. It's not fair."

Blaze leaned against the counter and hooked one foot behind the other. The cheese and chips were part of their no food dyes, higher protein diet, but she'd yet to discern a change in her sister. Except for the growing resentment.

Mercy filled a glass of water, then swept up her snack and stomped to the living room. The TV blared.

Blaze counted to ten before following. She paused Mercy's show and stood between the couch and the TV. Her sister slouched deeper into the cushions.

"I need to understand what happened so I *can* make a fair decision. If I don't know I can trust you, I won't know if medication is best. What happened with your report?"

"I did forget." She pursed her lips in an angry scowl. "When I remembered, it was too late, so I said it was done."

Mercy hadn't claimed to be done with the report until Blaze asked the afternoon before the due date. "You could've worked on it another hour or two that night. I asked you before dinner."

"Do you know how long it took to do the rest of it? Way longer than that. It was hopeless."

Mercy had camped out at the dining table most of an entire weekend, working on the paper. Then again, Blaze had seen her reading and surfing the internet a few times when she'd passed through. If Mercy had been able to focus, she might've finished the whole thing.

"Thank you for being honest with me."

Mercy knotted her hands together and kept her eyes down like a convict awaiting punishment.

"You need to finish the report and ask your social studies teacher if you can have an extra credit assignment to make up for the lost points." Blaze toyed with her hair, weighing her options. "I can see your schoolwork is still a struggle, and I do want that to get better, but I don't want you to learn you get your way when you lie."

Mercy's gaze lifted in jerks until she met Blaze's eyes. "I'm sorry."

"I forgive you, but I want you to clean the bathroom as a consequence."

Mercy nodded.

"After you clean the bathroom, we can go fill the prescription."

Mercy's posture straightened until she had the poise of a pageant contestant.

Blaze held up a hand of warning. "Remember that the medication takes time too. It might be a few more weeks before anything changes."

"Yeah. Okay." Mercy bolted for the bathroom.

For better or for worse, they'd be picking up the prescription within the hour.

16

*D*espite its flaws, Blaze had to appreciate her brain's capacity for multitasking. She processed Anson's arrival at her Thursday night show without missing a note.

He chose a table and sat alone.

As far as she could tell, he'd been a recluse for the three weeks since she'd cornered him after Rooted. She hadn't seen him talking one-on-one with anyone for more than a minute or two. Any interactions with her at Rooted or church had been strictly business, like the Sunday he gathered all of the youth leaders—including Sydney—to ask about the sleeping bag. Sydney appeared as surprised as everyone else, suggesting Anson hadn't told her about it previously.

Had they broken up?

Blaze's song wound down, and she took a swig from her water bottle to camouflage a peek at her watch. Anson once said he couldn't attend Thursday shows because of a work meeting, but that might have wrapped up. It was after nine.

She kept tabs on him through her last set. Song after song, he stayed planted. His former high school coach's widow, Gabby Voss, stopped at his table for a while. Then, he played on his phone. He watched the stage. When Blaze smiled directly at him, uncertainty shifted across his features. She ought to dedicate a song to him to get a reaction, but she couldn't risk him running before she could satisfy her curiosity.

As she bade The Signalmen good night and gathered her things, she figured he'd disappear.

He did not.

She crossed the deserted dance floor and took a seat at his table, leaving one empty chair between them. "How are you coping with the breakup?"

His lips tightened. His Adam's apple bobbed.

That was all the confirmation she needed. "You want to talk about it?"

"I don't." His glass was empty, save for some brown-tinged water at the bottom. Still, he stared at it like it held the mysteries of the cosmos.

Music streamed over the speakers. Everyone else in the venue left their tables, likely headed home or to the bar. Yet Anson stayed.

"How's the situation with Eric Newsome going?"

He exhaled long and slow. "I shouldn't have told you about that."

"Why not?"

"Because telling people about it could stir up dissension."

Dissension? She was one person, and she hated the rumor mill more than most. "I haven't repeated what you said, but I don't understand why he blames your leadership for Carter's issues. And the attendance goal started long before the canoe trip."

"He wants to grow the church. With families leaving, the budget is tight. The idea is that the more kids who have fun at our youth group, the more parents will choose to join us for Sunday morning."

The church was in financial trouble? Between her habitual tardiness and her wandering mind, Blaze might've missed some details at the last church business meeting. "Youth group can't carry all the pressure of increasing attendance." She sifted through hazy memories of weekly announcements and bulletin notices. "How else is the church reaching out?"

"We're raking leaves for people in the community in two weeks."

Now that announcement she remembered, but not from a Sunday morning. "I thought that was a youth event, like the corn maze."

"Adults aren't invited to the corn maze, but there's a sign-up sheet for the whole church to help with raking. We'll see who volunteers." He turned his glass. "So. Mercy got her ADHD diagnosis. Does it feel good to be right?"

He remembered? Her heart did a giddy twirl.

"It does." About the diagnosis and about Anson and Sydney. Not that she wanted or expected them to break up, but at least she no longer had to feel guilty over her wayward feelings.

"But?" he asked.

"Huh?"

"You said you were happy you were right about Mercy, but you don't look happy. Why not?"

"Once we had the diagnosis, we tried lifestyle changes,

but Mercy was still struggling in school, so I ..." She drew a deep breath. Anson watched her, attentive. "I took the doctor's suggestion to put her on meds. The trouble is, the non-stimulant can take months to make a difference—if it's even going to—and in the meantime, Mercy isn't sleeping or eating enough. She's always been a scrap of a kid, you know? I don't want to see her lose weight. I'm torn between seeing it through, giving in to see if a stimulant makes a quicker difference, or going back to the way things were. She'd hate me for that last one, of course. She still believes medication will solve all her problems."

The corner of his mouth pulled down. "A kid doesn't know best."

"I'm not sure I do either, but I'm trying. It's just hard." This was a lot to dump on an acquaintance, but she couldn't stop herself any more than she could've saved herself from the river. "My appointment is coming up, but if it's this much of a hassle to get Mercy settled, do I want to deal with a second diagnosis and prescription? It's overwhelming as it is."

He took a measured breath, studying her. "Sometimes things have to get worse to get better."

She waved her hand. That saying was peskier than a housefly. "The doctor said that too. I'm just not sure better's in the cards for us."

He chuckled. "Since when do you consult cards?"

She sighed. Of course she'd said something theologically wrong.

"'I believe that I shall look upon the goodness of the Lord in the land of the living.' Psalm 27:13." Gentleness marked Anson's voice. "God's goodness doesn't always show up in the form of an effective treatment, but, then again, He does answer an awful lot of prayers through modern medicine."

But her prayers? The few answers she'd seen lately didn't outweigh the years of unanswered pleas. Most of those involved her mother's alcoholism, though—did that count as many disappointments or one big one?

"Seriously." Anson rested his arms on the table and leaned closer. "Have a little hope."

"I have a *little*."

"But not a lot?" He was one surprise after another tonight. Even at their friendliest, he hadn't shown this willingness to linger with her and discuss hard topics.

Her silly, dancing heart tugged with the desire to leap into his arms. She twisted her ankle around a rung of her chair to keep herself from acting on it. "I usually have to fend for myself. Not that God's not there, but people fail. All the time."

He tapped his thumb on the table, and she imagined how that strong hand could cover hers. "You've had a lot of disappointments."

"You were one of them."

His eyebrows furrowed. "When?"

She pressed her tongue against the back of her teeth. Maybe she shouldn't have said that. If he wouldn't acknowledge his mistakes, this fledgling friendship would fail, and they'd be back to mostly ignoring each other. But better to find out sooner than later whether the safety she felt around him was real. "You were friendly my first day of high school and too good for me the next."

He winced. "You're right. I was young and immature."

She considered pressing until he told her which of the rumors had changed his attitude, but she didn't want to hear again the worst of what others said about her. Especially not from him. Instead, she posed a question that had haunted her almost as long. "What about the time my mom forgot to pick me up after that game, and I asked you for a ride home?"

His jaw shifted. "I was the team captain, and you reeked of alcohol. I couldn't get in the middle of a situation like that."

She rolled her eyes. "Why? Giving me a ride would not have gotten you in trouble."

"Probably." He shook his head. "As a kid, that didn't occur to me. But I've always been against drinking, so I wasn't going to make your choices easier on you."

A harsh laugh rose, and she didn't suppress it. "You wanted me to learn from the consequences, huh?"

He barely nodded as though concerned about where this was headed.

"A friend poured a beer on me because I was trying to get her to stop drinking." Saying the words felt like lugging a heavy suitcase onto the table. At least she wasn't carrying them anymore, but the consequences still had to be unpacked.

"Oh." He rubbed his mouth and dropped his gaze.

"After you refused to help me, I had to walk in the sleet with just a jean jacket to keep me warm. Guess what happened on the way home."

His eyes cut back to her. "What?"

"Some older man—thirties or forties?—circled past a few times, then stopped and told me to get in. When I didn't, he followed me until I hid in someone's bushes." On occasion, the stranger still rolled through her nightmares, ever pursuing her.

Anson grimaced. "I'm sorry, Blaze." The sincerity in his voice crashed through her memories and brought her back, safe and sound, to the present. "I made a bad call. I should've helped."

The grudge lifted. She squirmed. She hadn't realized how defenseless she'd be without it. "We were kids. You maybe even more so than me."

"What's that mean?"

"As we've established, I've been taking care of myself from a pretty young age."

He leaned back in his seat and lifted an eyebrow. "And my life has been all roses?"

"I'm sure losing Coach Voss was traumatic."

"You don't know the half of it." If it weren't for the quiet way he spoke, as though more to himself than to her, she wouldn't believe him.

"So tell me."

"You tell me the story of your nickname, and I'll tell you a story about me."

This was becoming a habit, him changing the subject away from himself. "I already told a story. It's your turn."

The tendons at the corner of his jaw flexed. "All right. One story, but don't believe this is the only one I have."

He had the perfect parents. Excellent grades. Athletic ability. And now the exact jobs he'd set out to land. Not exactly a life of difficulty.

"We lost a game we should've won." His voice slowed and deepened. "Piers Overton refused to pass a few times, and most of us blamed him for the loss. On the bus ride home, Nolan got into it with him."

"Nolan?" The friendly, happy-go-lucky Rooted leader? "I forgot he's a Lion too."

Anson's hand curled into a fist on the table, then relaxed. "He and Piers started shoving each other, so Coach moved to the back to break up the fight. Minutes later, a semi blew through a stop sign into the side of the bus. One second, everything was normal. The next, we were thrown into seats, walls, windows, equipment. Two or three seconds of chaos changed everything." He massaged his shoulder.

"The bus landed on its side. My arm was just hanging there. I'd never had a dislocated shoulder before. Didn't know it could be fixed. Honestly thought my basketball career was over. But survival was the important thing. The other guys—everyone was bleeding. A couple of them confused words or couldn't see straight. Gray couldn't walk. Sam's arm was ..." Anson blew out a breath. "... visibly broken."

A staff member started flipping up chairs on the far side of the room. Anson stared in that direction, but his eyes were still, not following the movement. "Working together to get everyone out kept us busy until first responders arrived. Then I realized how much worse the back of the bus was. Ambulances started taking us to the hospital immediately. Word didn't reach me that Coach had died at the scene until an hour later. I ... was more upset about that than I'd been about my arm."

Lines etched his face, and she wondered how that moment had played out. Who'd been there to comfort him? And should she reach out now?

Probably not. She intertwined her fingers. "He meant a lot to you?"

"He was like a second father. Losing family is never easy."

He was right. Even when the family member was troubled, it hurt. "Who else did you lose?"

"Huh?"

"You said it's never easy, like you've been through it more than once."

His mouth opened, then closed with a frown, and he studied the table. When he lifted his gaze again, his lips hooked up playfully. "You sure that's the story you want in exchange for you telling me about your nickname?"

His sudden levity suggested it wouldn't be worth the trade. But could she trust the change in demeanor? Or was his initial thoughtful hesitation a better clue to the significance of his story?

Before she could decide, he brushed his hand over the table as if to wipe away crumbs and stood. "Maybe next time. Good night, Blaze."

How could he walk away so suddenly? This conversation had unlocked a whole new dynamic between them, and she longed to explore.

She rose. "You play it close to the chest, don't you?"

She stood close enough to hear his exhale and smell hints of cedar and amber from his soap or cologne. He put his hands in his pockets and didn't answer.

"Thank you for telling me about the accident." She squeezed his arm in reassurance. The firm muscle under her fingers suggested he could more than look out for himself.

"I'm glad you told me what happened too." A notch appeared between his brows. "That couldn't have been easy."

"Easier than carrying it longer than I already have." She collected her purse, and he walked her out.

She hadn't believed him when he'd said he had more stories to tell, but as she drove home, replaying their talk, she was no longer sure. Her guess? His sudden joking tone when she'd asked about who he'd lost was a defense mechanism, hiding something even more formative than the team's accident.

Maybe the reason she'd always assumed his life was perfect was he projected that image. Tonight, he'd given her a glimpse of the truth.

17

"Who wants to help with raking?" Anson clapped in a bid to rally enthusiasm.

The middle school students sat facing forward, yet not one of them met his eyes. Only Mercy and Hadley had signed up. Blaze probably didn't give her sister a choice, and Hadley never missed an activity.

The others treated the three-hour event like a prison sentence. A total of six students between both youth groups were on board. Meanwhile, eight adults—not counting youth leaders—had signed up for something that was supposed to be a youth service project. The leadership board wasn't happy. "The more of you who come, the more fun we'll have, and the more people we can show God's love by helping with their yards."

"I'll be there." Nolan lifted his hand.

None of the kids followed suit.

"You guys know it's a competition, right?" Blaze's question drew everyone's attention. "After we work, we'll come back here for pizza *and*"—she stretched the word, despite

Anson's motion to stop inventing plans—"whichever team rakes the most yards gets to throw a pie at the leaders."

The kids traded wide-eyed looks.

So much for the students serving the community to show God's love to their neighbors. Pizza wasn't in the budget, and the leaders hadn't agreed to be pied.

Blaze was lucky he liked her.

He cleared his throat, because even the thought rang too loud.

Blaze was not the woman for him. He'd gone to The Depot last Thursday figuring if he had a real conversation with her, he'd see for himself all the reasons they were poorly suited for each other.

The plan had backfired. He couldn't get her out of his mind. He even missed a pass during game time because he'd been watching her instead of the ball.

"How many people on each team?" one of the boys asked.

Blaze scrunched her mouth in thought. "As many as you want, but there are only three leaders, so there will only be three pies to throw."

There would also be two Branching Out leaders, but Anson didn't mention it. Three pies were more than enough.

As the boys conferred, Hadley twisted in her seat to face Blaze and raised her hand. Once Blaze pointed at her, she asked, "What kind of pie?"

"Whipped cream." Looking pleased with herself, she added, "It'll be very messy."

An eighth-grade boy gave a definitive nod. "Okay. We'll come."

At least the leadership board would be satisfied. Anson

handed over the sign-up sheet. They passed it around, adding three names.

"Can we be on teams with high schoolers?" asked a girl whose sister attended Branching Out.

Finally, Blaze's bright eyes looked to him.

He found himself nodding. The girl and her friend committed to come. At the end of the night, the kids picked up permission slips on their way out the door.

As they filed out, Blaze bumped his arm with her shoulder. A whiff of floral perfume followed. "Wouldn't it be great if they all followed through?"

"Sure." Anson rubbed his neck. A glance from her had made him forget his hesitations. Why did she have such a strong effect on him?

"You don't think they will?"

"They might."

He'd always thought her face symmetrical, but her hairline was higher on the left than the right, and that eyebrow tended to arc slightly higher as well. Her nose was a touch off-center, and the right corner of her mouth sat a fraction higher. Instead of taking away from perfection, the differences rendered her face more interesting. More uniquely hers.

The lips he hadn't meant to study stretched into a mischievous smile. "You just don't want a pie in the face."

He turned away under the pretense of cleaning up. "A kid almost broke my nose with a pie a couple years ago. We'll have to put the whipped cream on paper plates and set up a line they can't cross."

"Wow. That's intense. Yeah, paper plates and boundaries." She popped into his peripheral vision, straightening chairs. "What else do we need to do to make this work? I can tell you're still not a fan. If that's because of the pizza, I'm buying."

He held up one hand. "I can't let you do that."

"I'm pretty sure you're supposed to let me give money to the church. In fact, you're supposed to encourage it." A tease brightened her tone.

"Not if it's for the wrong motives."

"What do you think my motives are?"

He checked for listening ears. Mercy and Hadley had their heads tipped together as they watched something on a cell phone. Nolan chatted with the only other remaining student by the door. He stepped closer to her. "You're trying to save my job."

Blaze feigned a horrified gasp. "How awful."

His failure with the kids ought to bother him. Instead, he pictured catching Blaze's hand and tugging her closer. He returned to straightening up, but the kids hadn't left much of a mess. He collected his Bible and notes from the lectern.

Blaze's voice followed. "Did a lot of high schoolers sign up?"

"Four, but it's not just the numbers. The kids' motives matter too. I want them to serve without strings attached."

"Ah. Well, learning how to make work fun is a helpful life skill. And you know what's not fun? Watching a group of preteens shut you down." She poked his chest. "I bet helping people was enough motivation for you, even in middle or high school. Most kids aren't that generous. Or maybe they have a hard time picturing how big of a difference their help can make."

He laid his Bible on the counter and picked up his coat from a nearby chair. Blaze's was underneath, so he passed it to her. "We can't throw pizza at them every time we want them to show up."

"Once in a while, though ...." Her smile bloomed. "And technically, you won't be throwing pizza at them. They'll be throwing pies at you."

"Even worse." He pulled his coat on.

"It'll be great. I promise."

"If it's not, do I get to throw a pie at you?"

"There will be enough pies flying as it is." She winked.

A smile fought past his defenses. He could endure a disturbing amount of teasing when it came from her.

Nolan came up behind her. "I don't remember signing up for a face full of whipped cream." He put a hand on her shoulder and mimed squishing a pie into her pretty features.

Jealousy slithered through Anson's chest, but he couldn't touch her like that. He could barely keep his wits about him as it was.

With a playful shrug, Blaze slipped away. "At least I didn't say dunk tank—and I could have. The dealership owns one." She donned her coat and motioned the girls to follow her. "'Night, guys!"

Giggling and echoing the carefree farewell, Mercy and Hadley followed her out as they slid into their own coats.

Nolan chuckled and shook his head. "That one's trouble."

"Yes, she is."

THE FOLLOWING TUESDAY AFTERNOON, Blaze left work early for her doctor's appointment. Instead of multiple appointments and assessments like Mercy had gone through, the doctor had her answer two pages of questions.

His frown deepened as he read her answers. He set the page aside and folded his hands loosely in his lap. "The trouble, Blaze, is that your assessment isn't definitive." His tone remained conversational, but his words slashed through her confidence.

She wasn't even good enough at having a disorder?

"ADHD is a lifelong disorder, not something that crops up in adulthood. That, combined with your symptoms, leads me to suspect anxiety instead."

Her mouth went dry. Was twenty minutes long enough to come to a conclusion, let alone such an unexpected one?

She'd always liked her doctor. He'd treated her iron deficiency, a UTI, and a nasty upper respiratory infection. She hadn't felt misunderstood or rushed those times.

"I'll write you a prescription for an antidepressant that's often effective in treating anxiety and a referral for talk therapy." He gave a perfunctory smile. "Between the two, I believe you'll start to find some real relief."

"Anxiety ...." Enough to require medication and therapy?

The doctor adjusted his glasses as he peered at his tablet. "Diet and exercise can also significantly impact your overall well-being. Exercise increases serotonin, reducing feelings of stress and anxiety. Meanwhile, changes to your diet, such as including more protein—"

"I changed my diet a few weeks ago to include lots of protein, fewer processed foods, and a lot less sugar." Getting up in the morning had become slightly easier, and the jeans that used to bite into her stomach were no longer uncomfortable. Her office and the reports that awaited her there, however, were.

A Surefire Love

He straightened his lab coat's lapel. "Your caffeine intake is higher than I like to see. Four to five cups of coffee per day could contribute to an inability to focus and anxiety."

That word again. "I don't have panic attacks or feel nervous all the time."

"You reported worrying 'often' about your job performance, how people perceive you, and your parenting. Worry is a synonym for anxiety."

She rubbed the growing tension in her shoulder. "I'm forgetful. I have trouble concentrating on tasks I need to do, like reports for work."

"Anxiety can cause that, especially when triggered by stressors like a promotion. An anxiety diagnosis is good news. ADHD can be treated, but it's incurable. Anxiety, on the other hand, sometimes goes away entirely with treatment. It may be a long road, but starting treatment can improve your quality of life immediately."

"Okay." She pressed her hands into the seat and scooted back. Immediate improvement sounded good. Mercy's appetite had finally returned, and she'd cleaned BunBun's area on first request last time, but the wait for change had been grueling.

The doctor handed her pages that recapped the appointment, his recommendations, and general information about anxiety. "What pharmacy would you like to use for the prescription?"

"Um ..." The antidepressant was so unexpected. How had she been right about Mercy and wrong about herself? But who was she to disagree with an expert? "The pharmacy here's fine."

18

*A*ttending Blaze's Thursday shows wasn't as fun as Mondays. Anson had switched to give Sydney space, but by the time he arrived, most of his friends were either on their way out or tired of talking over the music. They'd listen to him, but he couldn't delve into the trouble he was having at church. He couldn't discuss how, now over the shock of losing Sydney, he missed her friendship but not dating her. He certainly couldn't explain why sitting alone at a table near the back and listening to Blaze sing more than justified showing up.

At Rooted last night, she'd been quiet and withdrawn. Now, her tone was dull as she bade the crowd good night. She turned from the mic a little too quickly and disappeared in back.

The push and pull he felt where she was concerned was enough to tear him in half. His head argued she was a loose cannon that had landed him in a river, volunteered him for a pie in the face, and scolded him for how he handled Mercy. His heart focused on her depth of spirit and the tenacious compassion she—for reasons he couldn't explain—sometimes aimed at him.

She was unexpected and enchanting.

She reappeared, hugging her leather jacket closed, and made for the exit without a look in his direction. She'd proven she kept tabs on her audience, so she knew he was there. Even last week, she'd waved at Anson when he'd left while she talked with Philip. Why ignore him this time?

He abandoned his empty glass and caught up in time to open the door for her. "You were right."

She turned a hesitant gaze his way. She rolled her lips inward.

He propped the door open with his shoulder, since she wasn't rushing out. "Not many high schoolers were interested in raking. I was too focused on the ideal—that they'd want to pitch in out of the goodness of their hearts—to correct course by offering other incentives. Along the way, they might discover the joy of helping people, but until then, your idea was the right choice. I should've asked for your input sooner."

"Even a broken clock is right twice a day." She maneuvered past him and onto the concrete porch.

He stepped out after her. "Who's the clock in this instance?"

Lights strung from the overhang cast a soft glow on her features. Her dark hair fell between them as she descended the steps into the parking lot.

He followed. "If it's me, I'm not offended. I've been called worse."

"And if it's me?"

"Can't be." His certainty won him another glance. "You're not broken."

She exhaled a puff of air. "I have it on good authority that I am."

"I have it on the best authority that you're not. You're healed and new in Christ."

"And yet ...." She edged between parked cars, forcing him to fall back.

He jogged to catch up again afterward and touched her coat sleeve. The supple leather was cool against his fingertips, yet warmth radiated up his arm and into his chest. He lowered his hand. "Why do you think you're broken? Did something happen?"

She hit her key fob. A row away, her taillights flashed. "Anxiety. Apparently."

Anxiety happened? "I'm gonna need more to go on."

"The doctor says I have anxiety, not ADHD." She yanked open her back passenger door. Her purse landed on the seat with a dull thump. "He said to quit coffee and start meds, and it's two days in, and I haven't felt this awful since my wild days."

"What did those entail?" Now, more than ever, he craved the details of her story.

"Six to eight months of bad choices before I realized I was becoming my mother, hated myself—and the constant hangovers—and landed in church."

The sip of information didn't quench his curiosity, but he cared more about her present well-being than her past. "You did what your doctor advised, and you're back to hating yourself and feeling hung over?"

She crossed her arms, hunched like he'd once again sent her out into a cold, wet night. "Something like that. My head is killing me. I can't focus. I feel like ...." She pressed her fingers to the bridge of her nose. "I'm going to go." She pulled open the driver's door.

"Blaze."

She paused, one hand on the roof of her sedan.

"You quit coffee cold turkey?" The question seemed trivial in the face of the upheaval she'd expressed, but he wasn't sure what other help he could offer.

She nodded.

"I only have one or two cups a day, but if I skip it, I get a headache too. If you're used to drinking a few cups a day and just quit, it's no wonder you're feeling bad. Starting anxiety medication at the same time has to be a lot for your body to process."

"It's not even anxiety medication. It's an anti-depressant. I guess that's the go-to, and it's not that I think anxiety's worse than anything else, I just ... Is that me? I never thought I was anxious—at least, not abnormally so. But he says that's why I can't focus or meet deadlines. And why do I want a disorder so bad anyway? But anxiety's a disorder too, so I win after all."

"Blaze." He reached out again. Found himself taking her hand and dipping his head to look her in the eyes. When her fingers curved around his palm, protectiveness sparked within him. "I don't know what the answer is, but I do know you need to give yourself grace. And maybe a cup of coffee."

"Is that the best you can do, Pastor? Coffee and Jesus?" She freed her hand from his. Her helpless tone softened the challenge in her question. "I'm pretty sure I could get the same advice from a T-shirt."

"Yeah, but you'd have to pay $24.99 for it." He smiled. "As a pastor, I consider it my duty to dispense unwanted platitudes free of charge."

She sighed. "It's not unwanted. It's just ... I don't know. Too easy. I can't ignore the doctor and continue as I have been when there's a fix."

"It's never been easy, so continuing as you were isn't a cop-out. But I also didn't mean to ignore him entirely. Just taper off coffee."

"Maybe." She rubbed her temple. "I wanted answers, and now that I have one, I hate it. It doesn't seem to fit."

"Doctors and tests can be wrong. You know yourself better than anyone. If you're concerned about your diagnosis, get a second opinion."

"I don't even know how to do that."

"Call a different office and make an appointment?"

She stared off over the roof of her car.

If only he could drive her home and set her up with a cup of coffee and a blanket. He'd tell her that she wasn't broken and she deserved answers, that she was worth any effort.

"I think the best thing for me right now is bed." She forced a smile and dropped into the driver's seat.

"Let me know if there's anything I can do. I'm praying for you." He eased her door shut.

She waved meekly and drove away.

His offer of prayer shouldn't have been such an afterthought, but he didn't want to leave her only in the Lord's hands. He longed to comfort her himself.

"IT'S NICE AND QUIET, RIGHT?" The cheerful voice blared from the passenger seat.

Blaze blinked and found herself driving through a

sparsely developed industrial district on the edge of town. Her mind had been elsewhere, exploring questions about anxiety, Mercy, Anson, and coffee.

Coffee. Was Anson right? Should she make herself some? If it helped her focus, she might owe it to everyone else on the road.

She squinted at the rural highway. Following the route the dealership used for test drives, she'd turn left at the next intersection, if her trainee remembered to instruct her to.

"I get it." Selina, dressed in a Portofino top and on-trend dress pants, chuckled. "So easy to get lost in the drive when it's this smooth and effortless, isn't it?"

"Yes." Blaze spared her newest salesperson a placating smile.

Selina was a quick study. That, or the furniture store she'd worked for had trained her on the benefits of getting a customer to say yes repeatedly. Studies showed that if a prospective buyer got in the habit of agreeing, they'd be more likely to agree to purchase. Although, psychological studies were also the reason Blaze tested as anxious instead of distracted.

"I'll have you turn left at the next intersection. See that sign there?" Selina lifted a long, manicured fingernail.

Blaze looked at her own short, unpainted ones on the steering wheel. Last time she did her nails, she forgot the second coat on three of them. The uneven color had bothered her every day, yet it took a week until she remembered to remove it.

"It's a beautiful country road, and"—Selina drew out the word playfully—"it has a couple of twists that'll give you a feel for how this beauty handles. Sound good?"

A quick study indeed. "Sure." Blaze flipped on the blinker.

As part of her training, Selina was walking Blaze through the entire sales process. Blaze ought to pose a question to mimic a client. Something about safety features or mileage.

"Is this a test?" Selina half-whispered.

Blaze hadn't managed a question yet, so what did Selina mean? Oh. Blaze had passed the intersection without turning. Where was her head today? Since it ached, it must still be attached. She tamped down the impulse to apologize. "Always expect the unexpected."

Blaze coached Selina on how to adjust the test drive route when a customer wanted a longer turn behind the wheel, then they headed back toward the dealership. Selina slid back into her upbeat sales persona, and Blaze managed a question or two about the car and one about financing.

When they parked, Blaze continued in her role as though she wanted to buy. Selina showed her to her office and motioned to a seat across from the computer. "Can I get you a coffee before we get to work?"

Blaze lowered into the chair. A wall stood between her and the single-serve coffee maker in the lobby, but her eyes fixed on the spot, so desperate for a caffeine fix she apparently thought she had X-ray vision now. "What could it hurt?"

"Great. Be right back." Beaming, Selina slipped away.

Would a cup cause a setback? Blaze woke her phone screen to ask, then saw a social media notification. An event had been created for the leaf raking project, and someone had asked if they needed to bring rakes or tarps.

"Here you go." Selina passed her a steaming coffee and set two prepackaged creamers and two sugars on the edge of the desk before circling to the chair behind it. As she dove into the next stage of the sale, Blaze eyed the cream and sugar.

She'd gotten distracted and missed the minute she had to research the effect of caffeine on anti-depressants.

Distracted. Forever distracted.

You're not broken.

Would Anson say such things if he knew her twisted, dead-end thoughts?

She blew out a long breath, drawing a quizzical glance from Selina. "Is everything okay?"

"You're doing great." Blaze lifted her coffee in a toast, then took a long, slow sip as she prayed for her life to change.

19

Anson counted the rakes leaning against the exterior of the church. They didn't have one for each volunteer, but some of the students and adults milling around would bag and haul leaves once the event started.

Nolan added one more rake to the collection, then turned. His gaze hit Anson's chest, and he snorted. "I'm pretty sure my sister has that shirt."

Anson straightened the hem of his T-shirt. "But does she look this good in it?"

Nolan shook his head. "That's wrong, man." He walked off snickering.

Anson had known the shirt would draw reactions, but he'd take whatever ribbing came his way as long as the person he bought it for approved. Would she?

Immediately after his talk with Blaze, he'd ordered a *Coffee and Jesus* shirt. Though not tight or short, it might reveal too much. It showed forethought and obviously hadn't been free. It showed he was willing to sacrifice a little pride to make her smile. Combined, those things created a picture of the heart beneath the fabric. A heart eager to make her happy.

Her black sedan pulled into the lot, and nervous energy wound through his gut.

Mercy and Hadley sprang from the car and jogged over to the other Rooted kids. Blaze emerged more slowly. When she rounded the car, she carried a travel mug. Good for her.

Her scan of the area stopped on him. She adjusted her path to head his way with barely a nod of greeting. Just when he thought she'd forgotten all about their talk, her step hitched and her head tilted. A smile bloomed across her face, and confetti-like satisfaction swirled in his chest.

"We're all set for pizza later?" Sydney's appearance beside him sucked the confetti up faster than a vacuum. She propped her hands on her hips, where she'd tied the arms of a flannel. He appreciated that she hadn't let their breakup change her commitment to Branching Out, but he could do without her having glimpses into whatever this was with Blaze.

Blaze might feel the same way, because she stopped to talk to Nolan.

"Pizza's all set to be delivered at twelve fifteen," he said.

"Okay." She checked her watch. "The last Branching Out students are here."

So were all the Rooted kids. Some adults still hadn't straggled in, but it was the scheduled start time. For the youth group competition, each leader would go with a different team of students. He probably wouldn't get to talk to Blaze until after raking. Possibly not until after pizza and pies. Her smile would have to tide him over.

Had he ever been this anxious to talk to Sydney?

He stole a glance at her. She was still pretty. But what

he'd once considered dependability now struck him as playing it safe. Sydney was too much like him. Together, all they would've done was build a predictable life.

Blaze was all question marks and big emotions. He didn't know where they'd end up together—*if* they'd end up together—but she was already expanding his world, and he had no desire to go back.

THE NEXT FEW hours passed quickly as Anson helped his team, tried to make it fun, and connected with the residents who ventured outside. Back at the church afterward, the students dug into pizza, and Anson met with the leaders in the hall to collect final numbers.

Ray pulled a slip of paper and a stubby pencil from his pocket. "Dylan and company did nine properties."

"Nine?" Sydney threw her hands up. "That's three more than my team got."

Anson's team had only cleared five. "Can anyone beat nine?"

Nolan and Blaze shook their heads.

"Since Dylan's team is from Branching Out, Sydney, Ray, and I will face the firing squad. I'll let the kids know." He moved toward the classroom.

"You can't just *tell* them." Blaze caught his arm, fingers lighting sparks down his biceps.

Nolan grinned. "Definitely gotta make them work for it."

"Or at least announce it with a bit of flair." Blaze scanned the group, but no one offered ideas. "Okay, what if someone runs to the store for different pie fixings, instead of just using whipped cream? We'll set out empty plates. Whoever we announce first can add one ingredient. Then, every time we announce a new high score, that team can add another ingredient. At the end, the winning team gets to throw the pies."

Sydney and Ray exchanged hesitant glances.

Blaze's flair would excite the students, but she didn't have to endure the outcome. "Those will be quite the pies."

"I can make you ponchos out of garbage bags." She directed the offer at Sydney and Ray. Turning back to Anson, her gaze dipped to his T-shirt. "To protect your clothes."

"I'll run for supplies." Nolan backed toward the door.

"Of course you two are eager," Ray said. "You're not getting pied."

Blaze grinned and shrugged. Apparently that settled it for everyone else. Sydney and Ray carried a table outside for pie building. Blaze disappeared into the janitor's closet.

Anson tracked her path. Following her would allow for a private conversation, but it could also ignite a firestorm of rumors. He'd wait.

BLAZE HAD to hand it to Anson. For a man who didn't want a pie in the face, he hammed up putting on his garbage bag until the kids roared with laughter. Though it was covered now, Blaze couldn't help thinking of the T-shirt underneath.

Except when an event printed custom shirts, Blaze had never seen him in a graphic T. Until today. For her.

Her amazement over his choice bubbled up in the form of smiles and laughter and even a little extra energy—a relief because nothing else had reversed the energy black hole created by the prescription.

Once the pies were made, one of Dylan's friends slung a cherry-apple-whipped-cream-chocolate-pudding concoction at Ray. The wet plop elicited a round of cheers.

Dylan claimed Anson as his target, but before he threw his pie, the kids conferred. By their urgent tones, they disagreed about something. One of the boys pointed at Sydney.

Sydney also wore her garbage bag like a champ, but then Blaze had never spotted an ounce of negativity from the woman. Would that change if she knew the story behind Anson's shirt?

With his part of the ceremony over, Ray crossed to Blaze, who had the water bucket. She dunked a rag, wrung it out, and passed it to him.

Finally, Dylan announced the problem. "No one wants to pie a girl."

"It's okay, guys." Sydney smiled. "I signed up for this."

She hadn't, exactly. This had been Blaze's idea.

Anson stepped forward. "Throw the last two at me."

Now that was a sacrifice. Did he still harbor feelings for Sydney?

Dylan dove on the offer. He grabbed both pies and lobbed them at Anson.

The first hit his chest. The second splattered on his face. The kids jumped and squealed with delight as the fillings flew in every direction, including onto Sydney. The plates slid, smearing cream and fruit from Anson's face to the bottom of the garbage bag before tumbling to his shoes and rolling away. As students high-fived Dylan, Anson wiped his eyes.

Blaze moved forward with damp rags, giving Anson one first.

Sydney thumbed the smear of whipped cream from her cheek, tasted it, then shrugged away Blaze's offer. "He needs it more than I do." She tipped her head toward Anson, then walked off.

Anson pulled the garbage bag over his head, arching his body away from it. His T-shirt stuck to the bag, revealing a couple inches of skin around the waist of a man who spent his free time working out. Blaze's arm tensed, and her fingers dug into the rag. She *really* ought to look away. He tugged the hem into place as he dunked the soiled plastic in the nearby trash can.

Like a perfectly aimed and well-deserved pie, embarrassment splattered across her face. What was she doing, checking him out? And while they were working with the youth, no less.

Around her, kids and adults mingled. Hadley and Mercy scored the can of cherry pie filling and scurried off toward the shade of a tree, plastic spoons in hand. Sydney and Ray started picking up pie-making supplies. Nolan unspooled the hose and aimed it at the pavement, dissolving the sugary remnants of the projectiles. Anson flipped the rag he'd been using and swiped the clean side over his hair.

Blaze passed the remaining cloth from one hand to the other. He'd probably want it for his shoes or a second pass over his face and arms, but she wouldn't be the one to give it to him. Until her wayward hormones got the memo they were just friends, she'd keep her distance.

She draped the cloth over the edge of the water bucket and retreated inside.

20

Anson kept an eye on Mercy, who squealed as Hadley chased her around a tree. Blaze had disappeared, but she couldn't have gone far without her sister.

"I hope lots of people tell my dad how great this was," one of the kids said behind him.

Anson turned to find Dylan. "Glad you enjoyed yourself."

"Yeah. I mean, I got to throw *two* pies at you. Plus, the old lady at the last house was so happy we helped, she cried. We were going fast because we wanted to win. If it wasn't a race, we wouldn't have gotten to her house, but I'm glad we did, and not just because of the pie."

Anson clapped him on the shoulder. "Helping people feels good, doesn't it?"

Dylan's smile dropped prematurely. "I just wish I could help you more."

"Help me with what?"

"My dad says you're running the youth group into the ground. He wants to replace you." He looked toward his friends. "I think they had fun. I'm going to try to bring them to Branching Out tomorrow."

Carter had once offered similar help, but he hadn't repeated their dad's mission in such stark terms. A warning tone droned in Anson's ears. Eric might've grown more outspoken. "It's not your responsibility to help me with your dad. That's between us and the leadership board."

"But that's the thing. Dad talks to people about you."

Anson massaged his own shoulder. "You don't need to worry about it. God is in control, and I'm glad you brought friends so that they can know Him too. That's the important thing."

Dylan's mouth curved in a half smile, but before they could continue, his mom called him and his friends over to her SUV. Meanwhile, Ashley West parked. Hadley and Mercy bounded toward her and climbed in the car.

Anson helped Sydney and Nolan scrub pie toppings off the pavement and carry the table inside. One by one, the leaders said goodbye. Anson piled up one last load of empty pizza boxes and deposited them in the trash bin beside the building.

He could lock up and head home, but his SUV had company in the form of Blaze's black sedan. They could finally talk. Light steps carried him back to the building.

He checked the youth room first. Empty, but he'd left it unattended during the pie ceremony. He pulled the food stash out from under the couch. He checked it once a week, and nothing had changed since he'd first found it.

Today, however, an apple rolled into his hand instead of an orange. Some of the candy had been swapped out for other varieties, and the note with his phone number was gone. He scanned the room but saw no hints to reveal who'd stopped in. He hadn't seen any students snacking on anything besides pizza and pie filling during the event.

He rubbed his mouth, considering his options. All of them would require steps he couldn't complete now. He put the bag back and locked the room before setting off to find Blaze, if she hadn't already ducked out.

No one sat in the sanctuary. He swung by the offices, but all the doors remained closed. On his way to check the gym, he heard water running in the kitchen.

Blaze stood at the sink. Her jeans and long sleeves suited the cooling weather. Despite being in a ponytail, her hair reached the small of her back. What he wouldn't give to walk up behind her, slide his hand across the soft fabric of her shirt, and feel the ends of her hair feather across his knuckles.

She shut off the faucet and plunked a handful of serving spoons into the drying rack. Wiping her hands on a towel, she turned from the counter and jolted. Exhaling, she pressed a hand to her chest. "How long have you been standing there?"

Longer than he should've been.

She smirked. "Nice shirt."

"This old thing?" He tugged the hem for the hundredth time.

With a chuckle, she dipped her chin and turned away.

As she replaced the towel on its hook, he leaned against the counter beside her. "Was that coffee in your mug earlier?"

"I'm doing one cup per day until I can quit altogether." Lines bracketed her mouth, and light from the window above the sink glinted on her dainty gold necklace. Tendons shifted in her slender neck as she moved.

He could study her all day, but that was a bad strategy for connecting with her. "Despite asking everyone I could think of, no one knows how or why anyone is getting into the youth room. But the stash changed, so someone is."

"What are you going to do?"

"Set up a motion-activated camera. I don't think they're too pricey, and I need to find out what's going on so I can help if it's one of the students."

"Good." She shifted and assessed him without giving him the satisfaction of eye contact. She could leave, but instead she stuffed one hand in her pocket and settled her hip against the counter. "It's good, you know?" She spoke soft and slow.

"What is?"

She rubbed her thumbnail along the seam where the sink met the countertop. "That the kids have someone looking out for them. Invested in how they're doing."

"Because you didn't?"

She frowned and something flashed in her eyes.

Her stories waited beneath the surface, but he hadn't earned her trust yet.

"I've thought about that night when I didn't give you a ride home. I've always been a black-and-white thinker. Sometimes, like with Mercy and that bathroom situation, I get carried away with it." An example of how his head got him in trouble sometimes. Giving more sway to his heart might not be all bad. "Back when we were in high school, I was a lot worse. I apologized the other night, but I'm not sure you understood how much I meant it. I'm sorry I left you in the cold that night."

"Thank you." She hugged her arm across herself. "If it

makes you feel any better, it wasn't the first or the worst time someone did that."

"Made you walk home?"

"Left me in the cold." Her beautiful voice shivered.

How much had she been through? "Why would that make me feel better?"

She swallowed.

"But I do want to know."

Her lips parted, then sealed. After a long inhale, she said, "It's how I got the name."

When she bowed her head, he risked a guess. "Because you were cold, you started a fire. The one that burned the garage."

She returned to picking at the caulk around the sink. "I knew you'd heard the story."

"Not from anyone qualified to tell it. They left out the part about you starting the fire for warmth. And probably a lot more."

She didn't continue the story.

He understood the hesitance. He'd never laid out his story for someone so early in a deepening friendship either, but Blaze was unlike anyone he'd grown close to before. "My offer stands. If you'll trust me with your story, I'll tell you mine."

She assessed him and nodded. The deal was made. His soaring satisfaction set off ripples of concern that he'd promised too much. His story likely carried similar weight to the one he'd asked of her, but what if it changed how she saw him?

She hooked her hand behind her neck, eyes trained on the sink. "During Christmas break, I called a friend and invited her over. I listened as she asked her mom for permission, and her mom said she couldn't come because my mom drank so much. Until then, I didn't realize how different our family was or the connection between Mom's drinking and her behavior. I was so upset, I poured all her alcohol down the drain.

"When she found out, she was livid. Locked me out of the house. It was just me and my ... My kitten sweater had this big, black-and-white cat on it and a ball of yarn." She motioned over her torso. "I loved that thing, so I wore it even when it was way too hot. But that day, when I had nothing else against the cold ..." Pink shaded the whites of her eyes and the crests of her cheeks.

"A kitten sweater? You were young."

"First grade."

Little Blaze, huddled in her kitten sweater against the cold, not only abandoned, but pushed away by the person who was supposed to love her most in the world. His heart shattered at the image, and his arms ached to crush her in a hug.

She stared at her hands. "I banged on the door for a while, but it turns out I didn't get *all* the alcohol. While she was consoling herself inside, I found newspapers in the bushes by our front door and a lighter in the garage. My fingers were so numb, I could barely pull the trigger. But once I got it, I got it."

His stomach dropped. "The fire got out of control."

"Fast. The whole garage went up in flames. A neighbor called the fire department. I'll never forget how terrified I was."

"Were you trapped inside?"

"No. I hid behind a neighbor's house, watching. I thought

I'd go to jail for the rest of my life." The corners of her mouth lifted. "Instead, I got sent to the Blovers."

"What's that?"

"A foster family. I guess the neighbors saw me pounding on the door, wandering the yard, and running away from the fire. They're the ones who sent the police looking for me. I confessed the whole thing, thinking it was my fault for making Mom angry and burning down the garage. I thought the police officer would put me in cuffs and haul me away. And I *was* whisked away, just not to jail. It took a year for Mom to get me back."

Even that might've been too soon, given Anson had never heard her tell a good story about her mom. Hopefully, the foster parents gave her a glimpse of how family ought to work. "Were they good people?"

"The Blovers?" She shrugged. "Sure. I remember a lot of fresh baked cookies and dinners around a table. But I also knew I didn't belong. I missed my mom. I spent the year homesick. When I came back to Many Oaks, the kids started calling me Blaze. It caught almost as fast as the garage did."

"That was wrong." The urge to reach out was so strong, he shoved his hands in his pockets. After all, he'd taken her hands when she'd told him about her anxiety diagnosis. If she wanted that kind of comfort from him, she ought to know he was within reach, waiting. "The kids sold you short."

"With the nickname? I'd say I earned that."

"No one deserves to be branded for trying to stay warm." He couldn't help the little girl in the story, but he could help the woman before him. "We can change it back. I'll never call you Blaze again if—"

She held up a hand. "Jenny went up in smoke that day.

She's the before, the naive girl who didn't know how much heartache the world holds or how to handle it. Blaze is the survivor. All that's left."

Christ had carried her through the fire, Anson was certain. Someday, the Lord might breathe new life into the trusting and optimistic Jenny, but in the meantime, Anson's allegiance rested with the phoenix named Blaze.

How had he ever believed his classmates' stories about her? He should've befriended her. Should've given her a ride that night when she'd asked. What else might he have seen about her sooner? "I can't tell you how incredibly sorry I am —for what you went through, for believing the stories."

"What's done is done. " A wisp of hair fell along the curve of her cheek. "I don't want pity."

"Good. Because what you have is my respect."

Her wide eyes snapped to his.

"You once said surefire failure is your thing, that your nickname was connected with that idea. I should've argued on the spot, but Blaze, please hear me now. The deck's been stacked against you your whole life, but you've made something of yourself—*Christ* is making something beautiful of you. Surefire failure isn't your hallmark. The surefire love of God is."

She pulled a lock of hair over her shoulder and twirled it around her finger.

"You are tenacious and capable and compassionate, and no matter how many times you've been hurt or disappointed, you keep opening yourself up. I suspect you do it every time you step on stage. You do it when you stand up and fight for Mercy. You did it when you volunteered for Rooted. You did it when you dared to ask a doctor for help and again by telling me your story."

Her velvety brown eyes scanned his face. Her gaze landed on his lips before rising again. "You promised to tell me a story in return."

"I did." He considered spitting out the facts without diving as deep as she had done, but that would snuff out their flickering connection. His only desire now was to fan the flames. "Would you like to know about my brother?"

"You have a brother?"

"I d—"

"Anson. Good. You're still here." Greg appeared in his peripheral vision. "We need to talk."

21

*B*laze dragged herself through the first half of her Monday night show. When she left the stage for her break, she waved to Sydney and her friends but didn't stop at their table. Her medication sapped her will to interact with anyone. Seeming to understand, Marissa didn't linger to chat before taking Mercy home. At a table by herself, Blaze mindlessly scrolled her phone.

"I owe you a story."

She looked up from her screen into a set of blue eyes that were fast becoming familiar. Her fatigue-heavy body suddenly felt lighter. "Since when are you back to attending on Mondays?"

"Since I had a debt to pay."

When he hadn't texted her Saturday or sought her out at church Sunday morning, she expected him to renege.

Yet here he was.

Satisfaction and anticipation unfurled in her chest. "I'm kind of in the middle of something." She motioned at the stage.

"Don't let me stop you." He pulled out a chair at the table and dropped onto it. "We can talk after."

If she stayed late again instead of going straight home to relieve Marissa, her friend would grill her for information. Already, she kept putting air quotes around the word *friends* when referring to Blaze and Anson.

He rested his forearms on the table and dipped his head to catch her eye. "That work for you?"

"Beggars can't be choosers, I suppose."

Anson's brow furrowed, but Philip passed and pointed at the stage. Time to get back to work. She tucked her phone into her pocket as Anson studied her. He didn't understand the power of his full attention to crumble her defenses or he wouldn't keep turning that weapon on her. Would he?

"See you after." She escaped to the stage.

Except the platform didn't shelter her from him. Dozens of others filled the room, but he was the only person she saw. The only one she cared to impress. Questions about him swirled in her brain, distracting her from her own performance. When she finally replaced the mic, she wondered if she'd put on a good show or mumbled her way through it.

"Good work tonight, everyone." Philip lifted the strap of his bass over his head. "See you all Thursday at lunch."

The Signalmen had been performing together so long, they hardly needed the lunchtime rehearsals anymore. Hopefully, Philip's mention of it was routine and not a subtle jab at her performance.

She hopped off the stage and headed for Anson.

He stood when she neared. "You're not a beggar, Blaze. Choose."

A giddy exhale escaped. "What am I choosing?"

Sydney and her friends skirted their table on their way

out. Blaze's stomach clenched, but Sydney flashed her a soft smile.

Anson's focus stayed on Blaze. "When and where you want the conversation to happen."

She swallowed. Sydney was a living, breathing example that a relationship with Anson could go off track. That there were right answers and wrong answers, some that divided and some that connected. She desperately wanted to connect—wanted his stories, his attention, his affection. "What are my options?"

He shook his head. "I decline to influence your decision in that manner." Humor played at the corners of his mouth—that perfect mouth.

She passed her palms over the hips of her jeans. "I feel like a genie's granting me three wishes."

"Just one. And I'm no genie."

But he could make her wishes come true. She clenched her teeth to keep that one inside. "Well, I'm curious, so I'd rather not wait. We both know I have a hard enough time focusing without a juicy question distracting me."

"The prescription still isn't helping?"

She shook her head. "Unless you call turning me into a zombie helpful."

He winced. "I wasn't thinking about how tired you might be when I came here."

"Are you about to offer an option?"

He shut his mouth and mimed zipping his lips.

"I feel this way no matter the time of day, and it could be weeks before I get better, so for the foreseeable future, it's zombie or nothing."

"Then I'll take zombie." After a beat, a grin spread his lips.

"What?"

"Yet another way movies have steered me wrong. They led me to believe zombies were ugly, badly dressed, brain-eating monsters. You're as far from that as it gets."

Not exactly a straightforward compliment, yet she chuckled. "You could meet me at my house." The offer was out before she weighed the consequences. "Mercy will be there—sleeping—so we won't be entirely alone, if that's a concern for anyone."

"Your house it is." He gestured for her to lead the way.

His headlights hung in her rearview mirror across town to the split-level home she inherited from Mom. Blaze parked in the single-car garage and took the moment alone to consider what she was doing, inviting a man into her home after ten o'clock at night.

But this wasn't just any man. This was Anson. If he'd gotten the wrong idea about her intentions, he would've shot down any suggestion of meeting here.

Still, this was *Anson*. Her crush on him was as overwhelming as the river he'd pulled her out of, and she hadn't straightened up the house. She probably couldn't ask him to wait outside while she put things away.

She climbed from the car and met him in the driveway, then led him to the side door closest to the garage. It would have opened into the mud room, if it hadn't hit something.

"Hang on," Marissa said.

The two seeing each other was yet another inevitability she'd overlooked. Blaze glanced at Anson and prayed Marissa wouldn't pull out her air quotes.

A couple of clunks later, the door swung open, and Marissa appeared in the gap, zipping her coat. Her line of sight landed beyond Blaze, and her eyes widened.

Blaze bustled in. "Everything go okay with Mercy tonight?"

"Yup. Is everything okay with you?" She swung her attention to Blaze.

She steered Marissa toward the exit. "See you Thursday."

"Okay, *friend*." She snickered and stepped past Anson, who remained on the step outside.

Blaze motioned him in, then shut the door firmly.

"Friend?" His voice, rich with humor, filled the small space as she hung up her things.

"Don't worry about her." Cheeks stinging, she stepped into the living room.

How would their home look to Anson? Mom drank most of her money, so the house hadn't been paid off when Blaze inherited the estate, such as it was. Using her own resources, she hired carpet cleaners, purchased area rugs, and bought new used furniture online. The two chairs and couch differed in shades and textures, but aside from the clutter, everything was clean.

She scooped the junk mail, Mercy's backpack, and a throw off one end of the couch and motioned for Anson to sit. "Want something to drink?"

"I'm fine." His step forward halted, eyes trained below the coffee table. "Is that a rabbit?"

She leaned to spot the creamy brown fluff ball. "That's Cinnamon Bun, a.k.a. BunBun. He's Mercy's."

Anson squatted and stretched his fingers toward BunBun's twitching nose. After a few beats, the bunny shot across the room and down the stairs. A few seconds later, a distinct thud sounded. Hopefully Anson didn't know enough about bunnies to know that had been a thump to alert everyone in earshot of danger.

"Should I be offended?" He shifted over to the couch.

"It's a compliment he stayed as long as he did. Let me go check on him and Mercy."

She padded down the stairs. By the light of the hall, she spotted BunBun in his hutch. Mercy didn't stir in her bed. Blaze eased the bedroom door shut. BunBun would feel safer that way, and it lowered the risk of Mercy overhearing them. Whatever Anson's story entailed, Blaze's chatty little sister could not be trusted to guard his privacy.

She hesitated with her hand still on the knob. Why had she asked for this? The invitation to her home made their impending conversation too intimate. It was no longer a casual meet-up with a friend following a show. But it was too late to back out now.

She retraced her steps upstairs and lowered herself to the corner of the couch, leaving a good three feet between herself and Anson. If only they had a cat or dog, another distraction might've wandered through the room. But who was she kidding? A pet cheetah wouldn't overshadow her monumental awkwardness.

Her voice came out high. "You have a brother?"

LOGIC, Anson's former guide, told him to get out of there without answering. But his heart longed for the exhilaration of knowing and being known. Besides, he was determined to be a man of his word.

He angled toward her, drawing one of his knees up onto the cushions and resting an arm along the couch's back. But getting comfortable was a lost cause. His heartbeat rocked his ribcage. "My brother's name was Guriel."

"Your parents have a thing for unusual names, don't they?" She pulled her legs up onto the cushion and nestled into the corner. Then, she stiffened. "Wait. Was?"

He nodded.

"Oh." Lips parted, she leaned her elbows on her knees, shifting close enough that he could touch her shoulder if he straightened his fingers. "I'm sorry, Anson." Sincerity rang in her tone, as clear as any note she'd ever sung.

He rubbed his thumb against the couch cushion. "Carter reminds me a lot of him. That's one reason I've been trying so hard to reach him."

"How are they alike?"

"Gury was a popular athlete too." A chuckle rose. "He also had a pesky little brother who looked up to him more than he knew."

She smiled gently. "You're Dylan in this story?"

"Yes and no. Unlike Dylan, I've always been pretty serious and dedicated to the rules. But Gury told me once that I could be good or I could be cool. After that, being cool was my compass in all decisions related to him. I didn't tattle when he pulled pranks or came in after curfew. Sometimes, I covered for him.

"Mom and Dad found out some of what he was up to, though. That's how he ended up grounded toward the end of my seventh-grade year, his eleventh." Anson hesitated. He could share the version of the story he'd told before or the version he'd long since classified. He chose the familiar path.

"He snuck out anyway to go to a party at a state park. That area is known for some steep bluffs. When our family went hiking there, I remember feeling nervous on the overlooks. There's no fence or anything, just rocks jutting out until there's nothing but turkey vultures drafting on the air currents.

"A couple of hours after Gury left, I was up in my room when Mom made this noise unlike anything I've ever heard. It was a wail, I guess." He clenched his jaw as the memory played. His aching throat turned his voice gritty as he continued. "Gury fell from one of the bluffs. He was drunk. Goofing around. Died instantly."

"Anson. I'm so sorry." She reached across the distance and laid her hand over his forearm.

He stared down at her hand. He longed to hold her, but more than that, he wanted to be held so he wouldn't fall into the abyss of these memories. He swallowed hard. "You asked once who I lost. He's the answer."

She scooted closer, her knee resting on his thigh as she encircled his hand with both of hers. Her warmth convicted him. The cost of true connection was truth. He'd been alone or faked his way through relationships for too long. She deserved the whole truth. The full version.

"But it ..." He cleared his throat. "It gets worse."

Her hold on him tightened.

"When my parents discovered he'd snuck out—before the accident—they asked me where he was. I lied and said I didn't know, but I heard him and his girlfriend talking." Anson had sobbed as he confessed to his parents later that night. After more than a decade, he hadn't expected his eyes to sting over it. "If I'd told the truth—"

"No." Shaking her head, she wrapped her arms around his shoulders. Her cheek moved against his ear. "We'll never know the alternate paths our lives might've taken if some detail had changed, but your brother is responsible for his own choices."

She shifted back, placing one hand on either side of his face and forcing eye contact.

As if he could look away.

"Do you have any idea how many things I've done to be cool or to fit in or to not rock the boat?" Instead of waiting for an answer, she enveloped him in another hug.

And just like that, she joined him in the abyss with all of her light.

He dipped his chin to her shoulder and let his eyes shut as he inhaled. Her hair smelled like flowers, and her arms around him felt like lifelines. She rubbed her hand over his shoulder blade. Seconds ticked toward the moment the embrace had to end, and his gut churned in protest.

When she sat back and drew her hands into her lap, he clenched his teeth.

He wanted more. More than a hug. More than friendship. Did she?

"When we got interrupted on Saturday, I thought the deal might be off. Thank you for trusting me." Seated sideways, she tipped her head against the couch back. "What did Greg want, anyway? He sounded so urgent."

The question pulled him back from the brink of confessing his feelings. His emotions were raw and strong right now, prone to prompting actions he'd later regret. Besides, it was getting late, and Blaze had been tired to begin with. This was not the time to make a move.

"A few families have left MOBC. Greg and I both reached out, but when people leave a church, they don't tend to return pastors' phone calls. Eric Newsome had coffee with two of the men who left with their families. He met with Greg Saturday morning to relay that their coffee clutch determined I don't have the personality to be a good youth pastor."

Blaze's brow furrowed. "What?"

"I'm too serious and strict, and if I leave, they'll consider coming back."

She bolted upright. "As if church is what? A middle school playground?"

He didn't disagree. "It convinced Greg that Eric's trying to have me fired. Until now, he didn't believe it."

"What are you going to do?"

"I'm still praying about that. Initially, my plan was to double the youth groups like he wanted. I have to admit, watching the kids care for their friends is rewarding, even if that hasn't resulted in a huge numbers boost."

"I'll pray the leadership board sees the value you bring."

"Thank you." The clock by the TV turned to 11:00. He stood. "I might not need to say this, but anything I tell you about church leadership has to stay confidential."

She frowned even as she nodded. "Though if most people knew, they'd come to your defense."

"Defensive people can easily lead to church splits instead of de-escalations. That's why I usually keep these things to myself."

She rose and ran her hand down his arm. "Okay. Nothing leaves this room."

If only that were literally true and he didn't have to go. She walked him to the door and rested her hand on his shoulder as he stepped outside. The warmth from the contact cooled before he reached his SUV, but his feelings for her?

Those only strengthened the farther away he got.

22

*B*laze groaned at the estimate from the service department. If preparing the trade-in for resale cost this much, her salesperson had overpaid the client by almost a thousand dollars. How had he overlooked such worn tires?

She forwarded the invoice to the service department manager and asked if his team could watch for used tires in the right size. Swapping the nearly bald ones for a used-but-not-shot set would bring the bill back into the margins she needed if she hoped to improve her department's profits.

The email sent, her screen returned to the inbox view. She blinked hard, her body craving a nap right there in her office chair. This prescription was killing her. Staring at her screen would be so much easier than talking with the salesperson who'd made the mistake. But movement would wake her up.

She shook her head to rouse herself and pushed back from her desk.

Her phone buzzed in her pocket as she stepped onto the

sales floor, but she knew the dangers of distraction. Instead of checking it, she set her sights on Thomas, only to find him with a client. When he looked at her, she pointed and mouthed, *My office.* He acknowledged her with the slightest nod.

She treated herself to her phone as she headed back for her desk.

At Anson's name, her stomach swooped.

I set up a motion camera in the youth room. You'll have to let me know if you spot it tomorrow.

Hard to say whether she'd remember, but her brain did favor Anson. If she was going to remember anything at the right time, it'd be something for him. For example, she could replay almost every word they'd spoken last night.

Will do, she replied. *I'm glad it's up and running.*

The next most recent conversation was the one with Marissa.

After he left the night before, Blaze found a message from her friend. *Let me know how things go.* The string of kiss-blowing emojis had left zero doubt what kind of update Marissa expected.

We're friends, Blaze responded. *We had a good talk, but that's it.*

Her swoopy stomach needed that reminder today. If only, as they'd pulled back from that last hug, he'd cupped her face, been incapable of looking away from her lips, and asked to kiss her. Or, better yet, just gone for it.

He seemed like the type to ask, though. She'd heard that was the respectful, politically correct course, and he was nothing if not respectful and politically correct.

Not that it mattered how her friend—no air quotes—went about kissing people.

She rubbed her forehead and set the phone aside to tackle the paperwork her team had handed in that day. If she procrastinated, she'd fall behind again, and she lacked the willpower to fix it.

She lacked the willpower for anything these days. Even keeping her eyes open.

She exhaled as she rested them for a moment.

"Blaze?" a voice boomed.

Her eyes flew open. Her head swam with disorientation. Ten lines of 1s filled her screen. Had she fallen asleep with her fingers on the keys?

Thomas loomed in her doorway. A smirk tugged at his lips. "Sleeping on the job?"

She wiped her face. Ignoring the accusation might not be the best solution, but what could she do? Admit she had been? "I needed to talk to you about your latest trade-in." She clicked into the mechanic's report and turned her screen toward him.

He lifted an eyebrow as he stepped in.

She outlined what she'd done to correct his mistake.

He braced a hand on her desk as he leaned close to study the numbers. "Half of this is stuff no one would account for, short of having service go over it with a fine-tooth comb, which we don't do. As for the tires, you already arranged a fix. I don't get why I'm in here."

"*If* the service department obtains the right size tires with enough tread left, they can get us out of this bind. But it's better to use a tire gauge, like you've been trained to do."

He straightened and slid his hands in his pockets. "It's a common tire size. We'll have a fit for that car in three days. Maybe less. And don't forget this trade-in was tied to the purchase of a new car."

"We are not in the business of salvaging tires. Our policies exist for a reason. Can I trust you to follow them?"

"Sure, but when people take their business somewhere else, you'll know why."

"As a salesperson, it's your job to help them understand and appreciate the value you're providing."

Her phone vibrated against the desktop, and she jumped.

Thomas couldn't look any more unimpressed.

She forced herself to her feet, hoping to regain some of the respect she'd lost. "This impacts your margins, as well as the department's. If you need a new tire gauge, request one from the parts department."

"Sure thing." He rolled his eyes on his way out.

She couldn't say she deserved better. She dropped back to her seat. With her new, do-it-immediately system, she turned her reports in on time, but her department still wasn't meeting the financial goals. If they couldn't get there soon, she wasn't sure what her boss would do. Especially once he heard about her little nap.

23

On Thursday night at The Depot, Anson spotted David two seconds before he pulled out a chair at Anson's table and sat with his arms crossed.

On the high school basketball team, they'd been uneasy allies, bound to each other by their mutual goal of winning. These days, David seemed to favor only two attachments: his younger sister, Marissa, and his best friend, Sterling. Since Anson associated with neither, he couldn't imagine what common interest had inspired this visit.

David seemed content to sit like a ticking bomb, so Anson risked cutting the silence. "What can I do for you?"

David shrugged and looked toward the stage.

Blaze threw her head back, crooning a love ballad. She sounded good—a surprise only because she'd stayed home sick from Rooted the night before.

Anson asked if she needed anything, and she'd replied with two words: *Just sleep.*

Not sure if she'd take the stage tonight, he showed up

anyway. When her voice greeted him, the tension in his chest loosened.

"She tried out for the school musical once." David's eyes followed her across the stage. "They turned her down. Said she could sing but not act."

That was a weird piece of trivia to retain for ten years. "I'm sure she could act if she put her mind to it."

"Better than Prissy Johnston, anyway."

"Haven't heard that name in a long time." Anson wouldn't have remembered their school's biggest theater buff without the prompt. That David retained her name—and had thoughts on her acting skills—suggested he'd paid more attention to their classmates than Anson realized. "What's she up to?"

"Works for some production company in California."

"How do you know all this?"

David snorted. "Knowledge is power."

Knowledge about Prissy Johnston? "All right. I'm curious. Tell me about Blaze and the musical."

"I think the truth was, she was *too* good. She would've put everyone else to shame. Guess what else she's too good for." David raised his eyebrows.

Anson shrugged and shook his head. "Surprise me."

"You." David pushed his chair back and braced a hand on the table. As he rose, he paused to catch Anson's eye. "And if you don't believe me, it's even more true."

Anson opened his mouth to respond, but to say what? That he and Blaze didn't have that kind of relationship? That, maybe instead of either of them being too good for the other, they actually made sense?

David straightened. "Hurt her, and you'll have me to deal

with." He clapped Anson on the shoulder and headed for the bar.

～

WHEN BLAZE STEPPED OFF STAGE, Anson met her with a glass of water. She'd finished her onstage water bottle two songs ago, and his thoughtfulness made the drink that much more refreshing. "Thank you."

He smiled, and she wished he'd slide an arm around her. Wished their closeness on Monday, both emotionally and physically, were the norm and not the exception. Yet for all her wonder at their connection, they still had a lot to learn about each other.

She set the glass on the table. "I'm not sure I've ever seen you talk to David before."

Anson shrugged. "Other than graduating together, we don't have much in common."

They might have more in common than Anson realized. David tended to act careless and gruff, but for the right cause, he'd put the welfare of others ahead of himself. "You were in the same bus accident," she said.

"True. He helped haul people out." Anson focused on the middle distance. "At the scene, he seemed fine but I hear he passed out at home. Internal bleeding."

Blaze winced. The refusal to show weakness sounded like David.

"How close are you two?" Anson's voice lowered into a rumble.

Was he ... jealous? The idea was so far-fetched, she laughed. "He's Marissa's brother, so he was around a lot.

Their mom made him drive us places, since he got his license before we did."

Anson stuffed his hands in his pockets, eyes narrowed.

David had really done a number on him. "What did he want from you tonight?"

"He says you're too good for me."

A half-cough, half-laugh burst from her. David had a lot of nerve assuming they were a couple, let alone playing the older brother stand-in. But his concern for her, as embarrassing and misguided as it was, showcased a certain sweet loyalty. "And no one believes he has a soft side."

"He did end with a threat of violence." Judging by his tone, Anson wasn't worried. At least, not about David's threat. As he studied her, concern slanted across his features. "How are you feeling? I thought you might not sing tonight, since you weren't well yesterday."

"I'm sorry I missed Rooted." She motioned him to follow her as she stepped past an *Employees Only* sign. They passed an office, then the hall turned and widened into a coatroom with hooks and a line of mini lockers.

She shrugged into her jacket and spun the combination on her locker to retrieve her purse. "I've been exhausted. I fell asleep at work on Tuesday and struggled all yesterday. I was in bed before eight." She pulled the purse over her shoulder and turned to face him. "I hope you and Nolan managed okay?"

"Sure." A line appeared between his brows. "Is this still the medication?"

Embarrassment sent her toward the hall. It wasn't a true escape, since he'd follow her, but it spared her having to look at the pity in his eyes. "I'm not sure I'll last the however many weeks it'll take to make a difference."

"I'm surprised you're trying to last at all."

"At least the headaches are gone. Maybe one of these days, the fatigue will be too."

"Isn't it normal to have to fiddle with the prescription?"

Annoyance begged to fire off a sharp reply, but she forced a deep breath. "It's also normal to have to wait weeks to see whether it's working."

She might not have curbed her frustration as well as she thought because he fell silent. They passed through the event hall and the dining room. At the exit, he opened the door and they started down the stairs.

"The thing is," he said, "I missed you."

Her fatigue dropped away, and her feet froze on the bottom riser.

Anson didn't stop until two steps later. He circled back. His soft smile was hard to read. Apologetic? Inviting? Friendly?

"At Rooted?" she asked.

"Yeah. And I think Hadley missed both you and Mercy."

That must mean he meant "missed" in a casual, friendly way. Not the kind of pining that might happen if his recent openness with her meant he wanted more than friendship. She resumed her course for her car. "I'll do my best to keep it a one-time thing."

"Good. I don't like you feeling unwell."

Neither did she, but she chose silence so he wouldn't start challenging the doctor again.

"You deserve to be healthy. You know that, right?"

She let out a tired laugh. "There are so many people suffering much worse illnesses, and I'd never tell them our health is about what we deserve. It's not."

"True. How about this? You deserve an advocate who'll fight for the best care you can get."

She managed to suppress her scoff. "Who's going to advocate for me? You?"

"You. Are you asking Mercy to go through the same things you're experiencing?"

"For about a week, I did. Then her side effects started going away. We had to adjust her dosage, but she's doing well." Between medication and lifestyle changes, Mercy had managed to remember everything she needed for school each day for a week now. Their system wasn't foolproof, but the chaos—where Mercy was concerned—had lessened. And thank God for that, because Blaze could hardly keep dragging herself forward one day after the next, let alone find the motivation for someone else too.

They reached her car. She unlocked it and turned toward Anson to end the conversation and get herself home to bed. His scent reminded her again of their embrace and tempted her to step forward into his arms. He tilted his head, gaze roving her face.

Touched by his concern, cracks spread in a fragile web across her composure. One wrong move, and she'd shatter into a teary mess.

"It's okay if you can't do the corn maze this weekend," he said.

Was this Saturday November already? She slung her purse into her car with a sigh.

"You forgot?"

She couldn't hold back the tears and answer, so she hung her head.

"I have it covered. There will be enough other leaders there."

"But I agreed—" Her voice faltered.

Her hair shifted. Anson brushed a few strands back from her face, somehow without touching her skin. His hand rested on her shoulder. "Your health is more important. How can I help? There must be a way I can make this easier."

He could actually touch her face. That would distract her from an awful lot of problems. Or he could confess undying love and loyalty. Hey, she was sleepwalking through life. Who could fault her for dreaming a little?

She swallowed. "Not that I can think of."

"Then I'll think of something."

24

The gourds, scarecrows, and signs throughout the corn maze helped Anson keep his bearings. Based on the number of times Hadley and Mercy had led their party of four down the same dead end, landmarks weren't their thing. Anson brought up the rear, letting them have their fun because, as long as they wandered these dusty aisles, he had time to think about Blaze.

He longed to talk to her more—every day, multiple times per day. If he could, he'd become such a regular at her house that even the temperamental little rabbit wouldn't shy away. He'd risk any threat David or anyone else mustered if he could feel her snuggled against him for a movie. And if he ever did kiss her, he suspected his imagination would fall woefully short of reality.

Did she find him even half so intriguing?

Confessing his feelings would risk the friendship, but pining silently would undermine the openness they'd established. Each time they talked, he craved more connection, and he was tired of inching along.

He had to make a move.

The corn maze funneled them around another corner. Hadley, Mercy, and Jasper ran toward the blazing orange dead-end sign, as if they couldn't read it from ten feet back.

He needed a clear gesture for Blaze. Something as unique as she was. If only her fire-related nickname weren't tied to painful memories, he could show up on her doorstep carrying a literal torch for her.

"Are you laughing at us?" Hadley stabbed her hands onto her hips. "You're laughing at us."

He raised his hands in innocence. He was laughing at a pun, and he didn't need to give Hadley another reason to call him Dad.

Mercy assessed him, then pushed her thick bangs away from her glasses and looked down the path they'd just taken.

Jasper trudged back, retracing their steps. Hadley and Mercy giggled, then trotted past him and into the lead.

Anson fell into step beside Jasper. "So, how do you know Hadley?"

"School. She's in my gym class. And science. And English."

"That's a lot of classes. Which one's your favorite?"

"Science, I guess."

It wasn't much of an opening, but Anson took it by asking questions about the class's subject matter. He appreciated that Hadley had invited Jasper, but if he had to guess, a crush was involved, and she was too nervous to interact with him. That or she'd just wanted the Rooted hoodie, which she'd immediately layered over the sweatshirt she'd arrived in. She had to be roasting on a nice day like this.

Anson and Jasper trailed the girls another ten minutes until, finally, Anson spotted the exit.

Mercy giggled. "Maybe it's this way!" She turned away from the opening in the maze that showed a slice of the barnyard.

Hadley hopped to her side. "Yeah! Let's go."

Anson checked his watch. "We only have half an hour left. The longer we're in here, the less time you'll have to shop."

The girls froze and looked at each other.

"Shop?" Jasper groaned.

"Let's try this way!" Mercy sprinted for the exit.

As they stepped into the barnyard, Jasper fell to his knees and pretended to kiss the ground. Mercy's laughter rose over the bleats of goats and the chatter of the other children filling the barnyard.

Hadley grabbed his hands and pulled him up. "Come on. My mom gave me money for a pumpkin."

And the kids were off.

"Stay together," Anson called after them.

"Okay, Dad!" Hadley waved wildly without looking back.

Goats and miniature horses nibbled treats and grass in a pen beside a barn-turned-craft-store. The white farmhouse served as a café. Pumpkins blanketed the lawn of the former home. He counted nine MOBC students and two leaders, meaning one leader and seven students were either in the corn maze or exploring one of the buildings.

As long as the kids stayed in pairs, they didn't need a leader. Carter and his friend—one of the twins from the canoe trip—were the exception. Anson assigned them to stay with Ray, but Carter and his buddy slipped into the craft barn unattended. Anson followed at a distance. He didn't think Carter would shoplift, but he hadn't expected the student to drink on a youth group outing either.

A Surefire Love

While Carter and his friend tried on colorful knit hats they clearly had no intention of buying, Anson browsed the home décor. Would Blaze like any of this? A few nature scenes hung on her living room walls, and there'd been throw blankets and pillows on the couch and chair. But no knickknacks like they sold here. Papers and books covered most of the surfaces at Blaze's. Where would she even put a ceramic pumpkin?

The boys gravitated toward the candles. Carter popped the wooden lids off the jars one after another, smelling each before putting them back. Rarely, he offered one to his friend to smell. Did he actually want a candle?

Anson made his way up the aisle and stopped by the teens. "Who're we shopping for?" He picked up one labeled apple pie, but it didn't smell as good as canned pie filling, let alone the from-scratch delicacy his mom baked every autumn.

"Which one do you think my mom would like?" Carter set down *lavender charcoal* and picked up *hyacinth dreams*.

"She likes flowers?" Anson asked.

Carter shrugged.

Anson tried cherry blossom, but that smelled like baby powder. "What's the occasion?"

"Just want to get her something."

Anson chuckled. "Trying to get out of trouble?"

Carter shook his head, mouth tightly shut.

Obviously disinterested, his friend wandered back outside as Anson tried more of the food-scented candles. His hand hitched mid-reach in front of one labeled *peanut butter cookies*. The ivory wax didn't come close to recreating the aroma of Blaze's baking.

He tried another, then offered it to Carter. "Sugar cookie's not bad. My mom likes the ones that smell like vanilla like this."

Carter accepted the candle, inhaled, and chewed his lip. "It doesn't smell like soap like most of them."

"It's the thought that counts, right? She'll be happy you thought of her while you were out with your friends." Few teenage boys would. Some of the youth group girls browsed nearby, but none of the boys.

Except Jasper, who trailed behind Mercy and Hadley carrying a massive pumpkin. Poor kid.

As Carter started for the register, Anson considered getting a candle for Blaze. But again, fire. Plus, the peanut butter cookie candle didn't smell as good as the real thing. Maybe he should bake cookies for her. Since Blaze was tired, she probably wasn't spending much time in the kitchen, but she clearly valued homemade food.

Decision made, he caught up to Carter in line. "How's your mom been?"

"Okay, I guess."

"Just okay?"

Carter shrugged, his main mode of communication today.

"Is she still involved with the women's ministry?"

"Yeah." The line moved forward, and Carter put the candle on the counter. He didn't offer more details about why he thought a gift was in order.

Anson prayed Carter would talk to him if something significant had happened. With basketball tryouts starting Tuesday, they'd see more of each other. Maybe then he'd open up. "I'm getting a cider for the road. Want to come?"

Carter looked at the brown gift bag the cashier had

placed the tissue-wrapped candle in, then at his friends, then toward the van. "Yeah, sure."

Movement through the living room window drew Blaze's attention from the TV. A dark blue SUV parked at the curb. She made a living off cars and tended to note what makes and models people drove. Despite never having been inside this vehicle, she knew who drove it.

Anson.

She flung aside the blanket she'd draped across her lap. Bunny fur coated one knee of her black joggers. A ranch dressing stain marred her charcoal gray sweatshirt. She'd gone an extra day without shampooing her hair because she wasn't supposed to see anyone today besides Mercy.

Even that was limited. Mercy came home from the corn maze and then headed to the library with Amelia.

Anson stepped onto the front walk. She didn't have time to change, but she did snatch a hair clip off the coffee table. The thing would never manage to restrain all her hair, but it held the top half back.

As he rang the bell, she stabbed the button to turn off the *North and South* miniseries she'd been watching. Just seconds before the big kiss at the finale too. She paused a moment to breathe before swinging open the door.

Anson wore jeans and a flannel layered over a T-shirt. Autumn sunshine washed his shoulders and highlighted his hair. He held a thin produce bag and the container she'd used when she left him cookies. "Hey."

"Hey." She stepped back to let him in. "I heard you assigned yourself Mercy and Hadley at the corn maze—

brave choice. They didn't completely ignore Jasper, did they?"

"Not completely." He shut the door behind himself.

She crossed her arms, unsure why he'd come or what to do with him. She nodded toward the container he held. "Looking for a refill?"

"Nope. First …" He extended the produce bag. "This is parsley. The rabbit can eat that, right?"

She accepted the offering in dumbfounded silence. He'd shopped for BunBun? The bunny had been running laps earlier, but she didn't spot him in his usual living room hangouts now.

"You don't have to give it to him now or anything."

"Okay. Thanks." She folded the bag around the bunch of parsley. "And the container?"

He passed it to her. "Mom always said not to return dishes empty."

"That really wasn't necessary." The contents rattled as she accepted the gift. "Mercy and I have cut back on sweets."

"I remember. How's that going? The diet change and medication?"

"I decided to take your advice."

"How so?"

"I found a specialist for myself. I have an appointment Friday morning. They sound a lot more thorough." So much so, they'd suggested bringing a loved one along to provide insight into how she operated. When she said she didn't have anyone she was comfortable bringing along, they asked her if she could bring in short, written statements from people in three different spheres of life.

Maybe Anson …? No. She didn't want him thinking of

her as a patient with a problem. At least not any more than he already did.

She cleared her throat. "Anyway, even if it doesn't turn out to be ADHD, they diagnose and treat other disorders."

"I'm glad. You deserve to feel your best." He squeezed her shoulder, then stuffed his hand in his pocket. "As for the sweets issue, these don't have refined flour or sugar."

"What do they have?"

"Coconut flour, dark chocolate, maple syrup, a few other things."

A sweet, chocolaty scent met her as she popped the lid. "All right. Let's give 'em a try." She led the way to the kitchen, put the parsley in the fridge for later, and set the cookies on the counter peninsula that separated the kitchen from the dining area. She took a napkin for herself and offered one to Anson. He accepted, and they each took a cookie. Fat and round, the dough hadn't spread much in the oven.

Blaze took her first bite, and crumbles sprinkled onto her hand. The cookie sapped the moisture from her mouth. Bitter chocolate and arid coconut flour lingered on her tongue. She swallowed hard. Twice. Embarrassment flushed her chest and neck. What should she say? What if her face had already given away her opinion?

She risked lifting her gaze.

Anson held his cookie between his thumb and index finger. He chewed slowly and studied the remaining portion like he was deciding how to respond to an insult. He must not have tried one before bringing them over. What was it like to be so confident that failure came as such a shock?

A laugh escaped her throat. She lifted her hand to stop it, but he looked at her.

The corner of his mouth lifted. He parted his lips as if to speak, but instead he laughed rich and low.

Blaze set her cookie on her napkin and retrieved two glasses of milk. She passed one to him. "Anson Marsh, I do believe we've discovered the one thing in this world you're not good at."

He snorted and took a long drink. "Well." He set the milk on the counter next to their discarded cookies and cleared his throat. "That's a real shame, because I wasn't actually trying to bake cookies." He braced a hand on the counter.

"That makes more sense. If you were trying to make cotton balls, you're well on your way."

He nodded as if to say he'd deserved that. His smile relaxed as his gaze roved over her face. "I was trying to show you how much I care about you."

Her mouth went dry again. Did he mean *care* in a romantic sense? More likely, the miniseries he'd interrupted was fueling her imagination. "I value our friendship too. You're not who I thought you were. Or maybe you've changed since I made my initial judgments. I suppose I have too. Growing up will do that for a person." Was this how Mercy felt when she babbled? Blaze couldn't stop the words from spilling out. "And they say friendships are harder to establish as adults, but we kind of fell into this, and—"

"I'm falling for you, but not like that." Calm and steady, his voice conveyed none of the self-consciousness that zapped through her veins.

Paired with his serious expression, there was only one logical interpretation of his words, right? But ... "Not like that, how?"

"As much as I appreciate you as a friend, there's a lot more to how I feel about you."

"How do you feel?"

"Surprised." He shifted closer.

Closer than a friend would stand. Right? Shortness of breath might be depriving her brain of the oxygen it needed to interpret the situation.

His eyes flickered over her face again, halting her spinning mind. "Impressed." He slipped a lock of hair behind her ear. His finger traced the shell of her ear and sent tingles all the way down to her fingertips and toes. "Loyal. You've always intrigued me."

"Always?" Her voice shook. His tender touch was the realization of weeks' worth of hopes and daydreams.

"I was a fool to keep my distance, but I kept tabs on you through high school." If he weren't standing so close, she might have missed the color shading his cheeks. He was blushing? Over her? "When I came back after college, I tracked where you sat during services. I couldn't resist your shows." He winced. "Earlier this year, there was talk of you leaving to pursue a career in music, and the idea of you leaving was a gut punch."

"But we ..." She shook her head. "We weren't even friends then."

"Like I said, that's my fault. My failure to see what was right in front of me. I'm sorry I misjudged you. Can you forgive me?"

She'd never tried to break the ice either. She'd noticed his attitude toward her, written him off, and had been judging him for it ever since. Maybe *Pride and Prejudice* would've been a more fitting miniseries to watch today.

Yet there he was, openly admitting his faults. Seeking forgiveness. Humility skyrocketed to the top of the list of traits she considered appealing in a man—a list that hadn't mattered in years. But now Anson, the most upstanding guy she knew, was standing in her kitchen, laying out his heart.

For her. Blaze Astley. The girl who'd once burned down a building. The woman who couldn't seem to get her professional life together. The guardian who could barely look after herself.

He touched her hand where it rested on the countertop. "Forgive me?"

She tensed her arm, keeping her hand in place. This felt too good to be true. "I'm not Sydney."

His head tipped, kindness in his eyes. "I know exactly who you are."

The vow sparked hope in her chest.

"You are a survivor. An overcomer. A creative thinker. The best voice Many Oaks has ever heard—"

"What about Michaela?" Philip's pop-singer wife was internationally famous, and for good reason.

"You're better."

She dipped her chin in disbelief. "Anson."

"You will never convince me otherwise." He threaded his fingers between hers until their palms pressed together.

She could only swallow and wait, staring at their hands.

"You're a talented salesperson with a generous heart. You live a life of grace and kindness. If there's anyone you should've kept your guard up with, it's me. And yet you've shown me compassion and acceptance that I don't deserve. And my biggest problem with you ..."

She bit her lip and met his eyes again.

"My biggest problem with you is how you won't show yourself that same understanding. I hate seeing the hurt that causes, and I hate that I'm one of the people who treated you in a way that led you to believe you don't deserve the grace you give others."

She licked her lips, defenses and insecurities toppling. "What grace? I still haven't agreed to forgive you."

A slow smile pulled at his lips until a dimple appeared in his cheek. "Forgive me, Blaze?" He traced her jaw until the knuckle of his index finger rested under her chin. His gaze fell to her lips.

He wasn't only asking for forgiveness. He was asking for a kiss—an entire relationship.

She longed to step into that with him, but all these hopes and dreams sprang from an ideal, and how many times had people let her down? Left her to fend for herself when she needed them most? Even Anson had failed her.

Was it safe to trust him with her heart?

Anson watched the war play out in Blaze's eyes. He'd already said all he could to convey his sincerity and convince her to see herself his way. The Lord would have to do the rest. The transformation wouldn't happen in a moment, but what better place for her to take a step forward than on an autumn afternoon in her kitchen, the scent of chocolate from his ill-fated cookies floating on the air?

She folded her fingers tighter around his hand, and he had to look to make sure he hadn't imagined it. His attention raced back to her face. She lifted her chin. Her lashes fluttered closed.

Victory sailed through him. He tugged her hand, and she tipped closer, free hand braced at his side as he lowered his mouth to hers. Her lips were soft and full and—

She leaned back, creating a sliver of space.

He clenched his teeth against groaning a complaint. He opened his eyes to find her studying him. He wanted to promise her that she was safe, but his thick throat kept him silent. It was hard enough to school his ragged breath as his heartbeat rocked his chest. He waited, forehead against hers, fingers on the smooth, warm skin of her neck. The hair he'd tucked behind her ear tickled his thumb.

Her head carefully still, as though to issue no accidental encouragement, her brown eyes peered into his. "You mean all that?"

"And more."

Her exhale brushed his chin. Trust settled in her eyes, and instead of fighting the rush of satisfaction, he relished every detail from her chiffon skin and floral scent to the way her breathing deepened and slowed.

He nuzzled her cheek, and she tilted her head. The fringe of her lashes eased to her cheeks as her eyes closed. This time, when their lips touched, she melted into him. If she was an inspiration on stage, in his arms, she was an epiphany. He was no artist at expressing himself the way she was, so he poured as much of "and more" as he could into each move and breath and touch.

When he broke the kiss, he brushed his fingers over her hair. Looking into the depths of her eyes, he swallowed so he could speak. "And even more."

25

Blaze squirmed on the couch in the youth room, feeling every bit like a girl who'd had her braces removed and was waiting for her friends to notice. The change between her and Anson was so obvious to her that she couldn't believe no one had commented on it.

The Rooted leaders' meeting gave her the perfect excuse to ogle him. His dress pants and black button-down complemented his athletic musculature. Or was her brain simply filling in details about his build gleaned from her time wrapped up in his arms? She once considered his mouth irritatingly close to perfect. Now that he'd kissed her, she could confirm—his lips were, indeed, perfect. But irritating? Hardly.

"For our next series, I'd like to have adults from the church share their testimonies. I think it'll help bring home some of the things we've been talking about this semester."

She nodded along. If Anson's acceptance amazed her, then God's was so far beyond her comprehension she'd never understand what saving her had cost Him and spared her. Healing had started the morning she turned her life over to Him, and she loved stories of grace interrupting people's lives. Loved their victories. She still had a long way to go, and their stories gave her hope that the best was yet to come. "Who are you going to ask to talk?"

"I thought we'd keep it in-house, at least for this semester."

"In-house?" She shot a glance at Nolan, hoping he looked as clueless as she felt.

Anson drew a circle with his pointer finger, including the three of them. "I'll go first to set the pace, then I'd like it if each of you would take a week."

Dread reverberated through her core. He wanted her to share *her* story?

"Sure," Nolan said. "If you think it'll help. Mine's pretty straightforward, though. I was in middle school, so it's relevant in that way, but I'm not sure it'll take a whole lesson to share."

"You can talk about your walk with Christ since your initial decision too. Your stories could help show them it's a lifelong relationship, not a one-time rite of passage."

Nolan nodded, and Anson's gaze settled on her, eyebrows lifted.

"Um." She smoothed her skirt. "I'm not sure I've really arrived at a point where my story would be helpful to the kids. I'm kind of the opposite. A long story before I got saved, and not all of it is middle-school appropriate."

"You don't have to mention anything you're not comfortable with. The goal is to tell about what *God's* done rather than what *you've* done. I trust you both, but if either of you want to run your testimony by me before you share it with the kids, my door's open. I'll give mine this week, then Nolan

A Surefire Love

the week after." He consulted his phone, presumably checking the calendar. "Blaze, that would put you the following Wednesday. Does that work?"

"Okay." She eyed the lectern where Anson stood so comfortably. She would take him up on the offer to review her testimony before she gave it. A narrative took shape in her mind, too long and complex to type on her phone. Hopefully she could remember the parts she liked when she got home.

The couch shifted as Nolan rose. Anson stuffed his phone in his pocket and picked up his Bible and notes. She snagged her purse and jacket, then stood.

As Nolan left, Anson stepped up beside her. "What are your lunch plans?"

She warmed, and she hadn't even slipped into her coat yet. "Just headed home for soup and sandwiches." She slid her arm into one of her coat sleeves and juggled her purse as she twisted to find the other sleeve.

Anson moved behind her and held the coat for her. "You and Mercy?" He settled the coat over her shoulders and ran his hands down her arms before stepping away.

"Yeah. She spent all day yesterday out, so she needs to buckle down and do her homework today. Historically, that meant I'd need to hover over her shoulder, but she's been doing better the last couple of weeks."

"So her medication is working."

"It appears so."

"And yours?"

She fiddled with her purse strap. "I didn't have the heart to take it this morning. I'm sick of being so tired. The new doctor can scold me if he needs to. But the prescription didn't resolve my original problem—distraction." She gave a sheepish smile. "Did you say anything in the meeting that I need to know? Other than that the sleeping bag owner hasn't been found and I'm supposed to give my testimony?"

"I guess you'll see on Wednesday." Smirking, he waited for her to step into the hall, then locked the door.

There was no guarantee she'd focus any better on Wednesday than she had just now. Maybe after her appointment on Friday, though. If it went well.

"Can you write a note for me?" The question slipped out before she'd vetted it, but after yesterday, she didn't feel nearly as self-conscious with Anson.

He rested a hand on the small of her back as they started down the hall. "A note?"

"For the doctor. It's helpful if he can get a take on me from a couple of different perspectives, different spheres of life." Her voice came out cheery because Anson kept his hand in place.

Given how reserved he'd always been with Sydney, she'd assumed any contact from him would only happen in private. Walking down the hall with his hand on her back felt almost scandalous. Granted, the last classes had ended half an hour ago. She checked over her shoulder. The hall was empty.

"The idea is to see how much of your life is affected?"

"Right. ADHD wouldn't affect just one area. I have Marissa and Philip each writing a couple of lines describing me. If you don't mind writing one, you can seal it in an envelope. That way, there's a chance I'll be able to resist reading it so you don't have to worry about hurting my feelings by being honest."

"And what sphere of life do you want me to speak to?"

His warm hand made her very aware of the sphere of life she most wanted him in.

"We still haven't gone very far into the personal sphere."

He frowned. "I have some pretty vivid memories from yesterday that suggest we're making progress."

She coughed. She must not be the only one with a replay looping through her brain.

He chuckled as he withdrew his hand. "I guess I'll keep it church related. When do you need it?"

"Any time before my appointment on Friday."

He dipped his chin. "Consider it done. And speaking of Friday, can I take you to dinner? Either Friday or Saturday?"

Inwardly, she squealed, and her voice came out breathy. "That sounds nice. Just don't say you want to go to The Depot."

"For our first date?" He pressed a hand to his chest. "Never. How about The Red House Grill?"

Date. She liked hearing him say it. "I've heard of Red House, but I haven't been there."

"It's an American grill with a few unique things on the menu. Casual, but the food's always good, and since it's out of town, we're less likely to run into people we know."

He had openly dated Sydney in Many Oaks. Now he wanted to hide his time with Blaze? She forced a teasing tone. "Are you embarrassed of me?"

"It's not that."

Her throat cinched. *It's not that* was a long way from *no*.

"People are going to have a lot of opinions about us. I'd like to keep this private for now, if we can."

She felt like black tar was spilling over her head and dripping toward her toes. "Opinions like how you shouldn't be with someone like me?"

He stopped walking in the middle of the hallway outside the offices and caught her hand. "Not long ago, someone told me to follow my heart, and do you know what happened?"

She shook her head.

"An avalanche of memories, all of them about you. I wholeheartedly chose you, and I have no regrets or second thoughts." He ran his thumb over the back of her hand. "But I do want to keep this private. My position here isn't as solid as it once was, and Eric's been aiming at any target he can find. I need to protect our relationship from that. I care for you too much to do anything else."

"I care for you too." The words felt like the first steps after a fall—uncertain and a little painful. "I'll get back to you on whether Friday or Saturday works best. I'll need to find someone to watch Mercy. Either a sleepover at a friend's house, or Marissa might be willing to hang out with her."

"Okay. Let me know." His lips twitched like he wanted to say more. Instead, he released her hand and tipped his head, motioning behind her.

She turned to find Mercy headed their way. No wonder he'd released her. If they wanted any semblance of privacy, Mercy needed to remain clueless.

Blaze rubbed her hand, already missing his touch. "I guess I'll see you Wednesday."

"Take care." He stepped away.

Pastor Greg came out of the main office and cut past with a curious glance on the way to his office. There really was something to Anson's theory about how much interest people would take in them.

When Mercy was close enough, Blaze looped her arm around her sister's shoulders. "Ready for some grilled ham and cheese?"

Mercy eyed her like she'd lost it. "Since when do you like grilled cheese so much?"

She tweaked her sister's nose instead of answering, because it definitely wasn't grilled cheese she liked.

As ANSON NEARED, Pastor Greg stood outside his office with his mouth hanging open.

Anson suppressed a chuckle. The memory of Blaze's wistful look as she agreed to the date sent endorphins splashing into his bloodstream. "Need something?"

Greg pointed after Blaze and Mercy. "What was that?"

Anson looked back, but the sisters were already around the corner. "What?"

"The office door was open. You didn't hear me in there?"

"Oh." Apparently, he'd been oblivious to anyone but Blaze. "I guess not. Why?"

"When the printer stopped, I overheard a few things I didn't mean to eavesdrop on." Greg stepped into his office, and Anson followed. The senior pastor dropped a packet of papers onto his desk. "I thought you and Sydney Roswell were serious."

"We were until we weren't."

Greg's surprise flickered over his face. "You broke up?"

"A while ago."

"Well, that was discreet."

"Didn't see the need for it to be anything less." The whole relationship had been quiet. Why broadcast the embarrassing part?

"And you and Blaze?" Greg sat on the edge of his desk.

Her name linked to him brought a warm flash of pleasure. He'd written off chemistry as something better left behind in high school or college, a dangerous experiment that could blow up a pastor's career. Unchecked, it could. But within the right bounds? Someone get him a lab coat, because he had a new favorite subject. "We're getting to know each other."

Humor played at Greg's mouth. "Is that all? If you didn't notice me clunking around in the office, you were pretty absorbed in each other's company."

Anson crossed his arms. "Is that a problem?"

Greg shook his head. "I'm glad to see it. You're something of a lone wolf."

A lone wolf raising multiple packs of pups, maybe. Anson laughed. "I'm *always* surrounded by people."

"How many of them really know you?"

He cocked his head. "There are some things I can't run around talking about. That's the job, isn't it? Surrounded, but not necessarily known?"

"I'm not talking about running around, talking carelessly. But isolation leads to a lot of unhappy pastors. Everyone needs confidants and accountability—friends in their corner."

He wasn't wrong. Anson could use more friends on the leadership board, but opening up about personal matters at this point would more likely draw fire than amass allies.

"Besides, a ministry is more effective when it's not only theologically sound but also has a beating heart, don't you think? How long's it been since you shared a sermon only *you* could preach?"

Again with the heart stuff. Why did this keep coming up? "I just made a plan with my team to share my testimony."

"Oh. Then I stand corrected. Keep following the Lord's

prompting. Sounds like He's already showing you what to share and when." He walked around his desk and turned on his computer. "Let me know how it goes."

Taking the cue, Anson retreated into his own office. After he shut the door, he paused. The uneasiness stirring in his chest drew his eyes to the rough-hewn cross on the wall.

The Lord had poured His heart out for His people, and He had a right to ask Anson to do the same.

Am I holding too much back, Lord?

Given the current climate in the church, sharing too much with anyone—besides, perhaps, Blaze—would be like walking into combat without armor. As he stared at the cross, his uneasiness settled. His mission was to share God's heart, and if he wanted to continue doing that, he couldn't afford to be any more vulnerable than he already was.

26

On Tuesday, Anson looked from his clipboard to the players lined up along the bleachers. Their voices formed a low murmur, punctuated by occasional laughter or the squeak of a sneaker against the maple flooring. These forty boys would compete for the twenty-four spots available on Many Oaks High School's basketball teams. Every player from last year's varsity team, save for those who'd graduated, stood on the sideline with one exception: Carter.

A senior so invested in basketball normally would've been first in the gym, bent on intimidating the lower classmen and defending his position as the first-string power forward. If Carter didn't show, Tommy Pine, who'd played on the JV team for two years, was primed to move up.

Anson slipped his phone from his pocket to check for messages from the senior. He found a text waiting for him, but it was from Blaze, confirming Friday for their date.

Even the excitement of that didn't temper his concern over Carter's tardiness. *Where are you?* he texted.

Coach Thierry blew his whistle and explained how the four days of tryouts would work. Then Anson stepped forward, introduced himself, and forced himself to focus on the students who'd shown up instead of the one who hadn't.

On Wednesday, Carter missed tryouts again, still with no word. That officially disqualified him from the team. First the drinking, then the candle, and now this? Anson suspected Carter was dealing with something big, and he'd counted on having the basketball season to get to the bottom of it. Now that his only interaction with Carter would be at church, a lot more rode on his testimony.

After practice, Anson stopped home for dinner before continuing to Rooted. Following a similar lesson plan for both youth groups meant sharing his testimony with the younger kids would help him refine his talk before Branching Out.

Except, the closer the evening came to the lesson time, the tighter a fraying rope twisted in his gut. He sent a prayer heavenward as he took his place up front.

Blaze's lips tipped up in an encouraging smile.

Mercy sat beside her, wide eyes blinking behind her thick glasses. Next came Hadley, who hadn't made a decision for Christ yet. He wasn't sure about some of the others.

As he looked at them, praying his story would help them, the room quieted. He peered at the timeline he'd jotted down to serve as his notes.

Greg had encouraged him to share about himself, and maybe his nerves proved just how overdue this was.

He eased into it with background about his decision to trust Christ as a child and discovering basketball in elementary school. When he mentioned how his dad's job had brought their family to Many Oaks, Blaze flinched. She alone recognized what he'd omitted—Gury. His story had enough impactful elements without talking about his brother. At least, that's what he decided when he wrote his timeline. He was too far into the story to second-guess that decision now.

"As a junior, I was offered a full-ride basketball scholarship by one of the best college teams in the country. Aside from my parents, my coach was my biggest supporter. He and his wife took me and my parents to dinner to celebrate. The food that night was amazing, but in retrospect, I wonder if what I tasted was the flavor of dreams coming true. I was on my way to playing professionally and beyond excited about it."

Wonder glossed over some of the kids' eyes.

"But it went to my head. My senior year, I was team captain. I believed I deserved to be, but the other guys didn't respect me. It got so bad, one of my teammates and I almost came to blows over it."

Hadley toyed with the long ends of her hair. One boy cringed. Another nodded.

"Coach Voss pulled me aside, and I couldn't believe *I* was the one in trouble. I argued I was doing everything right." He raised his finger the way Coach had. "'But your heart is wrong,' he said. Since he knew I was a believer, he talked about how God values our hearts and is a lot more gracious and forgiving than I was being with my teammates. I learned a lot from Coach Voss, especially that year. He had a bunch of little sayings he repeated like, 'responses trump reactions,' and 'go out trying.' Those pop in my head and guide me to this day."

A flood of bittersweet memories tightened his throat. He took a few extra beats, staring down at his notes before he trusted his voice. "But toward the end of the season, our entire team, myself included, was in an accident coming home from a game." Flashes of chaos and darkness rippled behind his eyes. "Coach Voss died."

Gasps sounded around the room. These kids would've been toddlers at the time.

"Everyone was hurt, some worse than others. My shoulder was dislocated and I was banged up, but the hardest part for me was the spiritual and emotional aspect. I still miss Coach Voss."

But Coach was gone, and these kids needed to hear the end of Anson's story. "At Coach's funeral, people kept talking about how well he lived his life. Former players and guys who'd been in his Bible study shared about how he helped them when they were headed down a bad path. That's when I realized I didn't want my life to be about basketball. I felt very strongly that God was calling me to pick up Coach's legacy and run with it. The athletic accomplishments I'd been chasing wouldn't last. Only a relationship with God does. I backed out of the scholarship and went to seminary instead."

He skimmed the last couple of words he'd scribbled down and abandoned the paper on the lectern. "These days, I work here, and I'm a basketball coach at the high school. I still don't get everything right. Just like Coach used to, God corrects me—usually through His Word or His people—and sends me back out to try again. Now, it's *my* honor to invite other people onto the team.

"But that metaphor can go too far. God cares about you

beyond simply wanting to make you better. He wants you to be part of His family. When you're in a scary or sad situation, you don't have to fix everything yourself. You can trust Him. He's a coach and a friend and a savior." Anson paused and surveyed his audience.

Tate, the most hyperactive of the bunch, bounced his leg, but even he watched Anson. Meanwhile, Blaze smiled.

"Does anyone have questions about my story?"

Hadley blurted out hers before he could call on her. "What was the fight about? The one with your teammate?"

"How to do a drill."

"Did you see your coach die?"

"No, I didn't." He pointed to another student, hoping he'd pipe up before Hadley reloaded.

The boy asked about the accident too, as did the two students afterward. He'd captured their attention, but perhaps he'd failed to point it toward the Lord.

Testimonies could be powerful, but this might not have been the time or the place for his.

BLAZE COULD LISTEN to Anson field the students' questions all night.

For years, he seemed too uptight to relate to anyone, let alone a child. Yet his talk had been inspiring. His commitment to building a heavenly legacy, one that involved these kids he had no familial connection to, made her breath catch.

She saw his dedication in action as he worked through their blunt questions about his hard experiences. He answered without chastisement.

"What does it mean to be part of God's family?" Jasper asked.

Anson's shoulders lowered a fraction. "I'm glad you asked that." He went on to answer with empathy and grace. And a Bible verse.

How in the world could she take that hot seat in two weeks?

Maybe Anson would help with the Q&A following her testimony. Or maybe that part could be optional.

"Okay." Anson's voice broke through her thoughts. "We're going to break into small groups. Girls, you're up front with Blaze. Guys, let's circle up in back."

And just like that, five middle schoolers pulled their chairs closer, as if she could teach them something. Blaze glanced down at the discussion questions Anson had given her and read the first one. "Anson talked about thinking of God like a coach. How do you think of God?"

Painful silence stretched.

Hadley chewed the corner of her mouth as she eyed the other girls. Mercy picked at her nails. The remaining three looked anywhere but at Blaze.

As a distant authority figure probably wasn't the kind of answer she ought to share with the kids. The Lord was more to her than that, but when Anson talked about God being more than a coach waiting for her to do better, she'd needed the reminder.

You don't go alone. You don't have to make situations better for yourself. You can trust Him.

Promises like those had drawn her to Christ in the first place. She'd been overwhelmed by her failures and the sense of doom that she'd end up like her mother. She'd needed a loving savior like the one Pastor Greg—and now Anson—described.

Blaze steeled her nerves, ready to muddle through an answer about being grateful for God as her savior, when Mercy spoke up. "Sometimes the Bible calls Him Father, doesn't it? I like that one."

"Father is a good one." Praying it wouldn't backfire, she risked another question. "In what ways is God like a father?"

She hadn't meant to put Mercy on the spot, but before she mentioned that anyone could answer, her sister piped up again. "Once, I was playing outside with a friend, and she said that if anything bad happened to her, her father would come rescue her. I didn't believe her, because we were all the way in my yard, not at her house, but she was like, 'I'll prove it.' And she screamed so loud." Mercy held a hand near her ear. "Then her dad walked out into her backyard looking for her. She waved at him and said she was fine, and he went back to whatever. And I was, like, kind of jealous, but that's the kind of dad God is, I think. He's always watching, and He'll take care of me."

"That's really sweet, Mercy." And heartbreaking, because Mercy had never met her earthly father—neither sister even knew his name.

"My dad wouldn't hear me scream." Hadley folded her hands and twisted her arms as if to turn inside out. "He lives in Alabama."

"I didn't have a good dad either," Blaze said. "He left when I was really little." Should she leave it at that or share more? "Mercy's right that the Bible calls God Father, but I think any of the things we compare Him to—like coaches or fathers—don't fully express who He is. If He's like any of those things, He's also better than we can imagine. When we believe in Him, He really does take care of us. Maybe not always the way we want Him to in the moment, but in the way that's best for us."

The girls fell silent, but their little smiles said they'd been listening. She resumed the pre-written questions. The boys finished up, and Blaze hurried to lead the closing prayer—she'd never gone longer than the boys' group before. Maybe she was finally hitting her stride as a youth leader.

After her "amen," the girls hopped up, and Blaze reached to get her purse from beneath her seat. When she straightened, someone bumped her arm.

Hadley. The girl had been seated across from her moments ago, but now she occupied the chair next to Blaze. "What if I want God to be my father too?"

Blaze almost choked on surprise and a fresh surge of insecurity.

"If you're right that He's better than any dad I can imagine, He's the one I've always wanted."

Blaze glanced at Anson. Should she hand this conversation over to him? But Anson had assigned the girls to her, and Hadley had sought her out.

Blaze cleared her throat. "You can ask Him to come into your life. You can trust Him with your heart and tell Him you want a relationship with Him. Want to pray with me to do that?"

Hadley nodded.

The youth room grew louder by the moment, but Blaze folded her hands and bowed her head with a reverence she hadn't felt since her early days as a believer. For the minute she and Hadley prayed together, holy ground spread beneath them. Hadley wouldn't be the only one walking away from this changed.

When Blaze opened her watery eyes, Hadley smothered her with a hug. As she returned the embrace, Blaze spotted Anson watching. She grinned and nodded, and when he dipped his head, she knew without a doubt that he was thanking God right along with her.

27

"What have you got there?" Anson slowed his steps beside Shirley Aaldenberg's ancient sedan in the church parking lot. Through the windows, he saw her wrinkled hands tugging on a box that must weigh as much as the senior saint did.

The woman's poof of white hair lifted, and her face appeared over the roof of the vehicle. "They're candles for the Christmas Eve service. That warehouse store in Delft is closing. I got us a great deal."

He grinned. "I bet you did."

He circled the back of the car and hauled it out. He was already a few minutes late to the leadership board meeting, but letting Shirley deal with the candles alone would be the greater offense. He started for the building, and she scurried ahead to open the church door.

"Where are these going?" he asked.

"Wherever you think there's space for them, as long as one of us remembers where they are come December." She lifted a penciled eyebrow.

"How about the storage closet by the youth room? I use that closet all the time, so I'll remember. And it's a logical place to check, since we keep other decorations in there."

"Perfect. Need me to get any more doors?"

"I've got it from here." He made his way across the building.

He'd found no signs of the youth room visitor since installing the camera. Maybe the person had noticed the device and switched to using the closet again? That was where he'd first found the sleeping bag.

He flipped on the closet light with his elbow. No food, wrappers, clothing, or sleeping bags stood out. He stowed the candles and jogged across the building to the conference room.

The board had already moved through the opening prayer, approved the agenda, and was discussing the first line item—which keynote speaker to invite for a conference in spring. Anson took a seat at the foot of the table, drawing glances from the six others in the room.

As the last item was resolved an hour and a half later, Anson folded his agenda and waited for Pastor Greg to begin the closing prayer.

Instead, Eric sat forward in his seat. "I'd like to hear an update about the youth group initiative. When we first discussed this, the youth groups were expecting eight to ten students. My understanding is the groups haven't even seen a fifty percent increase over that, let alone doubling. You're averaging maybe eleven? Twelve?"

Anson unfolded his agenda and reread the line items.

George Pelle, a retired businessman, spoke up. "We voted to add this topic at the start of the meeting."

Frustration at the ambush simmered, but at least he had

a success to report. "I'm glad you asked about the youth groups. A Rooted student accepted Christ last night."

Smiles lit up faces around the room.

Eric's faded first. "I'm glad to hear that. But let's not change the subject. A single student's decision is separate from the attendance goal. There hasn't been headway. It almost seems you've dismissed the idea altogether."

"I've geared everything this semester toward helping the kids talk about their faith more and invite friends. One or two new kids show up each week." Every regular attender to Rooted had earned a hoodie. One of the new students had too. Branching Out students were more hit and miss with bringing guests. "Last year, we had a lot fewer friends dropping in."

"If that many new students come, why are the groups barely bigger than they were?"

Six serious expressions awaited his answer. Greg's held a tinge of apology. Same with Ed Larsen, a fifty-something social worker. Paul Beck, a retired lawyer, must have mastered his poker face during his days in court. Mike Kaysen, the youngest of the group at forty, narrowed his eyes.

"Most kids who are committed to church life already have a youth group, and my goal has never been to steal students from other churches to come here. The students and I are focused on friends who aren't involved in a church yet and don't believe, in a lot of cases because they haven't even heard the gospel. We're reaching the lost in a way we haven't before, and I'm grateful for the initiative because it inspired that. I think all the kids are benefiting. Hence Hadley's decision yesterday."

Ed nodded as Anson spoke.

Eric's lips settled into a pale line. "My understanding is that Hadley has been attending since the start of the semester, before any changes were implemented."

"True." Although the observation raised the question of who was sharing details about attendance with Eric. Perhaps his wife, who worked with the younger kids on Wednesdays.

"The kids who visit would benefit more if they kept coming," Eric said, "and you're not doing what it takes to make that happen."

Anson eased a breath out. If he stayed calm, Eric might show his true colors for all to see. "What do you suggest?"

"Youth group needs to be more fun. Relevant. Don't spend so much time on dry material. Just give them a safe, fun place to hang out and they'll flock to youth group."

"Safety and fun are part of it, but if you limit our responsibility to those, we're running a daycare, not a youth group. We're called to so much more."

Mike leaned forward. "What I think Eric's trying to say—or maybe forgetting to mention—is that we set this goal because the congregation here is aging, giving is down, and the youth groups are shrinking. If we want to survive, we need to make changes to attract a younger demographic."

Anson scanned the room. Only Ed and Greg looked troubled. "We have made changes. But attendance can't be the priority over the gospel."

Paul interlaced his fingers and tapped his thumbs together. "I think we're all together in hoping that improving the numbers will mean even more students hear the gospel."

"How would they if we're not preaching it?"

"Maybe what Eric's suggesting is a different way of living out the faith," Ed said. "It's like what I do as a social worker.

Live out of love and be ready to answer for my hope if someone asks."

Anson nodded. "I respect that as a way to live out your faith in a secular workplace, but the church exists to point people to Jesus."

"A message they'll get on Sunday mornings, when they come with their families." Mike creased his agenda in half and motioned with it as he spoke. "And can you imagine what a difference eighteen new families would make?"

Anson's muscles tensed. "For the budget or eternity?"

"Both." Heat crept into Eric's voice. "God cares about the practical as well as the eternal, as should we. As a board, we've determined a course we believe honors God to grow the church, and we asked you to join us. I added this to the agenda because I'm saddened by the lack of response to what we've asked you to do. Your spirit of contention won't be tolerated."

"Because I haven't quit teaching the kids?" Anson leaned back in his seat. He struggled to breathe as a deluge of insults rushed to mind. He should quit.

Responses trump reactions.

Quitting would sacrifice his last opportunity to reach Carter. He couldn't do that, no matter how angry he was.

"Let's step back for the time being." Greg's words reached him like a voice from another room. "We are all interested in honoring God here. With that to unify us, we *will* find a solution, but we won't find it tonight. Let's all pray about it and reflect on this over the next week, then bring suggestions to our next meeting. Between us, surely we can discern how the Lord would have us grow the youth group—and attendance in general—while maintaining our mission of being a source of light and hope."

Finding a solution after a week's reflection would take a miracle, and Anson had seen far too few of those. Still, Eric didn't object to Pastor Greg's suggestion, so Anson held his tongue.

∼

"I WAS HOPING YOU'D COME." Blaze slipped into the seat beside Anson's at The Depot and bumped his arm with her shoulder.

His smile was lackluster as he slid her an envelope. "This is for the specialist. Do you want to know what it says?"

She gulped and shook her head. If the notes she'd collected only sang her praises, the doctor wouldn't get a true picture of her to aid in the diagnosis. But she was already too well aware of her flaws. Reading the exact feedback wouldn't help her any more than eating that apple had helped Eve. She fit Anson's envelope in her purse next to Philip's.

Before she put the purse back on the floor, she pulled out a folded stack of lined paper. As she set it on the table, Anson ran a hand over his face.

She brushed his forearm with the back of her fingers. "What's wrong?"

"The leadership board. I knew Eric wanted me fired, but tonight was the first time I realized he might actually get his way."

"What?" At her loud question, he glanced around. She lowered her voice, despite the sense of injustice ringing in her core. "That's ridiculous. I've never seen a better youth pastor."

The corner of his mouth lifted ruefully. "Have you *seen* any other youth pastor?"

A nervous chuckle caught in her throat. "Like, in person?"

He laughed and shook his head. "Anyway. Why were you hoping I'd come?"

She hesitated. With his job in jeopardy, her own concerns were far less pressing. Yet he seemed to want a distraction. She nudged her papers toward him.

"Look at us, passing notes." As he unfolded her pages, insecurity shivered through her.

"After hearing your talk last night, I went home and all of that poured out. It's my story. I know I'll cut things like you did to make it relevant and shorter and less ... personal. But I thought you could help me decide what to cut and what to keep?"

His gaze swung up from the pages. "This is your unedited story?"

He might as well ask if he was holding her soft, beating heart.

"Basically." She'd omitted certain details, but she mentioned all the significant events she could recall. Some of her admissions were more appropriate for a high school audience than a middle school one. Some, perhaps, shouldn't be shared with either. She didn't trust herself to know the difference, especially when she'd been so surprised by Anson's choice in his testimony. "You left out Gury when you gave your talk. I understand not diving into all the details, but you skipped him entirely. Do you plan to tell the high school students about him?"

His brow furrowed instantly, and he gave his head a quick shake.

"Why not?"

Leaving the papers on the table, he sat back and pushed his palms over his thighs. "A story like his might elicit an emotional reaction, but I want the kids to choose Christ based on something less fleeting."

"Isn't Gury's story about as deep as it gets? We all need to consider the afterlife."

"Sure, but Gury isn't the only person I lost. Eternity comes into my testimony through Coach Voss too."

Feeling a little like a confused Rooted student, she persisted. If she couldn't understand this, how could she give her own testimony? "It's not always as impactful to students when an adult dies. When it's a student like them—"

"It wasn't the time or the place." His tone was firm. "The message that needed to come across did, or Hadley wouldn't have chosen Christ."

The reminder of Hadley soothed the sting of his interruption. "I haven't prayed with anyone like that since Mercy, and she was quite a bit younger at the time." Blaze bit her lip, looking at her papers. "I'll need your help deciding what to keep and toss in mine, then, because I definitely would've voted to mention Gury. I put in pretty much everything."

Letting him read her unabridged testimony served a double purpose. Not only could he give advice on how to present it—if he still believed her qualified to speak to his students—but she could also quit wondering if knowing the truth would change his mind about her.

He unfolded the papers, but after a moment, he extended the packet toward her. "I want to hear it from you."

She lifted a hand in refusal. "I wrote it out."

"It's different, reading versus hearing." Hope brightened his expression. "Besides, I love your voice."

"Flattery will get you everywhere, huh?" She accepted the papers back and scanned the words she'd hurriedly scrawled last night. In this lighting, she hoped he couldn't discern the tremor in her hand.

Laughter from the bar echoed through the event hall. With the evening's entertainment over, the room had mostly emptied. The few who remained were a good fifteen feet away and engrossed in their own conversations.

She'd asked Marissa if it'd be all right for her to not come straight home, but she couldn't dawdle forever. She cleared her throat and bumbled through the facts about her parents, the fire, and her stint in foster care. "By the time I got home again, I knew my mom wasn't like other moms, but she reminded me often that she'd worked hard to get me back, so I needed to be a good girl or I'd have to go away again. Maybe the reason all the kids believed I'd been sent away as a punishment was because that's what I thought. I was really lonely and scared." Her voice hitched. Wow, that was harder to admit than she'd expected.

Anson's touch on her elbow reminded her of how times had changed.

She flashed him a grateful smile, then refocused on her paper. "Then, one day, I woke up, and Mom was different. She made me breakfast. She touched my hair and called me sweetie. I was in high school by then, and I remember her affection and interest so clearly. I didn't trust it, but day after day, she stayed sober and interactive. She actually showed up for one of my choir concerts. Afterward, she hugged me and said, 'I know I haven't been there for you, but things are going to be different because there are going to be two of you, and I want to give you both the world.' And that's how I found out I was going to have a sister."

She licked her lips and swallowed, lifting her attention to Anson. "I'm not sure how much I should get into this part, since it involves Mercy."

"We can talk about that." He rested his arm along the back of her chair and trailed his fingers up and down her shoulder—right there, in public. "For now, if you don't mind telling me, I haven't heard this before."

She leaned into his side as she went back to the page. "Turns out, Mom had gotten sober when she found out she was pregnant with Mercy, and after a few months, I stopped worrying about her relapsing. My sister was born. At first, I thought Mom was kind of crazy for naming her what she did, but she said she liked the sound of mercy." Blaze could still hear her low, rough voice saying as much. "Mom wasn't a believer, but it did seem like mercy had been extended to us. I finally had a good mom and a sister, and between the two of them, I wasn't lonely anymore."

The memories of those days shimmered like a mirage, thin and unreliable. "One morning, as I was rushing out the door to school—late again—I heard Mercy wailing. She'd had a diaper blowout, and Mom wasn't anywhere to be found. I cleaned Mercy up, but I couldn't leave her alone when Mom wasn't in the house. A couple of hours later, Mom showed up with bits of grass stuck to her and dirt on her face. She reeked of alcohol." Grief pulsed in Blaze's chest. "Seeing her walk in that way was the biggest heartbreak of my life. She gave up her sobriety, and she never reclaimed it. After that, it was up to me to look after myself and Mercy."

"How did you care for an infant with school?"

"Mom had a job at that point, so she paid a neighbor to watch Mercy during the day. From then on, I was the one to drop her off in the morning and pick her up in the evening. Since Mom spent so much on her habit, I got a part-time job after school until Mercy needed to be collected, then I'd take her with me to buy groceries and stuff."

"How did you afford all that with a part-time job?"

"I used Mom's cards whenever I could. When those ran out, I used my money, so I could never save more than a few hundred dollars. Because Mercy's care was almost entirely up to me, leaving for college was out of the question. Besides, there was no money for it, and I'd never been a good student anyway. At eighteen, I got a full-time job selling cell phones and plans. I was good at it, so I made decent money, but I also watched my friends launch into adulthood with a lot less baggage than me.

"I resented having to take care of Mom and Mercy, and I started seeing a guy who said it was time someone took care of *me*. Man, I fell for him. He was a few years older. He had his own house, and he seemed like my knight in shining armor. He drank, but he never lost control the way my mom did. We got pretty serious. Or, I did, anyway. I lived at his house more than at home." The confession burned her face because Anson would know what that meant. She didn't dare look up.

"But over time, I saw his dark side. He *did* drink too much and missed work. He expected me to tend the house, throw parties for him and his friends, and contribute to the household finances. Meanwhile, I was still funding Mom and Mercy, even though I otherwise kind of left them to their own devices." She shook her head and sighed. But for Jesus, she was no better than either of her parents.

Clinging to grace and her last shred of dignity, she continued. "As if that wasn't bad enough, I'm ashamed to say

I'm not the one who broke it off. He got a fine from the town for not mowing the lawn, and he blamed me for not taking care of it. He got really ugly."

"Violent?" Anson's voice was low, and his hand curved around her shoulder.

She toed the ground, and her chair scraped against the floor. "Shouting. Nothing physical. He called me ungrateful and told me to leave. I moved back home with Mom and Mercy. I was paying the mortgage by then anyway. I was angry though. Resentful. I felt like I'd been dealt a bad hand. I got involved with another guy and started drinking. Did all kinds of things I regret." She peeked at him, her bottom lip clamped between her teeth.

Anson's mouth tightened, but he resumed rubbing her shoulder.

Bolstered, she continued. "I spiraled. I've always had trouble being on time for things, and with partying in the mix, I became the one who lost control. I missed work so much, they fired me. I went home and Mercy met me at the door and asked me for money so she could go to the grocery store because there was nothing to eat in the house." Tears collected in Blaze's eyes, and she read through the sheen. "That just about did me in. She was only six. She never should've had to ask that question. Realizing I was putting her in the same position Mom always put me in, I hated myself right into a church service."

There. The worst was behind her. Her neck relaxed. "I'd listened to the Christian radio station a few times over the years, accidentally at first, then trying to figure out what it was all about. They talked a lot about hope and change, so when I needed help changing, I knew I needed a church."

One of her few happy childhood memories surfaced, and

the tension released from her shoulders too. "I chose Many Oaks Bible Church because, once, years before that, during Mom's sober period, she took me to a mother-daughter tea there. That day, I felt like all the other girls. Everyone was so nice and so happy to see us."

She chuckled, thinking back. "Of course, since the tea party was my only experience with church, before I attended a service as an adult, I went to a thrift store and got a kind of ridiculous dress because that was what all the ladies at the tea wore. When I showed up at church and saw most people in jeans, I almost turned right back around. But I needed help too much, so I swallowed my pride and went in.

"Pastor Greg preached about grace and hope and mercy, and I craved it all. I prayed that morning to accept Christ, and I felt changed. Like I had some hope that God could turn it all around. I quit drinking. Quit going out with my friends and stayed home to read my Bible. Within a week, I landed a job at the dealership. I got some counseling. Caring for Mercy became more of a privilege than a burden, though I'm not sure I ever struck the right balance of boundaries with Mom."

Not for lack of effort, though. Blaze spent hours hashing through options and situations with her counselor. The woman helped significantly in some ways, not so much in others. "Whatever the case, there were some decisions I couldn't make for her. She was visibly unwell a long time before she finally saw a doctor. When she did see one, she refused to tell me what he'd said, but she got worse and worse. It was liver disease. She might've had a chance if she'd given up drinking, but she refused. In the end, her kidneys gave out first.

"I shared my faith with her again while she was in the

hospital that last time, but the only serious topic she'd discuss was Mercy's future. She signed the paperwork to name me as her guardian." Mom's hand had shaken as she pressed pen to paper. The wish of a dying woman who liked the sound of mercy but hadn't wanted to talk about it.

Blaze fiddled with the edge of her own papers as she braced herself to admit the next part. "It was both hard losing her, because it meant Mercy really was my responsibility, but it also felt like a fresh start. I know that sounds selfish."

"It sounds honest."

"Honest good or honest bad?"

"Good, Blaze. You went through a lot, but you tried to give her the best gift you had. I hope, in the end, she took it."

"Me too." Blaze sat with that for a moment. "I won't say this to the kids, but does it sound crazy to say I wonder about generational curses? I feel like I'm living under the shadow of something—despite Jesus, despite Mom being gone for years already."

"Childhood trauma affects a person." His hand covered hers even as she held her pages. "But through Jesus, you're not doomed to repeat anyone's mistakes."

"Maybe not. Maybe this whole journey into learning about ADHD and anxiety is about freeing us up a little more." She skimmed the rest of her notes. "That's basically what I wrote. That God is the reason Mercy and I have hope. He's the only reason we've made it this far."

She pushed the pages a few inches away, and Anson pulled her into a hug.

Her eyes sank closed. She hadn't felt so secure since he'd saved her from the river. "So, you liked it?"

"No."

Her stomach sank, and she shifted back.

He kissed her forehead, then tucked her to his side. "I don't like that you went through all that. And that was just a couple of pages of your stories. I'm sure you could fill a book with events that would ..." He sucked a breath through his teeth. "Probably break my heart and make me want to go on a rampage."

She tipped her head against his shoulder. "You still want to associate with me?"

He laughed, rich and low. "I want to do a lot more than associate."

She gasped and clutched at non-existent pearls. "Anson Marsh, whatever could you mean?"

"At the moment, I was thinking of walking you out to your car and stealing a couple of kisses."

"There's a commandment against stealing."

"You're welcome to give them to me instead." When he smiled at her like that, how could she resist? She followed him out to her car.

28

Blaze hadn't realized she'd chosen such a young specialist. Dr. Van Blair's bio included a thumbnail-sized picture, but she'd scrolled past to read about his approach to his practice. With only faint lines by his eyes and on his forehead, he might be in his thirties. A doctor his age couldn't have much experience. Had she made another mistake?

Lord, please give this man wisdom. I can't keep doing this.

She produced the envelopes. "Since I had no one to bring with, I asked some people to write about me. Philip is my boss for my singing gig." She surrendered his note first.

Dr. Van Blair hummed a few random notes to himself as he read. "Next?"

"Marissa. A longtime friend."

Her thoughts must've been brief, because he barely hummed two bars before he eyed her last envelope.

"Anson is my church's youth pastor." Her heart lurched as she passed it over.

The doctor withdrew the paper and read it as quickly as

the others. Afterward, he dove into questions about her work, her family, her experiences in school, and her life. Then came the assessments. Her confidence wore thin. If, after all this, he handed her another anxiety diagnosis, she'd be in tears. Which would probably confirm what she didn't want to believe about herself—that her problem was, indeed, anxiety, and all her other struggles stemmed from laziness or incompetence.

Two hours later, Dr. Van Blair looked up from the latest set of results. "Good news. Coffee isn't the problem."

Blaze bit her lip, unsure how to take that.

"Instead of leading to jitters, in people with ADHD, caffeine can adjust dopamine to a more normal level that helps with concentration. Heavy caffeine use was probably your way of self-medicating."

"Self-medicating?" Was he saying she had ADHD? Or ... "Isn't self-medicating associated with addiction?" The last word came out in pieces.

"It is sometimes used in that context. That's not the way I meant it, but"—he nodded—"there *is* a link between ADHD and addiction to alcohol and illicit drugs. Since ADHD is genetic and both you and your sister have it, it's likely one or both of your parents did as well. That may have contributed to some of their struggles in life. Left untreated, ADHD can shorten life expectancy, sometimes significantly." His mouth scrunched.

Blaze clutched the armrest. Her parents might have had more working against them than she'd known. Regret and *what-ifs* churned her stomach.

"But, back to the good news." Dr. Van Blair raised a pointed finger. "ADHD is also highly treatable. In addition to the lifestyle adjustments you've already made with your sister, the medications available are some of the most effective out there. Now that we've confirmed you have it, we can set about finding which medication and dose is going to change your life—and I'm not exaggerating. I think you'll see a huge improvement."

"I was told I had anxiety." The thought slipped out as a whisper.

The doctor inhaled loudly. "Sure, I do see some indications of that, and if it turns out to be necessary, we certainly can treat you for anxiety as well. But I believe what we're dealing with here are the secondary effects of ADHD. When we notice we're struggling, like you have been with ADHD, it's natural to become anxious or to have low self-esteem. If we treat the root cause, the anxiety might very well clear up on its own."

Blaze's eyes flooded faster than the canoe had. Tears dripped off her chin before she thought to catch them. "So I'm not just crazy?"

Dr. Van Blair passed her a tissue. "You're not crazy. More than that, you're not broken."

You're not broken.

Anson had told her the same thing, and she hadn't believed him. Had the Lord prompted Dr. Van Blair to repeat the phrase?

"ADHD does have downsides," he continued. "But again, they are treatable—very much so—and there are also benefits to the way your brain works. People with ADHD tend to be great problem solvers, creative, charismatic, and highly empathetic."

She chewed her lip. Was she those things?

The doctor tilted his head and narrowed his eyes at her, as though sensing he'd lost her. "It might take getting used to

A Surefire Love

after a lifetime of thinking differently, but your brain is a powerful asset, Jennifer."

She dabbed the tissue at a fresh cascade of tears. That little girl in her kitten sweater embraced the compliment like a long-lost teddy bear.

The doctor scrolled on his tablet. "For example, as a performer, you have the audience eating out of your hand—that's charisma." Philip must've written that. "You also showed charisma as a salesperson and again when you landed the management position. I think with the right treatment, you can happily stay in that position because, with focus, you can complete the administrative side of things in a timely manner. Then you'll be free to spend more time with customers and your team."

She took a deep breath. These were all good things. Better things than she'd hoped for. So much better, she almost couldn't accept them.

Thank you, Lord.

So much about her life made sense now. So many of the disappointments and judgments and struggles—all things she'd blamed herself for—lifted from her shoulders.

"There's still a process ahead of us." Dr. Van Blair set aside his tablet. "But since you've already made a number of lifestyle adjustments, what do you say we figure out where to start with medication?"

"We still have ten minutes on the clock." Anson motioned at his dash.

Blaze's eyes crinkled with a smile, and she nestled deeper

into the passenger seat beside him. "What's left to talk about?"

Night had long since fallen, and most of her neighbors' houses were dark. He and Blaze had been together for hours. Over dinner at The Red House Grill, they'd discussed everything from her diagnosis to caring for the rabbit. If Blaze hadn't promised Marissa she'd be home by eleven, he could've talked to her all night. How had they been in each other's orbits almost half of their lives without him realizing how special she was? How had he spent so long settling for sensible when magical was an option?

Blaze tipped her head against the rest. "The only thing I can think of is your job. How are you going to get the numbers the board wants?"

His chest tightened. He'd had a different idea about how to spend the last few minutes of their date, but at least he had an answer for her. "I'm going to propose something else entirely. Something you inspired." He reached across the center console and squeezed her hand because, yeah, he couldn't stop touching her.

Her eyebrows lifted. Even in the faint light of the streetlights, she was as captivating as a flame. "Me?"

"You came to MOBC because of an afternoon tea. We still have some events like those, but we don't advertise them to the community. I'm going to suggest we do family fun nights once a month with a marketing budget behind them. Game nights. Competitions. Crafts. Maybe there's some skill we can teach in a workshop, but..." He traced a finger over the back of her hand.

Blaze dipped her head and caught his eye. "But?"

He cleared his throat. He'd much rather focus on her than work. "No lesson. Maybe an opening prayer, but other than that, we'll just be there to connect with people so they know where we are when they need us."

"Like I did."

"We could use more people like you." He shifted his hand, and she interlaced their fingers.

"I never used to think you were that big of a fan—but if I'm not mistaken, you washed your car for tonight, and this is a new sweater." She smoothed her hand across his chest.

"You caught me." *In more than one way.* "You make me better, Blaze." The compliment earned him another grin and a lingering kiss before he walked her to the door and bid her good night.

Back at his own house, Anson was too keyed up to sleep, so he hopped on the treadmill. Afterward, as he plugged in his phone to charge, it buzzed in his hand. He limited late-night notifications, but he hadn't blocked them all so church members could reach him in emergencies. He lit the screen and squinted at the icon—an alert about movement caught by the youth room camera.

He scrambled to tap the app. The church lights must be off, because the live feed showed the youth room in the grayscale of infrared. Nothing moved. Nothing appeared out of place. He clicked over to the recording that had been captured two minutes before.

The youth room looked the same as it had on the live feed, except something moved past the narrow window in the door. He played it again. A person in a hoodie had walked by. He enlarged a still frame. With the hood up, he couldn't see enough of the face to recognize the individual, but that was definitely the start of the word *Rooted* printed down the sleeve.

The visitor was one of the students. Urgency pushed him back into his coat and to his car.

He found the building dark and still. "Please let me help whoever it is, Lord."

He approached the building and tugged the handles at both principal entrances. Locked. He let himself in with his key and walked through the entire building, turning on all the lights and trying all the lesser-used exits. All locked. Every room empty. Having played Capture the Flag and Sardines with students in the building, he knew kids could be hard to find, especially in the sanctuary, where they crawled under rows and rows of seats.

He took a second pass. And a third.

The kid might've left before he'd arrived. Or someone might really need his help and not want to admit it. If the student thought he'd left, he or she might come out of hiding.

He shut the lights off, went outside to move his car out of sight, and jogged back, staying in the shadows. A couple of homes stood across the road, and if someone spotted him skulking around the building, they might call the cops. It'd sure be fun explaining this.

He let himself in through a seldom-used back door and crept through the dark to the sanctuary. There, he waited. The heat kicked on. A distant siren sounded. A clunk turned his head, but when it sounded again, he realized it came from the ductwork.

How long would a displaced student hide?

Blaze might have ideas about what to do, given how often she'd been left to fend for herself, but was it worth waking her in the middle of the night when he was fairly certain he was here alone?

Probably not.

He stood in the darkness. "If you're here, I can help."

No one stepped through the shadows.

What more could he do?

Defeated, he dragged himself home and went online to order cameras for all the doors, including the emergency exits. He'd get the board's approval before he installed them, but he wouldn't ask the church to foot the bill when the budget was already tight. Helping a hurting student was worth a few hundred dollars of his own money.

He was comparing camera features when his phone vibrated. He pounced on the device, expecting another movement alert.

Instead, he found a message from Eric Newsome. At two in the morning? He tapped to read the text.

The church is on fire.

29

Blaze let her eyes sink closed as she stretched first thing in the morning. Her muscles responded with the languid ease of a sleepy cat. How long had it been since she'd slept so soundly? Weeks? Months? Ever?

For the first time in her life, she had a diagnosis and a plan for dealing with the symptoms that haunted her. She'd been on an amazing first date. Mercy was doing well too.

Her eyes eased open to sunlight glowing through the curtains. She rose and pushed the fabric back so the rays spilled over her. It was like Jesus had finally lifted the shadowy curse she'd described to Anson, and the future looked bright. It was almost like going back to before she realized her mom was an alcoholic. Before the garage fire.

Your brain is a powerful asset, Jennifer.

The compliment was flattering, but the use of her name had hit her more powerfully. She should've taken Anson up on his offer to call her by her given name, at least once in a while. Not the full name—she'd never gone by Jennifer—

but she was no longer the little girl who'd been called Jenny, either. Jen, perhaps?

Her stomach flipped at the thought of that name on Anson's lips. She turned from the window and headed downstairs to make coffee.

As she padded through the living room on her way to the kitchen, she spotted her testimony littering the armchair beside the couch. She plucked the pages up. She shouldn't have left such personal notes out for anyone to read, especially not spread all over Mercy's favorite chair.

Blaze straightened. She *wouldn't* have left the testimony like this. She'd left it on the coffee table to edit later. She hadn't thought Mercy would notice it next to the stacks of forms, bills, and junk mail. Blaze herself couldn't say whether the papers had been on the chair or the table when she'd come in last night.

She leafed through the papers. Several had been wrinkled. Mercy had definitely read the pages. Her gaze landed on a line near a newly torn edge: *I resented having to take care of Mom and Mercy.* Blaze's stomach rolled. She'd made her sister feel like a burden. How could she have been so careless?

Mercy was usually up by now, but if she'd read this, it was no wonder she hadn't shown her face yet.

Blaze went down and pushed open her sister's bedroom door. Light from the window spilled over the empty bed. On the nightstand, her sister's phone was still on the charger.

"Mercy?" She flicked on the light. BunBun froze with his mouth full of hay. After a moment, his nibbling continued. Mercy wasn't by the desk, closet, or hutch.

Blaze forced a deep breath. Maybe Mercy was in one of the bathrooms or the kitchen.

She hurried through the house calling her name. She checked the unfinished storage space and every closet. Dread grew in her stomach as, room after room, her calls went unanswered.

"Mercy?" She returned to her sister's room.

Nothing.

She ran to the mud room and hit the garage door button, then jogged outside. The November chill cut through the thin flannel of her pajamas. No Mercy in the garage or yard.

This could not be happening.

Panting, she returned to the house. She needed to call the police. No, first, Mercy's friends. And Marissa, who might know when Mercy had read the papers and how she'd acted afterward.

Now where had she left her phone? She spun a circle in the living room. Still in her room? She took two steps toward the stairs when the door opened behind her. She whirled around.

Mercy stepped into the mud room with a blanket huddled around her shoulders. The hood of a sweatshirt covered her head, and jeans and shoes stuck out from beneath the blanket. She froze on seeing Blaze.

Blaze floundered in a swamp of impulses and emotions. She stopped in the doorway between the living room and mud room. "Where were you?" Though low and calm, her voice rasped.

Mercy let the blanket fall, revealing that she'd layered a winter coat over her hoodie. She shed the coat and hung it up, and she looked so small. Vulnerable. She held a coat hook for balance as she toed off her shoes. "I didn't think you'd care."

"Of course I care. Where did you go? When did you leave?"

Mercy slipped by Blaze into the living room, on course for her room.

"Mercy!" Her voice cracked.

Mercy turned, her shoulders stiff. "You resent me, right? And you *never* loved Mom. You were glad I was gone, and now you're mad I'm back." She glared.

"That is not at all true." A tremor kicked up in her chest, and her nose stung. How could she fix this? "I love you, and I'm sorry my testimony hurt your feelings, but you can't sneak out."

"Sure, I can! I was gone all night, and you didn't even miss me, did you? You don't love me!" She broke for her room and slammed her door.

All night? Blaze's breath rolled fast, and she couldn't seem to focus. She braced her hand on the couch and melted to a seat.

Because of her own free-range childhood, Blaze made sure Mercy wasn't home alone for extended periods, even though other eleven-year-olds sometimes were. Despite all her care, Mercy snuck out, and Blaze had been oblivious.

The realization caught fire and spread. What if this wasn't the first time? It wasn't the first time Mercy had been upset with her, and if she coped by sneaking out, Mercy could be the child who camped out at church sometimes. The building was four miles away. A middle schooler could make it by bike. Though Blaze had checked the garage, she hadn't noticed whether Mercy's bike leaned against the back wall.

On trembling legs, Blaze descended the stairs.

Mercy sat next to the hutch, feeding BunBun his breakfast pellets from a bowl. A tear trail ran down her cheek.

Blaze knew rejection and loneliness, and she'd never wanted to cause her sister either one. She sat on the bed. "Let's talk about my testimony."

Mercy passed her wrist over her damp cheek.

"I'm sorry my story hurt your feelings. I didn't mean for you to read it. It's not ready yet."

Mercy set the bowl on the ground and scooted back. "Mom wasn't like what you said."

"What do you remember about her?"

"She was fun. She laughed and danced with me in the kitchen." Her voice grew animated. "We had singing competitions to see who could be loudest. She drew on the sidewalk with me. We made a fort together. Once, we made breakfast for dinner, and you came in all mad about the mess we made. When you left, she laughed and said you just didn't understand." She peeked at Blaze.

She nodded. She didn't remember the specific incident, but Mom and Mercy had often been partners in crime.

"Then she got sick. She was tired and crabby all the time instead of just sometimes. I couldn't always make her feel better, but sometimes I think I did. I remember lying down next to her and she kissed me." Mercy plopped her palm against the side of her head. "Said I was a perfect angel and she loved me more than anything."

Anything except alcohol. But even that Mom had set aside to give Mercy a healthy start. "I have some good memories of Mom too. She could be goofy and fun, couldn't she?"

Mercy nodded.

"The thing is ..." Blaze hesitated, but the truth needed to be told or they'd repeat this conversation every time Blaze was honest about her childhood. Besides, eventually, Mercy would have to deal with Mom's impact on her own life. "Mom was actually sick the whole time. Do you know what alcoholism is?"

Mercy shrugged. "People who drink too much. Like that guy who fell into me at The Depot and sprained my ankle. I know you think Mom was one."

Blaze patted the bed and waited until Mercy sat beside her to continue. "When people hurt, they want to feel better. Drinking can help them forget and have fun. At least that's what they tell themselves. Sometimes they believe it so much, they don't see how their drinking hurts other people, so they don't see how much they need to change. That was Mom, and it could've been me."

Mercy stole a sideways glance at her. "You?"

"That's what I was writing about. I was angry that I needed to take care of things Mom should've taken care of. And that's the truth. I shouldn't have had to. But drinking wasn't the answer—it made everything worse. I just couldn't see that until one day, God used you to show me how much pain I was causing."

Mercy's lips pursed, and her brows lifted.

Blaze wrapped an arm around her. "If it wasn't for you, Mercy, I don't think I would've gone to church or decided I wanted Jesus. I'm really grateful for you. You saved me, and I love getting to share our lives. Most sisters don't get to be as close as we are."

Mercy hugged her back. "I'm sorry I got so angry."

"I forgive you. And I'm sorry I was so careless."

"I forgive you."

Blaze took a deep breath. "Can you tell me about last night? When did you leave? Where did you go?"

Mercy played with her hoodie zipper. "I waited for you to come check on me when you got home, but you didn't. You just went to bed. So I left. I read a book in the gazebo and then came home."

The gazebo in the park was about halfway to the church. Nighttime temperatures dropped near freezing this time of year. "Did you go anywhere else? Maybe the church so you could warm up?"

She shook her head. "Nope. Just the gazebo. I put the blanket over my head, and it wasn't so bad."

Blaze's suspicion spiked. She'd assumed a streetlight near the gazebo had provided illumination so Mercy could read one of her paperbacks. "How did you have enough light to read, then?"

Mercy stuck her hand in her backpack and drew out a small light with a clip. A book-light Blaze hadn't gotten her.

"Where did you get that?"

"Amelia's mom gave it to me."

"Okay. Um … how did you get there? To the gazebo?"

Mercy snorted. "Don't worry, I didn't steal the car."

Blaze rubbed her temple. That thought hadn't even occurred to her. "What about your bike? Did you ride that?"

"No, I walked. I didn't think of my bike, but the blanket would've tangled with the tires."

That made sense. "Was last night the first time you snuck out?"

Mercy nodded. "And I don't think I will again. The gazebo isn't very comfortable."

Knowing Mercy had left the security of home wasn't very comfortable either. Blaze would have to be more vigilant. "It's also not safe for a little girl to be out all night by herself."

"I'm not that little."

"*I* would've been scared outside like that in the dark."

"Guess I'm just braver than you." Mercy grinned up at her. "So. Wanna make pancakes?"

Blaze scoffed. "Not so fast. It's not okay to sneak out. You're grounded for the next two weeks."

"Grounded?"

Blaze nodded as if she wasn't making this up as she went along. She'd never grounded Mercy before. She'd never been grounded herself. But this seemed like the kind of situation that required a responsible guardian to assign consequences. "You scared me really badly, and that was so dangerous."

Mercy brushed her bangs back. "I knew you'd be mad, but two weeks?"

"Don't argue unless you want me to make it longer."

Mercy jammed her lips shut, but they curved with a frown.

Blaze rose. "Breakfast is up to you. We can do pancakes if you still want."

Mercy's frown deepened.

"Think about it." Blaze returned to the living room and lowered onto the couch to replay the conversation. Mercy probably wasn't the kid breaking into the church, but if she was? That'd be embarrassing at best, dangerous at worst.

Then again, if the camera in the youth room had caught Mercy last night, Anson would've called. She could probably rule out a trip to the church. But that didn't mean her sister would never wander out again. For added peace of mind, she borrowed Anson's idea and went online to find doorbell cameras for both the side and front doors.

As she finalized her order, Mercy stepped into the living room.

"Pancakes?" Blaze asked.

Mercy nodded.

"Good." They could use the sister time. She left her phone on the coffee table and turned for the kitchen.

"Oh. Your boyfriend's here."

Blaze's stomach jolted. She pivoted, and sure enough, out the front window, Anson's SUV was parked at the curb. "I—I don't have a boyfriend."

Mercy pushed her glasses up. "You said you were going to dinner with a friend last night. And then Anson picked you up, and he's a boy, isn't he?" The corners of her mouth tipped up. "Your *boy*friend."

"Going to dinner doesn't mean he's my boyfriend."

"But you keeping him a secret does." Mercy giggled, apparently recovered from the morning's tension.

Anson started up the front walk.

Blaze couldn't answer the door in pajamas with tangled hair and unbrushed teeth. "Can you let him in? I need to go change."

"Okay, but I'm gonna tell him you *lo-ove* him." She skipped to the door.

Blaze scampered up the stairs and out of sight. "You can say *like* if you want, but not *love*."

Was she falling in love? Possibly, because her uneasiness over Mercy had evaporated at the sight of him.

30

Anson scraped his fingers over his unshaven jaw. He hadn't slept in over twenty-four hours and ought to sleep while he could, but restlessness had sent him back into the world. He'd ended up at Blaze's house. He hadn't considered that she might not be the one to answer the door, but Mercy stood in the narrow opening.

"Yes?" She scrunched her nose and pushed her glasses up with a finger, guarding her entry like a happy little troll.

Could trolls be happy? If not, did that make her something else? A fairy, maybe.

Debating such a question proved that he should've gone home to sleep. He barely had the strength to stand upright, but he craved the comfort of Blaze's soothing voice, understanding demeanor, and unwavering belief in him.

"Is your sister home?"

Mercy poked her head farther through the opening. "She likes you." Her stage whisper was not discreet, and the fact that Blaze wasn't rushing to interrupt suggested she wasn't nearby. Mercy's closed-mouth smile might be mistaken for smug if not for her comically wide eyes and raised brows.

Were her glasses amplifying her expression? Or his fatigue?

Wait. Mercy wasn't supposed to know about him and Blaze.

Maybe she was bluffing to get information. "I'm not sure she'd appreciate you saying that."

"She said I could." Mercy stepped back into the living room.

She wore her Rooted hoodie. Ten to fifteen remained in the box in his office, so hers was just one of about forty in circulation. Some who'd bought them when he'd first ordered didn't even attend Many Oaks Bible Church anymore, and who knew how many kids had given theirs away. Tracking them all down was out of the question.

Mercy cocked her head, staring at him.

At a loss, he rubbed his hands and prayed for Blaze to appear. "Blaze is awake?"

Mercy crossed her arms, staring at him. "Mm-hm."

Footfalls on the stairs saved him. Blaze stepped into the living room, beaming. A gust of emotion tempted him to close the gap between them and wrap her in his arms.

Mercy turned toward her sister. "We can still make pancakes, right?"

Blaze's smile faltered. She laid a hand on Mercy's shoulder but stayed focused on him. "Is everything okay?"

"Ah, no." He hadn't considered that he might be the one to break the news. The fire had been so big, people from the surrounding neighborhood had crowded along the barricades, watching and posting on social media. "There was a fire last night. At the church. I haven't slept."

A Surefire Love

Was that last one an important fact? He cleared his throat and pulled his phone from his pocket. A few taps later, he passed the device to Blaze, a video of the church playing.

Mercy pressed against her arm, gaping at the screen.

Blaze inhaled sharply. "Oh, no. This is …" She watched a couple more seconds. "This is a huge fire. I can't believe it. What happened? Some kind of electrical short?"

"It's a long story." He rubbed his temple.

"And you've been up all night."

He nodded.

Blaze looked at her sister, then focused soft eyes on him. "Have you eaten?"

He shook his head.

"We make delicious pancakes." Mercy bounced ahead of them to the kitchen.

Blaze passed the phone back. The joy she'd shown on seeing him had disappeared, replaced by concern. "I agreed to pancakes before you got here, but I can ask her to take a raincheck. We can talk instead."

"It's okay with me if she hears the story of the fire if it's okay with you. The little we know will be all over town before lunch anyway." He caught her hand, no longer able to tolerate distance. "She knows about us?"

"She guessed. We can swear her to secrecy. Or try, anyway."

He couldn't muster concern about whether that would work. People at church would have enough to talk about with the fire. They wouldn't care about their youth pastor's dating life. For now.

"Hey." Blaze touched his cheek, and he refocused. She frowned, then wrapped her arms around his waist. With her head resting on his chest, he managed to take a few peaceful breaths.

When she pulled back, she went up on her toes to kiss his cheek. He'd come to the right place. She tugged his hand, and he followed her to the kitchen.

A large measuring bowl sat on the counter peninsula. Mercy had piled bags of flour and sugar and a carton of milk beside it. She consulted a recipe card, then whirled around like a tornado, sucking up the additional ingredients and spilling them onto the work surface.

"Do this a lot?" he asked.

"Yup." Mercy skidded in her stocking feet. "Just sit down while we make the magic happen."

Blaze spared him an amused smile, then joined her sister.

Anson took a seat on one of the stools across the counter from where they worked. "If you put the ingredients in, I'll stir. How about that?"

"Sure." Mercy brandished a measuring cup Blaze had supplied and scooped it into the flour. "Dry stuff first, then you make a well for the wet ones and mix again."

"Got it."

Mercy doled out the dry ingredients. Blaze pointed her back to the recipe and issued occasional quiet directions. He hadn't felt a sense of home and family like this since the last time he'd been at his parents' house. Contentedness replaced some of the fatigue. The family he'd dreamed of having for himself had never had faces before. Now, it did.

Blaze took a break from supervising long enough to eye him curiously.

Right. She wanted details on the fire. "Eric Newsome texted me early this morning that there was a fire at the church. He lives a mile or two down the road, so I'm sure he heard the sirens. It was big enough that they had to call in backup from surrounding areas."

"That's awful. Just seeing a video of such a big fire …." Blaze shook her head. "How much damage is there?"

"The sanctuary is a total loss. That's where they think it started. It spread to Greg's office and the kitchen, and ate through the wall between the sanctuary and the gym. I'll be surprised if anything on that side of the church is salvageable. Smoke and water probably did in whatever the flames didn't."

Her face paled. "Nothing was saved?"

"The classroom wing, but that won't give us enough space for services." He checked his watch. "I'm surprised the leadership board hasn't called a meeting yet, but I'm sure they will soon. I'll have to go when they do."

He accepted the mixing bowl from Mercy and whisked together the dry ingredients before passing it back. She made the well and poured in the milk.

Blaze took a bottle of vanilla extract from a cabinet. The scent wafted over as she measured out a spoonful. "And the cause?"

"I have a theory, but the clues aren't definitive."

"Clues?"

He reconsidered getting into it in front of Mercy, but she'd hear all of this eventually. Better for it to come from him with Blaze here. "The motion camera in the youth room went off last night. Someone walked by the window in the door. We don't have a shot of the person's face, but they were wearing a Rooted hoodie." He pointed toward Mercy's sleeve. "The word *Rooted* is partially visible."

Mercy's lips froze in an O, then her head quivered back and forth. "It wasn't me. I didn't start the fire."

"Don't worry. I know. There are a bunch of those sweatshirts around. Which is a problem because we don't know much else about the person. Because they didn't come into the room, we don't have enough detail to know if it was a boy or a girl or their exact height. Best guess is they were short—five feet, give or take maybe four inches."

Blaze studied her sister for a few beats. Anson waited for her to tell Mercy to leave, but instead she asked him, "Between the hoodie and that height, it was probably a student?"

"Seems likely to me," he said. "Anyway, this was before the fire. When the camera went off, I went and searched the building and didn't find anyone. I locked up and went home. About half an hour later, a 911 call originated from one of the landlines inside the church. No one responded when the operator answered, so they dispatched police. Officers found the main entrance unlocked and the sanctuary so full of smoke they couldn't see the flames. An extinguisher was lying in the lobby. The theory is whoever started the fire tried to put it out. When that didn't work, they called 911 and bailed."

Blaze braced a hand on the counter. "They're sure no one was trapped?"

"As sure as they can be."

She brushed stray flour off her fingers. "Thank God for that, at least."

Mercy held an egg suspended by the bowl but didn't crack it.

He gave her a reassuring smile. "Sometimes, kids hear

things before adults do, so if you hear anything from any of the students, let me know."

"I don't know anything." She shook her head so hard, the arm holding the egg trembled too. "I've never gone there when I wasn't supposed to."

He looked to Blaze to reassure her, but Blaze turned away and opened the refrigerator.

It was up to him then. He tried another smile. "I know it wasn't you. I'm just saying if it was a student, whoever it was might talk about it with their friends."

Blaze put a small bowl of butter in the microwave for a few seconds.

"Then what'll happen?" If Mercy paid that egg any less attention, she'd drop it. "When you find whoever it is, they're going to be in big trouble."

"Mostly, I want to make sure they're okay."

The microwave beeped, and Blaze returned with the melted butter. She surveyed the ingredients strewn across the countertop as if she no longer knew what to do with them.

Realization flashed over him. Mercy wasn't the only one he should've been worried about. Blaze had a traumatic history with fires. He should've been as concerned about her as he was about Mercy.

He stood and took the egg from Mercy. "We can let you know when they're done."

"Okay." Mercy slipped from the room.

Blaze watched her go.

He cracked the egg into the bowl and tossed the shell.

"What happens to the child won't be your decision." Blaze poured in the butter and whisked.

He washed his hands. "True, but if I'm right and a kid

started it on accident, I can't see the church pressing charges. I think the focus will be on getting them help."

"How? Through child services?"

"I don't know. It's possible." He turned off the faucet just in time to hear the shudder in her breath.

He was making this worse and worse, wasn't he? He dried his hands and followed her to the stove, meaning to hug her, but she lit the burner without giving him an opening.

He rubbed her back. "I wish the signs pointed away from a student."

"Me too." Her throat shifted with a swallow. She sighed forcefully. "This whole thing must be hard on you."

"And you. I'm sorry it hits close to home."

She nodded but didn't speak as she oiled the pan.

As the griddle heated, warmth registered on his hand. He moved aside to allow her space to work and leaned against the nearby counter. "Eric's on a mission to hold me responsible."

"For the fire?"

"He says I should've done more to get to the bottom of the trespasser. And that I should've notified the police about the intruder last night instead of searching the building myself. Says that would've prevented the fire in the first place."

"You couldn't know they'd burn the place down."

"True. And technically, we don't know for sure that the intruder I saw started the fire. But Nolan was at the scene last night, and he thinks I should've called the police too. Said the intruder could've been an addict or a thief or someone in the middle of a mental episode." He scratched his neck. He did regret not calling the police, but not because of Nolan's theories or Eric's agenda. If his suspicions were right, some child needed help, and he'd failed to find them.

Batter hissed as Blaze poured the first round of pancakes. "So what now?"

He ached to sit, but moving away from Blaze would be more uncomfortable than standing. He stayed close. "An investigation. But that could take months, and who knows if they'll find who did it. It would help if someone came forward with information. The sooner, the better. Help us sort all these random facts and theories."

"Huh." She stared at the batter.

He rubbed her back. The building symbolized a way of life and had served as the setting for a parade of special moments between him and Blaze. The day she'd marched into his office to go to war on Mercy's behalf. The afternoon he found her in the kitchen after raking leaves. Watching her first connect with Hadley and later pray with the girl to accept Christ.

"Whatever the truth is, it's quite a loss. For you as much as for me."

"Hm?" Her face snapped toward him.

He shrugged one shoulder. "It was kind of a home away from home, wasn't it? It won't be the same, even once they rebuild."

"Oh." She fiddled with the spatula, then began flipping the pancakes. "I was just thinking, I really hope it wasn't a student. I can't imagine what it'd feel like to be responsible for something so catastrophic." An exaggerated frown curved her lips. "It's been twenty years, and I still haven't lived down a much smaller fire. I wouldn't wish responsibility for this on anyone."

"Me neither. But if it is a hurting kid, the only way to help is if we know."

Blaze angled away as she piled the finished pancakes onto a plate. "Who do you suspect? Hadley still?"

He hadn't even thought of her. "Considering her decision, I think you're right that she needed something, but not necessarily a place to stay. The only kid behaving in truly unusual ways is Carter. Trouble is, he's over six feet tall."

Batter sizzled onto the pan. He almost didn't recognize his phone ringing.

He fished it from his pocket and answered. "Hey, Greg."

"Can you meet?" The senior pastor's words were rushed. "We're trying to figure out what to do for a building for the foreseeable future."

"Sure. When?"

"Now. Eric texted everyone half an hour ago. I didn't realize he'd left you off the message until I parked at his house. Looks like the last of the others are pulling up."

Blaze laid a pancake on a napkin and smoothed butter across the surface. A little maple syrup and it'd be heaven, but he wouldn't get to taste it.

"I'm on my way."

"Good. I don't think the omission was an accident."

"Probably not. See you soon." He ended the call and traced Blaze's elbow with his fingertips. "I have to go."

She folded the buttered pancake in the napkin like a taco and offered it to him. "For the road."

"Thanks." Considering he was running on zero sleep, a few calories might help.

He told himself to go, but his body stayed anchored. He wrapped his free arm around her and pulled her in for another hug. Probably should've put the pancake down first, but ... he closed his eyes and inhaled. She smelled of flowers, and the aromas of vanilla and butter hung on the air. It blended into a sense of belonging. Home.

Did he have to leave?

She stepped back and retrieved her spatula. "It sounded urgent?"

Was she pushing him out the door? More likely, sleep deprivation was skewing his concept of time, and he was lingering too long. The less time he allowed Eric to address the board without him, the better. He lifted the to-go pancake. "Thanks. Enjoy your breakfast."

She nodded once. "Good luck. I'll be praying."

BLAZE STAYED STILL, listening, until the front door whooshed closed. Then, she braced her hands on the counter, lowered her head, and kept her promise, but mostly, she prayed for herself. For wisdom. Strength.

The hot smell of the pancakes forced her into motion. She flipped them as her mind turned over the facts Anson had shared.

Someone in a Rooted hoodie had been in the building last night, while Mercy had been out wearing a Rooted hoodie. Blaze's history testified that a hurt, displaced girl could easily start a destructive fire.

Soft footfalls sounded behind her. "It really wasn't me. I swear." Mercy's voice came meek and worried.

If only Mercy hadn't lied about that school report, her tone would convince Blaze. As it was, she peered over her shoulder at her sister and prayed for discernment.

"He doesn't think it was me, does he?" Mercy's bottom lip disappeared into her mouth.

"No." Though that might change if he knew what Blaze knew. Incapable of monitoring the pancakes, she shut off the burner and leaned against the counter.

If she told Anson about Mercy's outing, he'd report it. There would be follow-up. Mercy might be blamed whether she was guilty or innocent. After all, she was Blaze's sister. If people believed Mercy had followed in Blaze's footsteps, they might believe Blaze had taken after her mother and become an unfit guardian.

Mercy tugged her T-shirt. Goosebumps appeared down her arms. She'd taken off the hoodie.

Blaze forced herself to smile. "Anson doesn't think you were involved. Swear to me you weren't at the church?"

"I swear."

"Then don't mention to anyone that you left last night, okay? We'll keep that between us."

Mercy nodded eagerly.

Blaze's sense of danger didn't relent. "I'm going to finish cooking. Why don't you queue up one of your shows, and we'll eat in the living room, okay?"

"Okay." Mercy's voice quivered, but she left the room.

With three clicks and a whoosh, the burner ignited. Blaze poured four more circles of batter as she prayed some more. For herself and Mercy. For Anson, because she'd promised. For whoever was responsible for the fire.

And please, Lord, don't let that be Mercy.

31

Anson parked on the shoulder and walked up the Newsomes' driveway past the rest of the leadership board's vehicles. As he waited on the wraparound porch for someone to respond to the doorbell, he studied the distressed welcome sign beside the door.

Seemed fitting, since Eric's welcome was bound to be reluctant.

Carter swung the door open, dressed in joggers and a hoodie, his hair one big cow lick. "Everybody else let themselves in."

Everybody else had been invited. Anson didn't regret ringing the bell, since it gave him this moment with Carter. "I've been sending you messages. You didn't go out for the team."

"What's the point? You predicted this would happen. No college wants me."

"What I said was fewer than one percent of high school athletes end up on a Division I team their freshman year. There are plenty of other options."

"I haven't heard from any of those places either." The teen retreated inside.

"That's no reason to give up." Anson shut the door and started down the hall after Carter. "God can make some pretty awesome things happen, even when we think it's too late. And even if He doesn't miraculously open up a DI spot for you, there are so many alternatives that could turn out to be blessings in disguise."

They reached the kitchen. Warmth and the savory aroma of an egg bake met them. Samantha Newsome scrubbed dishes. Her smile of greeting was so fleeting, she wasn't even looking anymore by the time Anson tried to return it.

Carter grabbed a plate. "I'm still on my club team. More people get recruited that way than through high school teams anyway."

The basketball club offered a level of visibility, but not all clubs were created equal. "Your club doesn't practice. If you do make it onto a college team, you'll need the skills you could've honed on the Many Oaks team."

"Too late for that now." Carter scooped a square of the egg bake onto his plate and headed for the hallway that led to the stairs. "Besides, I could take any of the guys in my club —including the one who got an offer." He disappeared around a corner, and pounding footsteps ascended to the second floor.

"Help yourself to some breakfast." Hands buried in suds, Samantha pointed with her elbow toward the dish.

"I already ate." Normally, it took more than a pancake and butter to fill him up, but his disappointment and concern were heavier than a nine-course meal. "They're in the family room?"

She nodded.

A Surefire Love

With a prayer for help, he headed to the back of the house. A massive TV dominated one wall of the family room. Windows on another wall provided generous views of the backyard. The leadership team had spread out over the semi-circle of couches and chairs.

Eric perched at the edge of an armchair. "It could be months before the investigation concludes and we can rebuild. In the meantime, we have hard decisions to make regarding how to keep things going. I've brainstormed meeting places that are large enough for our church body." He lifted a slip from the coffee table that resembled the grocery list paper Anson's mom used to use. Decorative script at the top said, *Be still and know.*

Anson took a deep breath and attempted to apply the words. Whatever happened, God was still on His throne.

Mike and Greg moved down to make space on the couch, and Anson took a seat.

"The schools won't rent to a religious organization." Eric looked at the paper and pinched the margin as he read down the possibilities. "We can contact the performing arts theater, the movie theater, and the hotel."

Greg folded his hands and leaned forward on his elbows. "We could also ask if another church would allow us to host a service before or after their own."

"There's only one other church in town with a building big enough and beliefs that mostly line up with ours." Ed slid his empty plate on the coffee table, where there was already a collection of others. "Grace Evangelical."

The crease between George's gray eyebrows deepened. "If we meet there, what's to stop our people from deciding they like them better?"

"Relationships." Greg lifted his hands in a motion to

calm down. "Those have always been the core of the church."

"To maintain our distinct identity, we'd do best to stay away from sharing a building with another church." Eric shook his sparse list of options. "Hence the venues I suggested. The trouble is, any of these will charge to use their space at a time when I suspect we'll see a drop in attendance, due to being displaced from our building and routine."

As murmurs went up, Anson mentally ran through other options in town, places that could host a crowd and might be inexpensive. He'd been spending time in one every week for years. "We could ask The Depot. If we set up rows in the event space without the tables, the congregation would fit. The owner is a believer. He might give us a deal on the price."

Eric lowered his list and looked at Anson like he'd suggested meeting on Neptune. "We won't be worshiping in a bar."

"It's a full-service restaurant with an event hall. They serve alcohol, but so does the hotel on your list. As a bonus, Many Oaks residents are already familiar with The Depot. People who've been interested but intimidated by the church building might give us a try." He scanned the room, praying his enthusiasm would catch. "This could turn into a chance to build more of a presence in the community."

Greg nodded. "It's worth considering."

"All in favor of The Depot?" Eric surveyed the others.

Anson, Greg, and Ed raised their hands. One shy of a majority.

"Then I'll make calls to the theaters and hotel for price quotes and availability." Eric put the list back on the table.

"Perhaps someone can even make space for us as soon as tomorrow."

Greg shifted in his seat. "I finished the sermon on Thursday, but have you considered the other logistics? The worship team, especially, would have their work cut out for them. I'm not sure how many of their instruments were in the church. The sound system certainly was."

"The Depot has a piano." Anson spoke without thinking. Eric bristled, but Anson had already opened his mouth, so he might as well finish. "Philip must own a couple of guitars, and they have a sound system that's already up and running."

Eric took a deep breath. "For once, could you accept something this board has voted into place?"

Heat flashed over Anson's face, but he held still, waiting for Eric to backpedal.

Instead, he leaned over the coffee table and jabbed his finger as close to Anson's face as he could get without rising. "If you'd done your job, this wouldn't even be an issue. You failed to prevent a student from accessing the building. You failed to notify the police of a break-in. And, by your own admission, you were in the building shortly before the fire broke out."

Anson pushed his sleeves up and prayed for self-control. "I was in the building looking for a student—assuming it was one—but I didn't see, smell, or *start* a fire."

"Maybe not, but it's time Many Oaks Bible Church asks more of its youth pastor than *not* starting fires. I'm incredibly sorry I let things get this far before calling for this vote." Eric straightened his shirt cuffs. "It's time we face reality. Attendance and giving are bound to go down more than they have already, and we're facing extra expenses. Having a youth pastor on staff hasn't strengthened our church as a whole or our floundering youth groups. As small as our youth ministries are, we don't need the expense of another salary when those funds could be used toward more pressing needs. I move that we eliminate the position of youth pastor and allow volunteers to run the programs."

Mike lifted two fingers. "Second."

Ironic that now they'd follow the rules of order.

"Hold on now." Greg's normally reserved voice was gruff. "I deeply appreciate Anson as a partner in pastoring the church. Volunteers cannot preach every third and fifth Sunday. They cannot counsel parents and students in difficult situations the way he does."

"I work forty-five hours each week," Anson said. "Sometimes more. I'm always on call. Pastoring is an entire lifestyle, and volunteers don't have the capacity, training, or experience to do it."

"They don't have to," Eric said. "If the volunteers follow our suggestion of less teaching and more time hanging out with the kids, not only will it increase attendance, it'll cut down on preparation time."

"Even fun events take planning," Anson said.

Eric held up a hand. "You're not an unbiased observer. This will be the board's decision. However, since you're here, go ahead and make a statement before you leave us to deliberate." He waved his hand, as if giving him the opportunity to beg for his job was a favor.

Anson had known this was a possibility, but he'd underestimated how painful it'd be to have his life's work on the chopping block. What was God doing?

His hands shook as faces flashed through his mind—Coach Voss, Gury, Carter, Dylan, Mercy, Hadley. He gripped his knees. How was he supposed to persuade the board on no sleep, with the deck stacked against him?

His own words to Carter just minutes before came back to him. God could come through when it seemed too late. Anson believed God had more for him to do in Many Oaks, so he chose to trust that the Lord would control the outcome. "My belief in the importance of youth ministry started before I moved to Many Oaks, when a high school student died."

He hesitated. Blaze had encouraged him to share the story of Gury. He'd appreciated knowing her full story, and perhaps the fact that he'd lost a brother was meant to be shared as well. But if he broke his silence now, they'd question why he'd kept the secret so long. At best, it'd look like a play for sympathy.

"Once I got here, I watched Coach Voss help a lot of hurting kids, myself included. If the student who'd died ..."

The words sliced like a betrayal, demoting his brother from his rightful title. Anson tried again. "If Gury had had someone like Coach in his life, he might've made different choices. He might still be alive. Losing Coach showed me again that none of us know how long we have before we face eternity. I felt very clearly called to pick up where he'd left off as best I could.

"I sacrificed a promising basketball career, got a degree, and came back to continue his legacy. My work at Many Oaks Bible Church isn't done. Being faithful might not mean the numbers we'd all like to see, but Greg said it—church is about relationships. God will provide for our needs. He'll provide a place to meet. He'll provide the funding. It's our job to value and pursue the things He values."

Greg nodded.

Anson wanted to circle back, to expand on some of the points he'd made, but lobbying to persuade them would be as useless as trying to win an Internet debate. Either God already had enough board members on Anson's side, He'd change their hearts during the debate that would follow, or Anson had seriously misunderstood his calling.

32

"What do I say if someone asks about the fire?"

Blaze caught her sister's gaze in the rearview mirror.

This was what came of telling Mercy she'd sounded guilty yesterday when she'd randomly inserted into conversation with Anson that she hadn't started the fire. "If someone asks you a direct question, answer honestly. But don't volunteer anything they don't ask. Let's practice. How did you find out about the fire, Mercy?"

"Anson showed us a video. Am I allowed to say *that*?"

Blaze suppressed a groan. "Let's skip it, if you can. How about you say you saw it on social media and not mention who showed you?"

Many Oaks Bible Church was meeting in the performing arts theater a couple of blocks from the square this morning. As they got closer, trees, lampposts, and brick buildings lined the street.

Blaze tried another question. "Who do you think started the fire?"

"Some kid who did it on accident."

"Why do you think that?"

"I heard someone tried to put it out. Besides, who'd do that on purpose?"

"That's a great answer." Though it did little to assuage Blaze's worry. "No one knows you left the house, so don't mention that and it'll be fine."

"But what do I say if they ask why I'm grounded?"

"Say you don't want to talk about it."

"Oh. Okay, I guess."

Following a couple of other cars, Blaze steered into the theater's lot. She parked and twisted toward Mercy. "There are no classes this morning, so you probably won't end up talking to people anyway. You'll stay with me the whole time."

Staying together would also give Blaze an excuse to limit her conversation with Anson. Despite her curiosity about yesterday's meeting, she hadn't reached out because the more they talked without her revealing Mercy's early morning adventure, the worse her omission would be.

It'd be so much easier to tell him, but even if Mercy was exonerated, the questions would leave nasty rumors in their wake. The kind that could haunt Mercy for decades.

Anyway, if the meeting had gone badly, Anson would've contacted her. He'd probably been too busy helping pull off the change of venue.

Mercy and Blaze fell in with the flow of people approaching the theater's entrance. Other than the expected exchange with the greeters, no one talked with them as they found seats that mirrored where they usually sat in the sanctuary. Anson wasn't in the auditorium yet, but he'd know where to find them when he was free.

Ed opened the service with prayer and announcements instead of Anson. Maybe it was his week to preach? The usual worship team played, but an amp buzzed the whole time and Blaze struggled to focus on God. Thankfully, the team turned off the equipment when they left the stage, and the buzzing stopped.

Greg walked on stage to deliver the sermon. Still no sign of Anson. She did her best to scan the audience without making a big show of it. Didn't spot him.

Pastor Greg's closing prayer ended so abruptly, her eyes were still closed when he said, "The leadership board would like for all of our youth leaders to meet at the back before leaving today."

Was Anson sick? Regret churned in her stomach. She should've reached out.

Mercy followed her to the back of the room, and they fell in beside Nolan as a huddle formed.

"Do you know what this is about?" she asked.

He shook his head.

"All right." Eric Newsome wedged in and clapped his hands. "This everyone?" He looked around at the group of four youth leaders.

Sydney nodded.

Eric's gaze fell on Mercy and he frowned. She bumped into Blaze like she used to as a much younger child when she wanted to hide.

Blaze put an arm around her and aimed as sweet of a tone as possible at Eric. "What can we do for you?"

"We are going to need extra help with the youth groups moving forward, as we no longer have a youth pastor on staff."

A grunt of shock slipped through Blaze's lips. She

couldn't have heard right. Then again, it couldn't have been her imagination or Sydney's mouth wouldn't have fallen open. Nolan cocked his head. Ray shot a nervous look around the group. A dimple appeared above one of Mercy's eyebrows as confusion skewed her face.

Blaze held her tighter as regret swelled. She should've checked in with Anson yesterday.

"I understand this is a change." Eric jammed his lips together for a beat. "We'll take it one step at a time. Since we can't meet in the building, we're canceling youth activities for this week. In the meantime, talk amongst yourselves and pray, then get back to me about who will lead each group moving forward."

"That's a big responsibility." Ray stuffed his hands in his pockets.

"Don't worry." Eric's cajoling tone didn't reassure Blaze of anything. "We'd like the youth groups to be a place the kids can hang out, feel comfortable, and get a positive church experience that will keep them coming back. Whoever leads won't have to preach."

Sydney crossed her arms. "What will the responsibilities entail?"

"There's a series of five-minute devotional videos produced by a big church in El Paso with a thriving youth ministry. They're polished and entertaining. We'll have you play one of those each week as the teaching portion. Singing is optional. If you can get a great band together, perfect. If not, let's focus on other things. Any other questions?"

"No one else is going to ask?" Nolan rested his hands on his hips. "I will. Where's Anson?"

"Given the size of our church, we had to make a hard, fiscally responsible decision. I hope you'll understand." Eric rubbed his hands together. "As for new primary leaders, I'll need your answers by ... let's say Wednesday. That'll give some time to organize before restarting gatherings next week." He thanked them and walked away, leaving the shocked clutch of leaders staring at each other.

Ray ran a hand through his hair, sighed, and rejoined his family.

"I'm talking to Pastor Greg." Nolan stalked off.

Mercy peered up at Blaze.

Blaze lifted her shoulders helplessly as her stomach churned, queasy. She loved this church. She'd met Christ here. How could the leadership board have turned on Anson like this?

Sydney stepped closer and dropped her voice. "Do you know what's going on?"

"No." When he left yesterday morning, she'd known the meeting would be hard. She never expected them to fire him.

Sydney studied her. "People have seen you two together, and for some reason, they think I need to know. Like it's wrong for him to move on." She flipped the end of her ponytail over her shoulder. "For the record, moving on is healthy, and he doesn't have to stay away from Mondays at The Depot for my sake. I know he loves being there."

Blaze gulped. "He's been coming on Thursdays, after leadership meetings."

"I'm not surprised. Though I also thought you'd know what happened with his job."

Posing a guess, even an educated one, would be participating in the rumor mill Blaze hated so much. "I actually don't."

"Oh. Hm." Sydney's eyes narrowed. Finally, her expression relaxed. "Actually, that does sound like him. He's not very good about opening up, is he?"

Anson valued his privacy, but Blaze had thought he opened up to her. This omission did seem to suggest otherwise. Considering she was keeping a secret from him, perhaps she deserved to be on the outside this time.

WHERE COULD a displaced pastor attend worship? If Anson showed up at Grace Evangelical, people would recognize him and question his presence. If he went to the theater to join Many Oaks Bible Church, he risked upsetting the men who'd voted him out. And depending on how they planned to break the news of his departure, he'd face more questions there than elsewhere. Answering those questions could cause division in the body of believers he wanted to serve.

Besides, the Lord still hadn't answered Anson's questions about his dismissal: Why had God allowed it? He'd done what he'd believed the Lord wanted him to do. Why hadn't He blessed that effort? Anson might have made a misstep somewhere. He could've objected harder and sooner to the board's initiative. Or perhaps he was never meant to work at Many Oaks Bible Church to begin with. If he'd been wrong in either case, how would he ever figure out what he was supposed to do now?

He stayed home and spent the morning praying, studying the Bible, and reading a book on discerning God's will, which he'd started a few weeks ago.

The practices that normally led to a feeling of connection with the Lord felt empty.

Like he was the only one in the room.

A Surefire Love

Like maybe God wasn't present.

The silence eventually drove Anson to the gym. Even after working his way through the weight machines, his muscles crawled with unspent tension. He returned home to run on the treadmill until he collapsed.

Except when he pulled into his driveway, Blaze was sitting on the front stoop. They'd never spent time at his place before, but his address was in the church directory, so finding it would've been as easy as turning a couple of pages.

Relief and longing encouraged him toward her, but hesitation kept him buckled to his seat. He hadn't called her yesterday because he didn't want the loss to be true. He didn't understand what God was doing. Couldn't claim he liked it. He knew verses about situations like these, but applying them felt like finding comfort in clichés.

If the board knew he was thinking that way, they'd probably be happier they fired him.

Blaze stood. Keeping his pain and confusion to himself didn't make it less true or easier to bear. Blaze's presence might, so he got out of the car.

She wore dress pants and a blouse under a long green trench coat that rippled in the breeze as she approached. She must've come from the service.

His muscles protested as he pushed his door shut. His reckless pace at the gym could've injured him, and then what would he do with his spinning mind?

Blaze stopped on the other side of the hood with her head at an assessing tilt. The wind flirted with the ends of her hair, and the sun added highlights. "Not checking your phone?" Kindness, not recrimination, carried her voice.

He patted his pocket. He had left the phone in the car

during his workout and hadn't touched it since. "Purposely avoiding it."

"Ah."

He couldn't keep his head in the sand forever, though, so he retrieved the device from the center console. Then he escorted Blaze to the house and held the door open for her. "I should've called you."

She stepped into the entryway. "Ditto. I'm sorry."

Her simple response soothed the hurt he'd felt when she hadn't reached out. His eyes misted with unexpected emotion, so he turned away to shut the door. "Me too."

He ushered Blaze into the living room of his fixer-upper. A couch, TV, bookshelf, and coffee table filled the room.

"You seem like a dog person." Blaze reached out, as if looking for a head to pet. "A black lab, maybe."

"I thought about it. My parents had dogs when I grew up. I like them, but I'm not home a lot and they ..." He cleared his throat. "Pets never seem to live forever."

Blaze studied him. "None of us do."

Pressure built behind his eyes. He lowered himself onto the couch and rubbed his forehead. Blaze's coat rustled, the couch dipped, and her hand rubbed his back.

"I don't know why I'm upset," he said toward the floor.

"No?"

"I don't know why I'm *this* upset." Liquid collected in his eyes. He managed to blink it away. "It's not like there weren't signs they would fire me. I guess I didn't really think God would allow it. I keep wracking my brain, but I can't figure it out."

She rested her forearm along his spine, drawing circles with her fingertips between his shoulder blades. "I don't know what to do with it either."

He sat back and took her hand. "It's like, either they don't know God, or they don't care. How else could we come from such different places?"

"I don't know. The people on the board have been believers much longer than me, and I guess I had everyone up on pedestals." Her hands tightened until her knuckles paled. "But we're all just human, aren't we? The board included. And humans can be fully convinced even when they're only partially right, especially when it comes to a God whose ways aren't our ways." Her grip loosened as she spoke, but tension built in him.

"You think the board was partially right?"

Her eyes and mouth rounded like a student caught bad-mouthing a friend. She wet her lips. "I don't know what to think. These are people I trusted. I mean, I believe Eric could be off base, but how did he convince the whole board?"

Even she wasn't on his side?

He rose. Paced. Faced her. "The fact that they did something unbelievable doesn't make them partially right. I was trying to reach the youth spiritually. That should've been the board's focus too. Especially Eric's. If he believes what I believe about eternity, how could he lead a crusade against me when one of my biggest concerns was his son? What's going to become of Carter now? I just don't"—he clenched a fist and released it—"get it. Why did God allow this? And what am I supposed to do now?"

Her mouth tipped. "All you can do is trust God and stay faithful. Extend grace."

"Extend grace as Eric runs the church into the ground? This whole thing is just—" He growled. "Evil isn't supposed to win like this, but the whole leadership board is blindly following Eric because of money and numbers. How can they call themselves Christians?"

She worked her hands together. "Those are some pretty extreme accusations."

"If the shoe fits."

"Can't there be something in the middle? Like, maybe firing you was wrong, but maybe there's more to the story. And maybe you could've done some things differently too."

"I could've fought harder and sooner. Maybe looped in a few key people from outside the leadership board to help talk sense—"

She shook her head with quick jerks. "That's not what I meant."

"Okay...."

"You're ..." She opened her hand like she was waiting for a the right words to land there. Slowly, her fingers curled into a fist. "You're assuming the worst of them and acting like Carter's eternity and the future of the church depend on you. Like it's your way or the highway to hell, but does it have to be that extreme? I *do* think Eric's off base, but you're not perfect either. And you said it yourself. God allowed this, so he's still involved, right?"

In theory. He knew the sarcasm was wrong. God was always involved, even when Anson didn't understand what He was up to. Even when Anson was facing a critique from the one person he'd hoped would comfort him.

"Which of my imperfections do you think justified firing me?"

"It's not that I think their decision is justified, it's just, take care of the log in your own eye first, right?"

"The imperfection is an entire log now?"

Color rose in her cheeks. "I've wondered how in the

world to share my testimony the way you shared yours. So neat and tidy. Mine's not like that, and maybe yours isn't meant to be either. Maybe you would've gotten through to Carter and others if you'd told them about your brother."

"I was fired because I didn't talk about Gury?"

She lifted her hand and shook her head. "I'm just saying, if the board's human, maybe you are too. Maybe you could've handled the ministry differently while you had it. You were concerned about the kids' spiritual well-being, but even you put limits on what you'd do for them, didn't you? Why did you decide to keep Gury a secret? Did you think it would glorify God? Or are you ashamed to admit you kept secrets for him, as if we don't all have regrets that need forgiveness? Isn't God's grace enough for all of us?"

Guilt sizzled as it rained on the flames of his anger. He'd suppressed impulses to share about Gury, but he hadn't thought those came from the Lord. What if they had?

Blaze plucked her coat from the armrest where she'd laid it.

She was leaving? He hefted his reluctant body to stand between her and the door. "Why are you angry with me?"

She cocked her head. "The more I think about your silence, the worse it seems. You've lived among these people most of your life without showing the courage to be vulnerable. Why? So you can look better than us?" Her eyes glinted, tears lining her lashes. "Maybe with me, you can own up to things and still feel superior because I've got a much longer track record of messing up."

He opened his mouth but found no words. One of the things he loved about Blaze was her graciousness. Was he really so far off base that he deserved this attack? "Is that really what you think of me?" His voice turned raw.

"I don't know, Anson." She pulled on her coat and cinched the belt.

He dug his fingers into his own shoulder, unsure how they'd ended up here.

Without meeting his eyes, she motioned him to move aside.

Responses might trump reactions, but he could muster neither. He opened the door. She left without another word. A blessing, because the ones she'd already thrown would be stuck in his head for days.

33

She may have taken that too far. Blaze drummed her fingers on the steering wheel as she drove away from Anson's house.

Anson was an either-or thinker: everything was either right or wrong, success or failure. His convictions made him a man of integrity. A man she'd had up on a pedestal with all the other church leaders. Sure, she'd known they weren't perfect, but she had thought them better than her with her shorter walk with God, her messed up past, her dysfunctional upbringing.

But a disagreement this extreme meant anyone might have serious issues they needed to address. Anson had judged her too quickly back in high school. Remnants of that kind of thinking might still lead him to jump to the wrong conclusions.

Except Eric was probably guilty of something. He'd come up with one excuse after another until he'd finally found one that stuck. Which reason was real? And if his motivation had to be hidden under so many layers, was it valid?

Doubtful.

Why couldn't she have told Anson he was right? Why start nitpicking him?

Because getting him to recognize his own flaws might help him extend more grace to others instead of assuming the worst. If she could soften him up, maybe when she told him Mercy had snuck out, he'd start with trust instead of calling the fire inspector.

But even Blaze wasn't sure that trust was well placed.

Instead of skirting the downtown area to get home, Blaze flipped on her blinker and turned. A couple of blocks later, she found a parking spot on the square and started down the path toward the gazebo. Many of the oaks retained their leaves, brown and rattling overhead.

A text pinged as she passed the chinkapin oak, and she found a message from Nolan. *If they want a leader for Rooted, I vote they bring Anson back. I'm not going to take his place.*

Great. If she didn't lead, there would be no Many Oaks Bible Church youth group for Mercy. She ought to say she'd pray about it, but her testimony had done so much damage already, and she hadn't even given it yet. She didn't belong on the youth ministry team at all, let alone leading Rooted. Given how messy everything had become, maybe no one was qualified.

Where did that leave them? In God's hands. Where they'd always been. She'd found that truth more comforting before the Lord had allowed the board to fire Anson.

They might just bring in a new volunteer to lead, she replied.

That's fine. MOBC isn't the right place for me anyway if this is how they operate.

I'm sure Anson appreciates the support. She sent the

message, wishing she'd been the one to give it to him, and put the phone away.

Ahead, late autumn had rendered the vines on the gazebo frail and sparse. She stepped up into the shelter and scanned the bench that hugged the perimeter. Not even a stray wrapper lay on or beneath the white slats. No signs that Mercy had been here. Not that her presence in the gazebo would definitively rule out a trip to the church.

Blaze drove the shortest route home, the one a girl on foot would choose, though it meant slower driving with more stops. It was quite a distance for an eleven-year-old to walk in the dark, and the church would've been another two miles.

In the garage, she stopped by Mercy's bike. They'd upgraded her children's bicycle to a small mountain bike last summer, and Mercy had zipped around the neighborhood with her friends. Once the weather had cooled and school started, the bike had been more or less forgotten. Blaze squeezed the front tire.

Totally flat.

Would Mercy ride it that way?

Her phone pinged. Expecting another text from Nolan, she pulled it out.

Anson.

Her eyes instantly watered, and with weak fingers, she opened the message.

I'm sorry we fought. I'm not in a great headspace. Haven't slept much since Thursday. Can we try again in a day or two?

I hate this. I miss you already.

Unexpected and sweet, the messages twisted her stomach. She wasn't in a great headspace either. Her fight with Anson had mostly sprung from her defensiveness about

Mercy. But no one knew she'd been out. As long as Mercy kept quiet and no proof indicating her surfaced, reconnecting with Anson shouldn't be as hard as Blaze was making it.

Her legs ached from squatting by the bike, so she straightened to compose her reply.

I'm not in a great headspace either. A day or two sounds good. I'll be at The Depot tomorrow. Otherwise, I'll be home Tuesday night.

She'd heard couples needed to learn to navigate conflict, but it would've been nice if she and Anson could've made it past their second date before it crashed in on them.

Monday's basketball practice served as a much-needed mental break for Anson. One that ended abruptly as he left the gym and his phone went off with a call from Nolan.

Anson stopped at the exit to answer, looking out through the glass at the high school parking lot. The clouds hung low over the smattering of cars. "Hey, Nolan. What's up?"

"It's ridiculous, firing you. And then to say we're not teaching anymore, except with these five-minute prerecorded devos? Aren't we a church anymore?"

"Yeah, I—"

"I'm not standing for it." Nolan was more fired up than Anson had ever heard him—except perhaps during the fight on the bus all those years ago.

Uneasiness crept through Anson's aching muscles.

"I'm going to bail if they don't bring you back with a raise and a huge apology. I'll get members to vote. You'd get your job back by a landslide, and we could elect a new board."

"Hold on. Back up." Anson clenched and released the hand that wasn't holding the phone. In theory, he'd wanted someone to feel this way—everyone, actually—but a fight had cost Coach Voss his life, and this time, it could split the church. The damage to individuals' spiritual lives could be devastating. Blaze had been wise to shy away from pointing fingers and toward extending grace.

"I don't know all the factors that went into the decision. Let's go slow, assume the best, and prioritize the ministry." The words tasted like spoiled milk.

"What ministry?" Nolan demanded. "They're ruining it. And what are you going to do for work?"

Excellent question. He wasn't qualified for much besides coaching and pastoring, and he wouldn't find a full-time job in either role in Many Oaks. He rested his hand on the cold metal bar on the door. "I'm not sure yet, but God will provide for me and the church." The statement still didn't feel one-hundred percent true, but he knew it was. If he kept saying it, hopefully it'd sink in. "I don't think He's going to let the ministry die. I'd appreciate it if you'd help keep it alive, unless you're confident you're being called somewhere else."

"You don't think all this is a sign?"

"Responses trump reactions."

Nolan grunted. "How am I supposed to *respond,* Coach?"

"Take it slow and pray. Let God work. That's what I'm trying to do."

"We can't take it too slow. They want to know who's going to lead Rooted by Wednesday so we can start up again next week. You really want me and Blaze taking over without you?"

"I trust you both."

Nolan exhaled heavily. "Fine. But I don't like it."

"Me neither."

When they ended the call, Anson's bag of equipment felt twice as heavy as he shouldered through the door and into the lot. He'd head home and pass the time until Blaze's show browsing job listings. Or not. Just walking to his car drained his energy. It seemed he'd finally exhausted himself.

Footsteps slapped the concrete behind him. "Pastor Anson! Hey!" The runner pounded to a stop at his side.

Anson shifted his duffel bag higher on his shoulder. "Dylan. What are you still doing here?"

"I'm a stagehand for the musical. And, unlike my brother, I didn't bail."

That's right. Carter had volunteered for the theater department to clear his suspension. "Why did he join the crew if he wasn't planning to go out for basketball?"

Dylan shrugged. "Maybe he thinks I'm cooler than he lets on and he wanted to hang out with me."

Anson had to smile. "That must be it."

"He acts like he can't stand me, but ..." His shoulders rose again. "He's actually not the worst."

Anson chuckled. "High praise."

"Hey. So." Dylan pulled his hands into the sleeves of his hoodie. "What's the deal with the fire? You went when my dad texted, right?"

"I did." Eric had been at the scene, but he never explained why he'd texted Anson and then failed to invite him to the leadership meeting.

"I heard it was an accident."

"That was the theory, the last I heard." Presumably the investigation was underway.

"You ever figure out who was on the camera? You have video of the person?"

A Surefire Love

The question confirmed one of Anson's suspicions—that nothing about the fire was secret. At least not from the students. Dylan might've heard something the adults hadn't, though. "Who do you think might be in the video?"

"How would I know? I just heard you had a picture. My mom says I'm nosy." His face lit. "It could be Silas. He's kind of weird. I bet he likes to play with fire."

"Silas is introverted, not weird."

Dylan wagged a sleeve-covered arm at him. "You can never trust the quiet ones."

Anson dismissed the accusation with a head shake. "I turned the video over so it can be used in the investigation."

The humor disappeared from Dylan's face. "I suppose you had to." His forehead wrinkled. "So, why can't we have youth group this week? I heard the youth room is fine."

Anson took a breath, started to answer, stopped. Was it possible Eric hadn't told his own family the decision he'd instigated? "The room was spared, but I believe it still has smoke damage."

"Ah. Okay. Good. 'Cuz someone said it was because you quit."

Anson had wanted to let the leadership board tell the congregation what happened, but he couldn't let that slide. "I don't work at the church anymore, but I didn't quit."

Dylan cocked his head like a puzzled puppy. "Huh?"

"They let me go."

Dylan froze, mouth open. "No." Somehow, he managed to not move his jaw.

"Afraid so."

"Because of the fire?" He was back in motion, balling his hands under his crossed arms.

"No." Although during that last meeting, one of Eric's

talking points had been his prediction about the fire decreasing giving. "Not directly, anyway."

"Then it was because of my dad?"

"The leadership board made the decision together." Hopefully that was diplomatic enough.

"My dad is such a ...." Dylan clenched his jaw.

Part of him would've loved to finish the thought, but he took a page from Blaze's playbook instead. "The board is doing what they feel is best for the church."

"So, no more youth group?"

"My understanding is they're coming up with a plan, but if you want details, you'll have to talk with your dad."

"Carter's going to .... Are you sure this isn't because of the fire? It was an accident. You shouldn't be punished for it."

Dylan spoke with a little too much certainty.

"Is there something you want to tell me?"

"What do you mean? No. Why?"

"How do you know the fire was an accident?"

"You just said."

"I said that was the theory. You sound pretty sure."

"No, I'm not. I'm not. I just ...." His hands popped back out the ends of his sleeves. "Okay, so all I know is we sent you the text."

"What text?"

"The one about the fire. It wasn't from my dad. It was from me and Carter. Well, Carter, but he did it because I was worried about the church."

"How did you know about the fire that early on?"

"One of my dad's friends called and told him. The guy saw all the fire trucks and called because he knows Dad is kind of in charge or whatever. Carter and I heard Dad getting ready to go see what was happening, so we asked him what was going on. I was really worried. Carter said you could help."

"Why use your dad's phone?"

"We checked to see if he called you, but he only called Pastor Greg, so we sent the text. But we figured he might be mad about it, so we deleted it from his phone. He doesn't know he texted you. Maybe don't tell him? He'd be mad. But I guess you probably couldn't really help, huh? The fire was so big."

Spoken with the confidence of a witness, but Anson hadn't spotted him at the church. "Did you see it?"

"There were pictures online."

Suspicion needled Anson. "Is there something you're not telling me?"

"Sure. Lots of things. I aced my algebra test. In band class, Jonah hit Melody in the back of the head with his trombone." He mimed extending a trombone slider. "Mrs. Ratey was sick, and we had a sub for—"

"About the fire, Dylan."

"Oh. Then no."

Someone called Dylan back inside. With a hasty goodbye, he sprinted off.

Anson hefted his equipment bag onto the backseat of his SUV. Shrugging the kink out of his shoulder, he studied the school. Dylan knew something, but Anson wasn't sure he could find out what without crossing Eric or the leadership board.

34

"Your church is off the rails."

Blaze looked up from her phone to find David across the table. He wore the all-black of the waitstaff, so he was likely serving in the dining room. She had five minutes left of her break, so she motioned to a chair.

Instead of taking it, he leaned against her tall table and scanned the room as if to supervise those gathered for the Monday night show.

People sat at every table. As she'd made her way to this spot, she overheard at least three conversations about the church. Word of Anson's dismissal spread right along with every imaginable theory about the fire.

It was no wonder David sought her out. He'd been disappointed when she became a believer. Had even called her a fool when she invited him to church. What was she supposed to say now, when the leadership board had proven to not be as trustworthy as she'd thought?

Then again, maybe David was talking about the fire. "Off the rails? How so?"

He scoffed. "Come on. Even the legendary Anson Marsh can't make it work? That guy's been a teacher's pet and a religious fanatic since the day he got here. If he wasn't good enough for them, how judgmental are those people?"

Her nose tingled with impending tears. If she admitted the truth—that she couldn't defend the board's choice—she'd be a blubbering mess. That'd probably scare David off, but how would that represent Christ to him?

God, help.

"The focus is on being more relevant." Anson, as confident and immediate as an answer to one of her prayers had ever been, stepped up beside David and set a soda on the table. "*Less* fanatical."

David straightened like a gladiator eyeing a worthy opponent. "Here on a Monday? What's your ex think of that?"

"Not my priority," Anson said at the same time as Blaze said, "She's fine with it."

Both men turned her way.

Rather than add fuel to the fire, she shrugged. She didn't mind filling Anson in on her conversation with Sydney, but David had come looking to stir up hard feelings. Best not to give him more ideas. Besides, she wanted to hear what Anson had to say about the church.

"Less fanatical, huh?" David lifted his chin toward Anson.

"That's my understanding. Maybe you should join us some Sunday."

"Us? I thought you were fired." David's question echoed her own.

"My beliefs haven't changed. I'm taking a couple weeks off, but once the dust settles, I'm planning to go back. As an attender."

She gaped. She'd encouraged Anson to lead with grace, but she'd never considered he might return to the same people who'd rejected him. She'd considered leaving herself.

David's lip curled. "If this place fired me, I would not come back."

"Maybe not if you only see it as a place to earn a paycheck." Anson turned his head, scanning the room. "But if you see the people here as family, my guess is you wouldn't stay away long." A smirk lifted one side of his mouth. "Unless you got yourself banned on the way out."

David snorted. "And you didn't?"

Anson tucked a hand in his pocket. "Guess I'll find out in a couple weeks."

"That's kind of crazy, man."

"Fanatical, you mean."

"Yeah, sure." David stepped away, but before his hand left the table, he paused. "You know, if you'd seen half the fanatical things people did in the name of religion that I saw overseas, you'd give the whole thing up."

Blaze's breath caught. According to Marissa, David never talked about his time in the military.

Anson took a beat, then nodded. "My schedule's wide open, if you want to talk about it."

"Nice try." David stalked off toward the dining area.

Anson's attention settled on Blaze.

"You're coming back to MOBC?"

"Someone told me to trust that God is bigger than this circumstance. To try grace first." He slid a hand across her shoulders, and a shiver cascaded down her spine. "I might not be able to stay, but until God tells me to go somewhere else, I'll hang around in hopes that He'll do something."

"Like get your job back?"

"If I go into it with that mindset, we all lose." Releasing her, he folded his hands, leaning heavily against his forearms on the tabletop. "I'll minister here while I can, even if it's only in the form of conversations like that one with David."

She picked at the label on her water bottle. "Is Eric going to be angry?"

"That's part of why I thought I'd better give it a few weeks. Right now, he's angry. *I'm* angry. Sad. Still processing why God let this happen. He might never tell me, but I'm waiting to go back to MOBC until I can honestly say I'm not hoping to stir up trouble. Ideally, I want to do the opposite." He braced a hand on the table, straightening. "If I stay at MOBC until I find a new position, it might calm down people like Nolan, who are angry enough to leave."

"You don't think they should?"

"The teaching and worship on Sunday morning are still solid. So no, I don't think there should be a mass exodus. If the Lord does want to adjust the youth group philosophy, He'll likely do it through faithful people who stay. And I do think most people there love God and want to serve Him." He turned his glass on the tabletop, and bubbles raced up the sides. "This whole thing could be a blip that lasts a year or two and then gets corrected again." His smile wavered.

She understood the conflicting feelings. As much as she found comfort in his perspective, she hated that someone so faithful had been pushed out. "Where do you think you'll work?"

There were other churches around, though most were

different denominations. He'd make a good teacher, but his degree was in ministry. Perhaps the Christian school a town over had fewer restrictions on whom they could hire than public schools.

He sipped his drink. "A church I interned with during college is talking about hiring an associate pastor. They're in Minnesota. Or a guy I went to school with is a lead pastor in Arizona. The youth pastor there accepted a position with a missions organization, so his position will need to be filled."

Her grip on the water bottle tightened. It hadn't occurred to her that he'd consider moving, let alone to such far-flung locations. "Out of state? Why not find something closer?"

"Many Oaks doesn't have any open pastoral positions. Even if it did, if I worked nearby, people might follow me. When I move on, it needs to be a clean break or it could cause a church split."

"Oh." She couldn't fault his reasoning, but could their relationship survive long distance?

"It's not what I wanted."

She nodded and dropped eye contact. Perhaps they could overcome her secret or his move, but both?

Philip and the other Signalmen made their way back onstage. She escaped the conversation, but that didn't stop her mind from circling the problem.

She'd challenged Anson to assume the best and respond with grace, and he seemed to be doing both. He had more integrity and resolve than she'd given him credit for. If only she'd realized the far-reaching implications of the board's decision, she wouldn't have been so nonchalant about the whole thing. They were running him out of town.

Someone needed to fight back.

She caught an amused glance from Philip. Maybe she'd let a little too much of her anger show in her performance, but at least this cover of an Awestruck song lent itself to the intensity.

As the night continued, however, her anger drained into a pit of grief. Anson was accepting the board's decision. Her only true option was to trust God with the church and to shore up her relationship with Anson as best she could.

Out in the crowd, Gabby Voss took a seat beside Anson. After a conversation that lasted three songs, she wrapped him in a hug and patted his cheek in a motherly way before leaving. Blaze needed to be supportive like that.

When the show ended, she gathered her things and rejoined Anson.

He stood as she neared. "You sounded good tonight. Especially so."

"Thank you. The new prescription doesn't make me tired, and it does seem to be helping." If only the medicine could reassure her of Mercy's innocence or mend the rift Blaze had created with Anson. Then it would truly be life-changing.

Anson studied her. "So, what now?"

Until she'd learned he would be moving away, she'd thought the next steps would be getting their relationship back to normal by putting some time between them and their fight, them and her secret. Now she wasn't sure. "You tell me. You've got a lot more up in the air than I do."

"Because I have to move?"

She managed a nod despite the aches building in every muscle.

"The job openings are months away. Most youth pastors

finish out the school year. Not always, of course." He pointed at himself. "I'll be around a while yet. Income from coaching and my savings can carry me a few months. I'll look for something temporary, so finances won't rush me into a decision about where to go next. I'm in no mood to have a repeat of what happened here."

"You say that like it was a mistake to work at MOBC, but I don't think that's true." She laid her hand over his.

At her touch, his eyes softened. "Thank you."

She gulped down the pride that would have her stop short of the apology she owed. "I'm sorry I wasn't on your side yesterday. I've seen how good you are with the kids, and I know how hard you work. You didn't deserve to be fired. Eric's gone too far."

He turned his hand and threaded their fingers together. "Your point stands. I can't change him. Only myself."

"Yesterday shouldn't have been about making points."

"Apology accepted. And, truly, Blaze, you said good things. I'm still not sure what God wants regarding Carter and Gury's story, but ..." He shrugged one shoulder. "What's new, right? I also don't know what He wants for us, but I plan to hang around until I find out. In both cases." He squeezed her hand. "These last couple of days, knowing we weren't on the same page was unsettling. I meant it—I missed you right away. I missed you before you showed up on my doorstep. I missed you when I got the call about the job. I let it go to voicemail. It took two hours to work up the courage to listen to it."

Her sympathy welled. "Why didn't you call or text? I could've come. Listened to it for you. Held your hand."

He lifted her hand and kissed it. "I was reeling. And

embarrassed. I'm sorry. You hit on something when you said I haven't shown the courage to be vulnerable. I hope you know I don't see myself as better than you." He waited for her to nod, then took a deep breath. "But in general, yeah, maybe my ego got in the way of being real. I don't like to fail, so I keep failures—like how I kept quiet for Gury or couldn't convince the board—under wraps. But it's more than that. I keep everything—from emotions to life events—to myself if I think there's a possibility for disappointment. But that's no way to live. Holding back can cause the very thing I'm afraid of because secrets are toxic to connection."

Her heart shuddered. She should tell him about Mercy. If she maintained the secret after that speech, she could never blame her silence on ignorance. He would want to know. He would want her to trust him with it.

He turned her hand in his. "I'm praying about how to apply that more broadly, but for starters, I say we forget dating quietly." His eyes, blue and loyal, fixed on hers. "I never want you to think I'm looking down on you. It's the opposite. You inspired me to turn around my whole way of thinking these last couple of days. I'm honored to be with you. I want everyone to know that. Especially you." He chuckled and lifted their intertwined hands. "Besides, I can't seem to resist touching you. Anyone with eyes has already seen the truth."

He gazed at her with the steady trust of a man who'd laid his heart out and had nothing left to hide. A man who'd come clean and couldn't fathom that she'd do anything less.

Secrets are toxic to connection.

Somehow, he'd imagined he was the only one who struggled to accept that.

But he wasn't dealing with Jenny, who'd blurted out her full involvement with the garage fire the moment she'd been discovered. He was dealing with Blaze, who understood that some truths could, at the least, pile rumors onto a little girl's shoulders. At the worst, they might take Mercy from her.

35

Aside from the hum of the furnace and Blaze's pleased laugh, the conference room was silent. She set her laptop at the head of the table and sent a picture of the eight empty chairs to Anson.

What am I looking at? he asked.

I'm first to arrive for a meeting! I don't think this has ever happened before.

Congrats. Lots of firsts for you today. I'm proud of you.

She read and reread that last sentence. There were only two firsts—this and tonight, when she'd share a pared-down version of her testimony with Rooted. Both would've been a struggle before the prescription.

With the medicine, distractions didn't make her late as often. And she'd been able to focus while planning her Rooted talk with Anson.

Movement at the doorway prompted her to lower her phone. Tony spotted her, peeked at the empty chairs, and stepped in. "I saw the leaderboard. Selina sold five cars last week?"

Blaze's chest expanded. "She's a natural."

He braced his hands on the back of a chair. "Actually, I ran into her in the break room just now. She says she had a good trainer."

Blaze had been half-asleep on the wrong medication while training Selina, but she had dedicated large blocks of time to her new hire. The Lord must've been helping Blaze even before the medicine had. "Whatever caused it, it's driving Thomas crazy."

Tony scoffed. "A little competition will do him good."

"Speaking of, I wanted to talk to you about reworking the monthly sales leader bonus to factor in some additional metrics. Some of the team cuts corners, like not accounting for bald tires on a trade-in. They still haven't beaten Selina that way, but with some adjustments to the bonus, we could give them incentive to be more careful."

Selina tapped on the open door.

Tony motioned her in. "You always were a good idea person, Blaze. You're on to something. Stop by my office after this, and we'll work it out."

She hadn't been this proud of her work since she'd won the sales leader bonus four months in a row. "Will do."

"Keep up the good work, ladies." Tony ambled out.

Blaze typed herself a reminder to follow up with him. By the time she finished, Thomas had arrived. Moments later, the rest of the sales team took their seats, and she stood to start the meeting. As she reviewed the first report, another first happened—she spoke with the calm confidence of someone who was thoroughly prepared. She followed an agenda, had answers for each question, and a vision for her team. And she couldn't stop smiling.

Anson's strategy to "run into" Carter at the community center might not work. He'd been fired almost three weeks ago. Most days since, he'd run drills on the center's basketball courts, hoping the student would show up. Still hadn't. Nevertheless, Anson had nowhere else to be on a Wednesday night as Rooted met without him.

Last week's youth group had bothered him less because Nolan had hosted and shared his testimony. Tonight, Rooted normally wouldn't meet since it was the night before Thanksgiving. A fact Anson hadn't mentioned when Blaze told him her plan to host the group and share part of her story. Despite knowing what she planned to say, Anson longed to be there. To support her. To watch the kids' reactions. Instead, he was on a basketball court, waiting on a student who might never come.

He dipped into lunges while dribbling. His body had borne the brunt of his unoccupied time since he'd been fired. The initial soreness had faded, and his muscles responded to the workout with ease.

As kids came and went on the other side of the court, he worked through single-person drills. His mind and heart weren't in it—they were wrapped up in prayers for Blaze and the students.

He took his first shot at the basket and missed the backboard entirely.

Walk me through the valley, Lord.

Even as he prayed, he fought doubts that this might not be a temporary valley. This sense of being adrift might be permanent. His new normal.

On second thought, God, you might need to carry me.

He sighed, rebounded the ball, and returned to the mark he'd been shooting from. A form appeared in the nearest doorway. He took his shot. It bounced off the rim. On his way to rebound, he checked to see who'd stopped.

Sydney waved as she stepped into the gym. She wore slacks and a plain black top, probably about to leave for the day. "You've always been fun to watch on a court."

He passed the ball from one hand to the other. "Thanks." They hadn't spoken in months, aside from conversations required for youth group. He hadn't expected a compliment to end the silence between them. "I heard you and Ray are stepping up for Branching Out. I'm glad."

She crossed her arms and nodded. "It seemed like the thing to do. I know your heart for the group and wanted the mission to continue, even if you couldn't be the one to do it."

"Careful." He returned to the line and shot again. This time, the ball went through the hoop. "My mission got me fired."

"Sometimes, that's what we're called to."

The ball bounced against the hardwood beneath the net, but Anson made no move to go get it. "Getting fired?"

"Or crucified. Or stoned. Or imprisoned. Or boils."

"Boils?"

"Like Job. If you think about it, you could've been given a much harder assignment."

He laughed and ran after the ball as he followed the idea. So many heroes of the faith had endured trials despite their obedience. He knew that, yet only now applied it to losing his job. Maybe he hadn't misunderstood God's leading. And if he hadn't misheard last time, he could listen again now with some hope of getting it right. With the ball braced between his wrist and side, he rubbed the heel of his palm against his eye.

"It's been a rough couple of weeks, huh?"

"Yeah."

Sydney smiled softly. "You'll be all right."

Maybe he would. He and Sydney had shared many talks like this one. Her take on difficult situations had steered him well the entire year they'd dated. "You're wise. You know that?"

She chuckled. "You're welcome to tell me. I don't turn down compliments."

"You said some good things the last time we talked too. I'm sorry I didn't see the truth about us sooner. And for the pain I'm sure I caused you."

She nodded slowly. "Me too."

He turned toward the basket, resuming his drill.

"You can't get by on your coaching wages forever. What're you going to do?"

"Not sure yet." He didn't like his options, especially after watching Blaze's face fall as he described them.

"I won't have any basketball coaching positions until summer, but we're looking for a facilities manager." Her voice lifted. As the director of the community center, she filled a few positions every year.

"Is that a janitor?" After a job with so many interpersonal dynamics to navigate, spending time cleaning might prove cathartic.

"More like a handyman and equipment monitor." She outlined a couple more details about the position, but another person arrived in the doorway behind her.

Dylan—with Carter in tow.

Joy swelled in Anson's chest, and a grin overtook his face. Dylan waved at him. Carter glowered.

Sydney stepped aside to let them in.

"Hey, Sydney?"

She looked over her shoulder.

"Thank you. I don't know about the job, but I appreciate the offer."

She waved and walked away as the brothers stepped onto the court.

Between clarity from their conversation and his gratitude that the Lord had brought the Newsome brothers to see him, Anson could take on the world. Or at least Carter and Dylan. He lifted the ball. "Two on one? Winner buys burgers?"

"You mean loser?" Dylan half-danced, half-strutted onto the court.

"Nope. Winner. For the record, that's going to be me."

"We'll see about that." Carter clapped his hands, demanding the ball.

"Pride really does go before a fall." Dylan's voice echoed around the court. "But we'll still let you buy us food anyway, right?" He smacked his brother with the back of his hand.

The basketball propped against his hip, Carter studied Anson. "You lost on purpose."

Anson lifted his hands. Dylan had served as a handicap for Carter, but as soon as the game started, Anson had been distracted by an idea. One he credited to God. After begging the Lord for direction, Anson couldn't very well ignore Him—even if the prompt meant doing something he had avoided for years.

"You won fair and square," he said. "But yeah, dinner's on me."

"We already ate." Carter passed the ball from one hand to the other in a slow, steady rhythm.

Dylan stood on his toes. "We could eat more."

"You drove here, Carter?"

The student nodded.

"Meet me at The Depot?" Only after the offer was out did he remember Eric's dislike for the place. "Just check with your parents first, okay?"

"I'll text Mom," Dylan said. "She won't mind."

"Maybe *I* do." Carter held the ball and looked between Anson and his brother.

"You promised." Dylan grabbed Carter's arm and pulled. "Come on."

Promised what? He'd ask, but the community center was closing. Perhaps he could figure it out at the restaurant. He led them outside.

At The Depot, they took a booth in the dining area. Dylan gleefully ordered more food than any one person—even one who hadn't already had dinner—could eat, but once the waiter walked away, he became as quiet as his sullen brother.

Anson considered diving right into his story about Gury, but something—the Lord, he hoped—prompted him to start with a question. "Did you come to the community center looking for me?"

Dylan shot a bright look at his brother, but Carter only scowled. Dylan pressed his hands on the tabletop and leaned toward him until his chest hit his wrists. "The fire inspector says someone lit candles in the sanctuary. They found what was left of them on the stage. They were supposed to be for Christmas Eve." He leaned back, jostling the seat and Carter in the process.

Anson absorbed the information. That the candles had been taken from the closet by the youth room enforced his suspicion that their repeat visitor had started the fire. When he'd stored the candles there, he'd checked for signs of whoever was sneaking in. Instead of helping, it seemed he'd put tempting flammables directly in his or her path. "Do they still think it was an accident?"

Dylan shrugged and nodded. "Do you think the person who did it will get in trouble? I mean, the candles were supposed to be burned in church, so it's not like it was wrong to light them."

They might as well be back on the court, playing two-on-one, only Anson couldn't afford to lose this match. He needed to find out what the brothers knew.

Carter rolled his eyes. "You're making him think you did it."

"What? No!"

"Western burger." A burger piled six inches tall with toppings landed in front of Dylan.

Dylan's eyes darted to the waiter who'd dropped it off, but the guy didn't miss a beat as he unloaded the rest of Dylan's order, including fries, a milkshake, and fried cheese curds. Carter accepted the plate with his onion rings. Anson had ordered the same.

Once the waiter left, Anson said grace, then the boys started eating. His own appetite having evaporated, he studied the brothers. "What do you know about the fire?"

"Nothing," Dylan blurted.

That elicited another eye roll from Carter. "Just what we told you."

"How did you two learn about the investigation? It's not wrapped up yet, is it?"

Dylan gulped down a bite of burger. "The leadership board keeps meeting at our house."

"Those meetings are supposed to be confidential," Anson said. Even without an ongoing fire investigation, the board covered sensitive topics—details about struggling members, conflicts within the body, and employment decisions.

"Yeah, but you should be included." A glop of barbecue sauce and mayo slopped over Dylan's pinkie and dropped to the table. "You shouldn't have been fired."

"Telling me what they're saying isn't going to change what happened."

"My dad's a bully. Nobody stands up to him but you."

Dylan's declaration drew a sigh from Carter, who rested his elbow on the table, his cheek against a loose fist.

"Who has he been bullying?"

Dylan lowered his gaze to the mountain range of food in front of him.

Carter studied his brother, the corner of his mouth tight.

These two had a secret, but as clearly as Anson had once felt the Lord directing him to give up his basketball scholarship, he knew it wasn't the boys' turn to talk. It was his.

"Did you guys know I used to have a brother?"

36

Blaze watched from the doorway as the last Rooted student hurried through the cold November night to hop into her mom's car. Nearby, Nolan waved before getting in his truck. As both vehicles pulled away, she shut the door and surveyed the living room.

Since the church wasn't usable, she'd decluttered her living room. Even with the paper plates and games scattered around, the place felt cleaner and calmer than normal. While Mercy sorted board game pieces into the appropriate boxes, Blaze collected napkins, plates, and plastic cups and tossed them in the kitchen trash. She hummed to herself as she closed chip bags until she heard the front door open.

Her chest constricted. As of yet, the doorbell cameras had recorded nothing suspicious, but what if Mercy was upset about her testimony again?

"Mercy?" She abandoned her work.

Her sister stood at the front door letting in a late November draft. Before Blaze could ask what she was doing, Anson stepped in.

Months ago, when they'd crossed paths at the park in the square, she'd assumed he'd never fall for a girl like her. Never look at her with this blend of gratitude and hope, like simply standing in her presence was an answer to prayer.

A soft smile lifted his mouth. "Hey."

"Hi." She wrapped her arms around herself and checked over the space again. She hadn't vacuumed yet, but this was the best her house had looked in ages. The best her life had been. But her continued fears about Mercy reminded her of the one thing she didn't have—a clear conscience.

"Is the rabbit around?" Anson lifted a bag of cilantro.

She opened her mouth but found herself speechless. He'd brought greens again?

"He's hiding. People aren't his thing." Mercy bounced back to the coffee table and the games. "He can't eat all of that at once because he already had his greens at lunch, but I can give him *some* of the cilantro."

Blaze had never heard that teacher-like tone from Mercy before.

Lips twitching, Anson laid the bag on the table near her. "All right. As long as you tell him it's from me."

"Sure." Mercy snickered and fit the lid on one of the games. "I'm almost done. Then I'll go to my room, even though it's *not* a school night. And *that's* why I'm thankful for Thanksgiving." She hammed it up like she was auditioning for a cheesy commercial.

Anson passed Mercy a playing card from the coffee table. "You missed one."

"Oh. Weird." She added it to the correct box.

When she leaned over to check for other strays, Anson plucked it back out of the pile and slid it toward her. "You missed one."

"Where was it?" She snatched it up and put it on the stack.

Anson shrugged.

Blaze didn't bother hiding her smile—her sister was too busy keeping up with Anson's game to notice.

Mercy peered under the coffee table.

He got the card back out. As soon as Mercy straightened, he dropped it to the carpet. Pointing, he said, "You missed one."

This time, Mercy eyed him leerily.

"I'll get it for you." He squatted, plucked the card from the floor, and extended it toward her. "Since I'm a nice guy."

Giggling, she accepted it and placed it on the pile.

While she was turned, Anson tossed another card even Blaze hadn't seen him palm. "You missed one."

"You!" Mercy snatched the card from the carpet and returned to find yet another card on the seat she'd just vacated. She shook her recent finds at Anson in mock outrage. "What do you think you're doing?"

"I had nothing to do with that last one. I swear." He lifted his hands.

Mercy turned to Blaze. "Did you see?"

Blaze shook her head. She'd made the mistake of taking her eyes off him. She'd glimpsed this side of Anson at youth group but had never watched him tease her sister.

"You have to believe me," Anson said. "I didn't do it. Here, I'll put them away for you." He held out his hand.

Mercy narrowed her eyes. "No way." She plopped the cards in the box, jammed on the lid, and covered the whole thing with her forearms. "Try getting more of them from me now."

Without taking his eyes off her, Anson pulled a stack of

cards from his back pocket and flicked the whole thing into the air behind him.

As they fluttered to the ground, Mercy's laughter filled the room. It expanded into spaces inside Blaze she hadn't realized were empty.

She and Mercy hadn't spent a lot of time enjoying themselves. Mostly, they bounced from damage control to disaster response and back again. They really needed to make more time for fun. Who'd have thought serious Anson Marsh would remind her of that?

He asked Mercy questions about her day as they finished packing up the games. The plastic bag crinkled when he moved the cilantro to check beneath it for pieces. Tonight was just one more example of how he cared for Blaze and every member of her little family. And she ... Did she love him for it?

They'd come a long way since their first meeting. And maybe someone who'd come that far with her could be trusted with the truth about Mercy. Except he was still Anson, and she was still Blaze. He'd be compelled to report Mercy's suspicious behavior and rumors—if not real, court-appointed consequences—would devastate the Astleys again.

They finished putting away the cards, and with more laughter, Anson stacked Mercy's arms full of everything that would go back in the game tote downstairs. She tottered away, as though the load prevented her from bending at the knees.

Anson turned to Blaze, humor still lighting his face. "Rooted went well?"

She nodded and motioned him to follow her to the kitchen. "Mercy and I always go to the meal Philip and

Michaela host at The Depot. I have to make a sweet potato and onion tart to share."

"You're like my very own cooking show." His fingers skimmed her back.

"I'll put you to work this time." At the counter, she ran her finger along the ingredient list. "We can make two so you can take one to your parents' house."

Anson's hand settled on her waist. "Or we could make one, and you could skip The Depot to join me at my parents' house."

She turned her back on the recipe to face him. "That's ...." She meant to write off the offer as impulsive, but the interest in his eyes held hers. Her voice faltered. "You want to introduce me to your parents? Now?" She shifted backward and bumped the counter. "I mean, we're not even exclusive."

He lifted an eyebrow. "Oh?"

She cleared her throat. "Isn't meeting the parents a big deal?"

He boxed her in with one hand braced on the counter on either side of her. "You are a big deal to me."

"But meet-the-parents big?" She rested her hands on his chest, mostly because he hadn't given her many other options. "You once said you chose me with your heart, but you don't have to throw logic out the window."

His eyes narrowed.

She smoothed her hands over said heart. "Have you even told your parents about me? You don't want to give them heart attacks by suddenly being like, 'Hey, remember Many Oaks's town drunk? I'm dating her daughter.'"

"I would never introduce you that way, and if they knew of your mom, I guarantee that's not how they thought of her. Weren't you telling me to assume the best about people?"

She dropped her gaze to his chest as embarrassment poisoned her air supply. She'd also told him to share the whole truth with people.

"As for the head versus heart thing, you've captured my heart, and logically, you help me follow Jesus better, so we make sense both ways. But ultimately? I don't want to follow my head or my heart. I follow Jesus. He loves you. The way I see it, I'm just following His lead."

Love? Sparks lit across her skin.

With a fingertip, he drew a line from her forehead, across her temple, and down her cheek, until his hand rested on her shoulder. He toyed with the hair at the nape of her neck. "Let's be exclusive."

Heat shot through her. She'd have stumbled backward in surprise if not for the cabinets. "Sure." Her voice wobbled.

"Sure?" He tilted his head, scanning from her eyes to her lips and back again. "That's all the enthusiasm you can muster?"

Yes, because her amazement floated on a pool of regret, and at the bottom of that lay her secret. For that to stay hidden, she had to do better. "I'd love that." She rested her fingers against his cheek, relishing the textures of skin and stubble.

His lips met hers in a kiss that should've turned her inside out. He was warm and solid and steady and deliberate, and she was hiding something from him. The kiss broke, and he studied her.

She smiled, but did it fool him? "Exclusive," she said.

He held her gaze another moment before he shifted away and rolled up his sleeves. "What can I help with, Blaze?"

Heaviness tainted his voice. After how close she'd come

to asking him to call her Jen, the use of her name stung like a paper cut.

She put him to work peeling sweet potatoes. She got out the baking pan they'd roast the vegetables on, then started slicing onions—her least favorite part of cooking, but she couldn't very well give him the worst job after all that.

"Tell me about Rooted?" Anson asked.

"I gave my talk like we planned." Her knife sliced through the end of the onion and clicked on the cutting board. "Since I kept it mostly limited to the garage fire and the church fire like we planned, the kids asked about Shadrach, Meshach, and Abednego. I offered the option of starting games right away or reading about the fiery furnace. They chose reading, so we spent an extra fifteen minutes on that. I figure since the kids chose to extend what was supposed to be a five-minute talk, Eric can't complain if he hears about it." She finished slicing the first onion and tipped her head away, trying to clear the sting from her eyes.

"Sounds like you did a great job."

Not *the best you could* or a *good* job—a great job. As soon as the satisfaction settled in her chest, it sank. Would he compliment her if he knew what she wasn't saying? If he knew Mercy had slipped by her and spent an entire night out on her own doing who knew what?

She returned to slicing. "Did missing it drive you nuts?"

"I knew the kids were in good hands."

Another compliment. Blaze sniffed and wiped her wrist over her watering eyes. The onions stung, but knowing how little she deserved his approval hurt worse.

"Here. Let me." He took the knife from her. His hand on her waist guided her away from the cutting board. By the time her eyes cleared, he'd cut the whole onion.

She washed her hands, then picked up where he'd left off with the sweet potatoes.

"I went to the community center." His knife scraped against the cutting board as he swept the onions onto the waiting pan. "The Newsome boys showed up."

"Speaking of things Eric might complain about."

"They said their mom knew where they were. I think something's going on with them that they're not saying."

"With Eric and Samantha?"

"With the boys." He rinsed the knife, then dried his hands. "I told you about Dylan acting weird when he caught up with me after practice that one day."

"He said it was because he and Carter sent you a text from Eric's phone."

He picked up the sweet potato. "Does this get sliced too?" When she nodded, he returned to the cutting board. "Now they say the inspector believes the fire originated from the Christmas Eve candles. Someone lit them in the sanctuary. I don't doubt Eric would talk about that in their earshot, but the boys have been in the thick of it since the night of the fire. And Dylan called his dad a bully tonight."

She paused peeling. Even his family would say such a thing? What was Eric like to live with?

Anson dropped the sliced sweet potato in the pan, turned toward her, and waited until she met his solemn blue eyes. "I told them about Gury, hoping they'd believe me that some secrets do more harm than good. They were stunned, but not into talking."

She gaped. "You told them?"

"I've thought a lot about what you said." He stepped nearer, taking the peeler from her hand so he could intertwine their fingers. "About how I shouldn't keep him a secret.

I'm going to start talking about him more in general, and when and where God calls me to, I'll tell the part about the secret I kept for him. The time seemed right with Carter and Dylan."

Could he possibly understand what a compliment it was that he'd listened to her? She'd only made the suggestion to keep the focus off herself and her secret.

"I was hoping they'd spill whatever they're hiding." His thumb caressed the side of her hand. "Carter actually looked like he might, but Dylan got antsy and insisted they had to go."

She still held the potato in her left hand. A sane person would put it down to concentrate on this vulnerable, caring man sharing his heart. Her grip around the vegetable tightened, and she resisted turning fully toward him. "Who do you think is hiding something?"

"Both. But who has more at stake? Hard to say." He released her hand and returned to the cutting board with another potato. "Dylan acts suspiciously, but I don't imagine Carter would come see me for nothing. He might've been along to make sure Dylan didn't blurt out anything incriminating."

That sounded like her watching over Mercy. "What are you going to do?" Her voice sounded shrill. She picked up the peeler and worked quickly, hoping the noise of it might distract from her tone.

"Wait and see if being honest with them prompts them to be honest with me."

"And if they had something to do with the fire?"

"I'll help them with the consequences."

The potato she'd been peeling slipped from her fingers. "Meaning what? You'd report them?"

A Surefire Love

"There's an ongoing investigation." A hint of incredulity rang in his tone. "Everyone needs answers. And I don't like the hints they've been dropping about Eric. Depending on what they have to say when the whole story comes out, child services might have to get involved."

She laid the last potato on the counter between them and braced her hands on the surface, keeping her face turned down and away. "I'm not sure I have so much faith in the system."

She heard the rustle of him move, but he didn't touch her. "Why not? I thought your experience in foster care was okay."

"I was still separated from my mom, and I missed home every day. When Mom got me back, nothing much had changed except she made it very clear there were things we couldn't talk about because we needed each other, but if people knew about our lives, they'd separate us."

"She never should've put you in that position. It's never good when an adult asks a kid to keep a secret."

Her breath rushed out, and tears flushed her eyes. Had she become her mother after all?

"Hey." Anson's hand on her shoulder guided her away from the counter. His thumb skimmed her cheek before he pulled her into a hug. "I'm sorry for what you went through. I'm sorry you needed help and were left to fend for yourself. I really don't want that for Carter and Dylan. I don't know if there is a problem in their family, but if one of them started the fire—"

"I don't want to lose Mercy. It's my greatest fear."

He stilled for a moment. His chest shifted as he leaned his head to see her face. "Why would you lose Mercy? You're doing a great job with her. She's happy and healthy and well-cared for."

Was she, though? Blaze bit her trembling bottom lip. She had been trying for years to break the cycle of dysfunction. She thought turning her life over to Christ would do it. She thought obtaining diagnoses and treatment would release her. But what if it wasn't about breaking the old cycle, but rather building a new one? One that rejected the old lies. One that followed Jesus's lead as Anson had said? And following Jesus's lead meant telling the truth regardless of the consequences, the way a scared little girl named Jenny had.

She took a deep breath, then straightened away from him. "When I got up—" Her lungs spasmed, but if she had to sob her way through this, she would.

She tried again. "When I got up the morning after the fire, Mercy was coming back in."

His eyebrows dipped, but his gaze held hers.

"I had no idea she'd gone out. She said she was upset because she'd found the first draft of my testimony and then I didn't check on her after our date. So when I went to bed, she snuck out. She was gone all night. She swears she didn't go to the church and has never snuck out before, and I think I believe her, but it's not like she has a perfect track record of honesty." Blaze's eyes slid shut, and two tears dropped to her cheeks.

She forced her eyes open. "She had just read my testimony. It might've given her ideas about starting a fire or about what would happen if she was honest. She might be lying, even to me, because she's as scared as I am of the consequences." She shuddered. All of that was speculation. She needed to own up to one last fact. "She was wearing her

Rooted hoodie when she came in. It looks so suspicious, I told her not to tell anyone, and I especially didn't tell you."

His mouth dropped open and he crossed his arms over his chest.

Unable to watch his anger replace his faith in her, Blaze lowered her face.

37

Anson felt the force of Blaze's words and the aftershock as he replayed them. She'd said she'd *especially* kept the truth from him. When she'd made him work to gain the promise of exclusivity, he suspected she'd withdrawn. Only now did he comprehend how far or why.

"Are you angry?" Her shoulders were as rigid as prison bars as she stared at the floor.

He was so much more than angry. Disappointment, pain, offense, and rejection all vied for control. He'd thought she prized honesty. He'd opened up to Carter and Dylan at her insistence. Meanwhile, she'd kept a secret. But before he could call her on the double standard, Coach's voice came back to him. *Responses trump reactions.* He planted his feet, steadying himself against the onslaught of his tangled emotions.

"Are you going to report us?"

"Report you?"

"To the authorities." Blaze looked up.

Stiff with shock, he could barely shake his head. "Why would I do that?"

"Because I don't know where she was. Some of the details line up."

He inhaled. Exhaled. "Do you think it was her?"

"Not really, I guess. But she could—"

He motioned her to stop. "Then neither do I."

She rubbed the back of her neck, then dropped her hand and blew out a breath. "Really?"

"Yes. When I was talking about reporting things, that was about acting on knowledge, not unsubstantiated possibilities."

Her shoulders relaxed and she nodded. "Thank you." Finally, she lifted her gaze. Her lower lip trembled. "But you are angry."

"I'm ..." He wasn't going to say he was disappointed. Disappointed sounded too much like a scolding parent. "I'm fine."

That was a lie he hadn't meant to tell.

The lines around her mouth deepened.

He clenched and straightened his fingers, as if the right response was something he could grasp. "You saw a threat and went into protection mode." That had nothing to do with his feelings, but maybe it'd give them a place to work from. She'd been protecting herself and Mercy from ... him. "I've let you down in the past. I know that. I just thought we put that in the past."

Red splotches appeared by Blaze's collarbone and crept up her neck.

"I wish you'd trusted me enough to let me in on it sooner. Instead, you thought it'd be better to let it eat you up like this? You must've really expected something terrible from me." He recalled what she'd said just before telling him the story. "Did you really think I'd try to have Mercy taken away?"

"No. Not on purpose. I just ..." She swept her fingers over her eyes, but more tears fell instantly. "I thought one thing might lead to another. But you're right. I should've trusted you."

His phone rang. He rubbed his forehead. Should've silenced the thing when he'd walked in, but he hadn't expected to end up in a serious conversation.

"You can get that." She backed farther from him. "It is kind of late. It might be important." Her gaze shifted to the oven clock. It was only 8:45—dark outside the windows, but not that late. She shrugged as if to acknowledge her error.

"Or it might be one of the kids planning to ask if my refrigerator is running." A much easier question to field than how to respond to Blaze. He shifted away from the counter to pull the device from his pocket. "Almost no one has reached out since I got fired, so the odds of them prank calling are low, but never ze—" He read the name on the display. Truth might be more contagious than he'd ever realized. "It's Carter. I need to take this."

She picked up a knife and the last potato. "We can talk Friday."

Friday. Because tomorrow was Thanksgiving, and she didn't want to join him. "I'm supposed to be at my parents' house until Sunday night."

"Oh." She worked her lips. "Monday or Tuesday then."

The phone kept ringing. He hesitated to leave at all, but he'd been working toward a breakthrough with Carter for years. He couldn't fail now. If the conversation went nowhere and ended soon, he'd come back, work through things with

Blaze tonight. For now, Anson passed through the living room toward the door. "Hey, Carter."

"Hey. There's something I've gotta tell you."

He closed his eyes a beat, a wordless *thank you* to God. But even as he stepped out of the house, he knew he also had Blaze to thank. If not for her advice, he wouldn't have opened up about Gury. He and Carter wouldn't be having this conversation. "I'm listening."

"My parents fight. A lot. Dylan hates it, so he splits whenever they get going. Mom and Dad don't even notice. If it's late at night, sometimes he doesn't come back home."

Anson climbed into his SUV as Carter's statement scattered his thoughts like a cue ball breaking the rack. "Fight how?"

"Yelling. Mom complains Dad's always gone. He says it's how we pay for everything. It doesn't sound that bad, I guess, but they're both pretty unhappy, and nobody seems to know how to fix it. I'm not sure they're going to make it. Sometimes I think it'd be better if they didn't."

Anson's parents had argued occasionally. Once or twice, he wondered if they'd work it out. Each time, the thought of divorce terrified him. To suspect his parents might be better off apart, Carter's home must be a battlefield. But Eric and Samantha were only background to what Carter was saying about his brother. "Where does Dylan go?"

"Friends' houses, sometimes. But Dad lost his church keys a while ago. He had to get someone to make new copies for him. I think Dylan's got the original set."

Anson replayed the meeting where he'd asked the leadership board about their keys. Eric had never admitted to losing his. Had he forgotten or lied by omission?

"I knew you were worried about a kid sleeping at the

church," Carter said, "but it didn't seem like a big deal until Dylan woke me up all worked up about a fire at church. He was in tears. He said you'd know what to do, but he wouldn't let me call you. So we texted. He calmed down some after that, but before the fire, Mom and Dad argued. I didn't see Dylan go, but when he woke me up, he was sweating and panting, and he smelled like smoke. I'm actually surprised Mom and Dad didn't notice."

Dylan wasn't driving yet. Whether he'd gone on foot or taken a bicycle, racing the mile or two between the church and the Newsome house would explain the sweating and panting. "He said your family learned about the fire when someone called your dad."

"He woke me up before that. We heard Dad's phone ring. He won't tell me any more than what I told you, but I think ..." Carter's voice grew rough. "I think my brother's in trouble, and I don't want it to get any worse, like it did with your brother. Dylan's too afraid of Dad to tell our parents what happened."

"Okay. It's going to be all right." He was still working out how that would be true, but reassurance seemed like the place to start. "Thank you for telling me."

"What'll happen?"

Anson sighed as he stared at the steering wheel. "I know you don't want to hear it, but you guys really need to talk to your parents."

"I'm telling you. Dad's ... look, he's the reason I'm not on the basketball team."

"What?"

"I wanted to be—that's why I did the whole stagehand thing. And now that I know about your brother, I get why you reported us. It was pretty dumb to begin with. I kind of thought if I got in trouble, Dad would stay around more to keep me in line or something, and Mom might be happy."

Anson's stomach churned. He never would've guessed that the acting out was a misguided attempt to save his parents' marriage.

"With Dad, either he's your biggest fan or your biggest enemy." Carter's voice faltered. "He's a fan of me, so he didn't believe I did anything wrong. All that happened was he got extra mad at you. He hasn't liked you since the day I told him what you said about the odds of getting on a DI team."

Frustration cracked through Anson's muscles, but he suppressed a reaction that wouldn't help. "He won't consider his own son an enemy."

"Why not? He thinks Mom's one."

Anson wanted to say he was sure it wasn't that bad, but how would he know? If the rift between Eric and Samantha had caused the kids to react in the ways Carter described, something major had gone off course. Knowing Blaze's upbringing reminded him that parents didn't always have their kids' best interests in mind. Were Carter and Dylan in danger? What about Samantha—or even Eric?

Before he could pose a question, Carter said, "With me, Dad wants to talk about college and basketball, and he attends my games and stuff. He started the Division I talk. That was cool for a while, but at this point, it'd actually be good if he believed in me as a basketball star a little less. Like, if he could be okay with me playing for a less competitive team and working on a degree that'll get me a job *after* college. But that's how he is with me. Total fan. With Dylan, it's different. Most of the time, Dad doesn't even see him, but that won't last if Dylan burned the church down. Dad would have him thrown in jail."

"That's not up to him." Anson didn't know who would decide, but Dylan was a minor. It likely was an accident. They wouldn't send him to jail for that, would they? "How's Dylan holding up?"

"He's mostly been in his room. I think. Maybe he's still sneaking out. He said something about running away, but he didn't mean it."

Anson rubbed his face. He'd underreacted to a kid breaking into the church. He wouldn't make that mistake again. "What's your family doing for Thanksgiving?"

"We're going to my aunt and uncle's house at, like, four."

Which meant the Newsomes weren't hosting and didn't have plans first thing in the morning. "Is everybody still up?"

"Yeah."

"Okay." Anson weighed his options one more time. The kids needed help. The sooner, the better, since it seemed likely Dylan had already made one devastating middle-of-the-night decision.

Is it my place to go have the conversation, Lord?

He'd already been fired, so he had little to lose by poking sensitive topics. Besides, Carter had chosen to open up to Anson, and neither of the boys seemed willing to talk to their parents alone.

"How about I come over, and we all have a talk?"

"Dad isn't going to want to see you."

"I'll invite Pastor Greg too." They'd need a mediator, and Greg was still an MOBC pastor who would want to be involved. "I imagine he'll be able to make it."

"Dad doesn't hate him so much, but I don't think he listens to him either."

Probably not. "I'm going to pray that God will smooth the way."

Carter was silent for a few beats. "You really think praying's going to help?"

"I prayed quite a bit before I told you about Gury, and God answered those prayers."

"Because I talked to you?" His flat tone suggested he wasn't impressed by the evidence.

"God cares about you and your family. I know things seem messed up, but I think you're about to have a front-row seat to watch the Lord in action."

Carter grunted. Still skeptical, then. "So you're on your way?"

"Let me coordinate with Greg. I'll text you when we're on our way."

"Okay. Then I'll get Dylan. And maybe Mom. She can handle Dad. Sort of." Carter disconnected.

Anson surveyed the dark neighborhood. If he'd been stumped over how to respond to Blaze a few minutes ago, he would be completely out of his depth walking into the Newsome house. They needed someone who could handle Eric, and Anson doubted he, Greg, or Samantha could. It would be up to the Lord.

38

*B*laze and Mercy spent from noon until five at The Depot. Philip and his family had pushed together enough tables to make a banquet table long enough for the thirty-some people who gathered. After the meal, Blaze and Mercy helped clean up and then worked on a puzzle with Philip's oldest daughter and a few others. As dinnertime neared, they carried their now-empty platters back out to the car and headed home.

"You know what I'm grateful for?" Mercy said from the back seat. "That they didn't have a kids' table."

Blaze chuckled. Mercy had been listing things she was grateful for all day. Blaze was having a harder time being so thankful.

"I'm also grateful we know about ADHD," Mercy said.

"Me too, kiddo." Blaze steered through town.

Mercy was keeping up with her chores, schoolwork, and friends. It'd been weeks since Blaze had had to drop off a forgotten lunch or instrument. And she was having an easier time at work. An easier time staying on top of the clutter. They'd even shown up on time for the meal today.

If only she could blame ADHD for the rift she'd created between herself and Anson. He'd been so shocked she'd kept a secret from him but so ready to believe Mercy simply because Blaze did.

She never should've underestimated him.

Of course, she'd had to do so right before a major holiday. How had his conversation with Carter gone? How was dinner with his parents going? Should she have accepted his offer to travel with him, or would he have rescinded it after she revealed her secret?

She pulled into their driveway and hit the button to lift the garage door. She should've texted him to check in—she'd thought of little else, even through all the conversations at The Depot—but she'd chickened out. They'd talk once he got back home, as planned.

"I thought you said Anson was at his parents' house."

"He is." She angled to see Mercy in the rearview mirror.

Her sister was looking over her left shoulder, back toward the street. "*Was*, maybe. He just parked."

Foot still on the brake, Blaze turned. Sure enough, a familiar SUV sat at the side of the road. A flurry of nerves swirled in her core. Blaze straightened in her seat and carefully navigated into the garage. "Sweetie, there's something I should tell you."

"What?"

"I told him you left the house the night of the fire." Blaze shut off the car and twisted to look directly at Mercy. "I was wrong to ask you to keep it a secret like I did. I don't want to put you in that position."

Mercy fiddled with her seatbelt. "I shouldn't have gone for that walk."

"I forgive you. Forgive me?"

Mercy nodded, then quirked an eyebrow. "How long are you going to make him wait in the cold?"

Blaze reached into the backseat to tweak Mercy's nose, but her sister dodged, giggling. They got out of the car and headed outside.

"I'm going to have to go to my room again, aren't I?"

"Anson and I do need to talk today, but you don't have to hide away from us all the time."

Mercy stepped into the gray afternoon. "You having a boyfriend is kind of boring."

Boyfriend. Did he still want that title? Her steps dragged as she and Mercy met Anson between the garage and the house.

His smile was muted, but when Mercy got close to him, he tossed her a purple-and-white vegetable the size of a baseball.

Mercy turned it in her hands. "For BunBun?"

He nodded. "Radicchio. You'll tell him who brought it?"

"You're kinda weird."

No, he was incredibly sweet.

Mercy scampered inside and to her room, presumably to give the bunny a snack.

Anson shadowed Blaze into the kitchen. She delivered the tart platters to the sink, but as she reached for the faucet, Anson's much larger hand covered hers, drawing her back to face him. "I left my parents' house right after the meal. I can't stand how we left things."

"Me neither." The trouble was, even as she studied their

linked hands, she wasn't sure she could stand where this conversation would lead them.

Still, it was a good sign that he'd come. A good sign that he'd taken her hands with such tenderness. "It's not too late," she said.

"For what?"

Tears dropped to her cheeks.

He released her hand to brush them away.

"To change your mind."

"About?" His fingertips rested lightly against her cheeks and neck as if she were a glass egg.

She could only blame herself for the fragile state of their relationship. "What we talked about before I told you about Mercy." She couldn't bring herself to say it more directly. He'd asked to be exclusive, but now that he had more experience with her, would he want that?

"I don't follow. Wait. You mean...?" He grunted. "I'm not sharing you." His voice came out gruff and possessive, but his touch was gentle as he threaded one hand into her hair and the other around her shoulders, pulling her into a hug.

A hum of relief escaped her as she laid her head on his chest and fit her arms around his waist. She inhaled his scent and relished the solid warmth of his body.

"What does that mean?" Mercy's voice was like an alarm, jolting Blaze from a dream. "'Cuz I'm a kid, and my sister's my whole family. You have to share her with me."

Blaze lifted her head, and Anson stepped away.

Mercy stood halfway between the doorway and the fridge, a slightly smaller head of radicchio in hand. Her lips and eyebrows both skewed with what Blaze assumed was worry.

Blaze put an arm around her sister's shoulders and gave her a squeeze. "And you're my family."

Anson crossed his arms and leaned back against the counter. His lips twitched like he wanted to smile, but he narrowed his eyes. "All right. I'll share you with Mercy. Beyond that, don't get any ideas."

Mercy tipped her head, resting it on Blaze's shoulder. "What's he talking about?"

A giddy trill fluttered in her stomach. "He's talking about being my boyfriend."

"I thought he already was." Shaking her head, Mercy crossed to the fridge. "BunBun says thanks for the radish."

"Radicchio," Anson said.

"Okay, that." She placed the remaining portion in the lettuce drawer and padded off again.

Still leaning against the counter, Anson's gaze rested on Blaze. A half smile lifted his lips.

She wrapped one arm across herself and twisted a lock of hair.

He pushed away from the counter and threaded their fingers together. "You look worried."

"I made a mistake, keeping my concern about Mercy from you."

"I've thought a lot about that. I wish you'd felt like you could've told me, but I understand why you didn't. You don't want to lose Mercy the way your mom lost you."

More helpless tears fell to her cheeks. "That's what I was focused on. Losing her. But I shouldn't have been. What I really want is to avoid hurting her the way Mom hurt me. By asking her to keep that secret, I was repeating one of Mom's mistakes. It's a tangled mess, trying to stop the generational curse from continuing. Trying to avoid something led me to actually repeat it."

"One mistake isn't the same as repeating all of them. You are not your mother."

"It's still a setback. I thought I was beyond all this." She massaged her forehead. "Before I got worked up about Mercy, I almost asked you to call me Jen sometimes. It's silly. Blaze is who I am. I know that. But the name came out of bad experiences, and before that, I was Jenny. I thought going by my given name sometimes would be like …"

"Evidence of a resurrection."

Her throat constricted, and she could only stare. He understood?

She tucked herself to his side and wrapped an arm around his waist. "I thought of her again when I finally told you about Mercy."

"I'm not surprised." His body shifted, and she felt him lower his face to rest against her head. "It's a gift to know you, Jen."

The name settled like warm sunshine. Like a blessing. She turned into him and peered up at his face. "So is knowing you, Anson."

"Since you know me so well …" He brushed her hair back over her shoulders, then clasped his hands behind her back. "Did you notice?"

She ran a split-second inventory, but he hadn't gotten a haircut in the last few days or started wearing glasses. "Notice what?"

"That you're not the only one in process. I was living out bad habits I learned from my parents too. Can you imagine the support they would've gotten if they'd opened up about Gury? But they didn't, and I didn't, and it hurt my ability to help the students. When I talked to Carter and Dylan the way you encouraged me to, they opened up in some very necessary ways. If I'd talked to them more honestly sooner, the church might not have burned down."

She stepped back. "I can't believe I forgot. What did Carter say last night?"

"He suspected Dylan was the church intruder and the one who started the fire."

This was going to be a long conversation. She motioned him to follow her to the living room. He sat in the corner of the couch, and when she lowered to the cushion next to him, he pulled her in, tipping her against his side. She settled in, her back against his chest, her shoulder under his right arm. He kissed the top of her head, and she played with his hand using both of hers.

"Because of what Carter was saying, I decided to go over there. He predicted Eric wouldn't be happy to see me." His voice vibrated against her back. "He was right, but Greg came along and managed to get us through the door. We were barely in the house before Dylan spilled the whole thing. He'd taken his dad's keys and went to church when Eric and Samantha were fighting. They'd had a huge argument the night of the fire. Dylan was there hiding when I checked the building. After I left, he lit some of the Christmas Eve candles. I guess it was supposed to be like the votive candles in Catholic churches. He thought they'd help his prayers for his parents."

"Oh, no." Those candles were thin, meant to be handheld during candlelight services, not to stand upright on their own.

"They were too close to an autumn flower arrangement with dried grasses. That caught and lit a banner. Dylan went for a fire extinguisher, but by the time he got back, the wall had ignited, and he couldn't figure out how to work the extinguisher. He called 911 and hightailed it home."

She tightened her hold on his hand. She knew the terror Dylan must've felt. The crippling guilt. "What happened when he admitted all that?"

"I talked with the boys for a while, and Greg worked with Eric and Samantha. Greg was still there when I left. I haven't read it, but he told me he, Eric, and Dylan typed up the story and emailed it to the fire inspector. Eric included a copy of that letter when he emailed Greg his resignation from the leadership board."

"He resigned?" Amazement fluttered in her voice.

Anson's chest rose and fell behind her with a deep breath. "Eric and Samantha have some things to work through. Samantha's been concerned for some time that Eric's out of balance. Between work and church, he spends very little time at home. That's been at the core of their arguments. When Eric found out Dylan had been sneaking off to church because of it, he was angry. But then Samantha said her piece, and Carter talked about his experiences, and Eric ... was not the man we've come to know."

"Do you think you'll get your job back?"

"Greg says the resignation letter includes a recommendation that the board consider reinstating me."

"Praise God." She laughed. "It's amazing He turned the whole situation around so quickly."

"Yeah." His voice was clipped and low.

"What is it?"

"Last night wasn't about that. I wanted to be there for Carter and Dylan. You predicted God would work through my story, and He did. I hope He's not done yet, because

Carter still hasn't made a decision for Christ, though some of the things he said last night were promising. I told him he'd see God move, and I think watching his dad soften was like witnessing a miracle." He rubbed her arm. "Carter's got some curses hanging over his head, but Christ is a curse breaker."

She settled her head against his shoulder. "I wish it were more of an all-at-once freedom than an ongoing process."

"It's both. The moment we turn to Christ, sin no longer determines our eternity. But being free to make the right decision doesn't make it easy." He stroked her hair. "That's one reason relationships are so important. We get to remind each other we're free when we forget to act like it."

Blaze tipped her head back to see him, but he still felt too far away. She rotated and propped herself right in front of his chest with her elbow on his shoulder, her hand where she could toy with the soft bristle of his hair. "Keep this up, and ..." She bit the inside of her lips, but she couldn't suppress the words. "I might fall in love with you."

His mouth pulled into a full smile, and she brought her hand around to run her thumb over those perfect lips. He kissed the pad of her finger as it passed. As soon as her hand was out of the way, he drew his arms tighter around her and kissed her lips. The thrill sank deep and fast into her core, the sensation of falling tempered by the security of his embrace.

He kissed the corner of her mouth, her cheek, then her forehead. His sigh skimmed her skin. "That's the goal, isn't it? What all of us want."

She traced a finger up and down his neck. "To fall in love with you?" She felt his laugh as much as she heard it.

"Love." Still holding her up with one arm, he brushed

her cheek with his knuckles. "What we need is love that's steadfast when we're acting cursed. That's the only surefire cure. God's first, then each other's."

"Steadfast and surefire." The words held her as surely as Anson's arms.

"That's what I want to be for you." His focus roved her face. "That's how I want our relationship to feel. I love you."

"I love you too."

He nudged her nose with his and leaned in for another kiss.

The moment before their lips met, she repeated it again, this new heartbeat for their relationship. The words she'd spend her life living by. "Steadfast and surefire."

Know therefore that the Lord your God is God, the faithful God who keeps covenant and steadfast love with those who love him and keep his commandments, to a thousand generations.
Deuteronomy 7:9, ESV

BONUS EPILOGUE

"All right, let's put those muscles to good use."

David deserved a medal for not rolling his eyes at Sydney, especially when she clapped her mittened hands.

Scratch that. He didn't need more medals to stash away and ignore.

Still, he could think of better uses for his muscles. They'd won basketball games, helped teammates out of the bus wreck, fought insurgents in the military, and participated in a few other activities that wouldn't be received well by the church people surrounding him. Carrying a couch? Low on the "good use" list, no matter how many times Sydney clapped.

Many Oaks Bible Church had been more-or-less homeless since one of the kids incinerated the place. Having a new building—even if it was a former preschool—was a big deal to members. Self-appointed move coordinator Sydney Roswell among them.

David squatted, fit his fingers under the edge of the

couch, and waited for his best friend to do the same. Sterling nodded, and they rose in tandem.

"That goes in Anson's office." Sydney consulted a clipboard. "The second classroom on the left, all the way through into the office at the back." As she eased the door shut behind them, she yelled, "Watch your step!"

He didn't respond. Another medal for the drawer.

Sterling smirked.

The guy rarely spoke above a murmur and usually sent his sentences out to face the world alone. Most died on contact. But a few days ago, he said, "My church got a new building. Help us move in on Saturday?" If Sterling was two-sentences-serious, who was David to say no?

Besides, Marissa's best friend, Blaze, attended here too. She was pretty serious about Anson, the youth pastor here, so by extension, moving this couch was one way of returning all the kindness Blaze had shown David over the years.

When David and Sterling came to the assigned room, they wordlessly turned. Inside the room, Anson was screwing the legs onto a table. He took the screws from between his lips and motioned toward the office off the classroom. "Bookshelf construction is underway in there. You can leave the couch by the door. I'm not even sure it'll fit."

David and Sterling did as they were told and set down the couch. As David straightened, he heard a familiar voice muttering in the office. He poked his head around the corner. Bookshelf pieces covered the floor of the rectangular office. Marissa sat at the epicenter of the parts explosion, her curly hair whipped into a frizzy disarray that indicated she'd been running her fingers through it.

"Who thought this was a good idea?" he asked.

Bonus Epilogue

Her lips parted in a gaping grimace. "Blaze was helping, but she got called away." Marissa struggled to hold a shelf in place while finger-tightening a screw that might hold—*if* she didn't bust the pre-drilled hole.

Finding open spots on the floor was like navigating a Twister mat, but David maneuvered close enough to grab the shelf from his sister. "I've got this." As her hold loosened, he lowered the F-shaped contraption to the carpet.

Sterling appeared in the doorway and stepped in far enough to offer Marissa a hand up. Like a hostage being led to freedom, she took it. Moments later, they were gone. David found the directions and sorted parts, vaguely aware of Anson leaving. Components for not one but three bookshelves littered the room. Marissa never should've been left unattended in there.

When he finally had all the parts in order, he worked on Marissa's F.

"Pastor Anson!" Footsteps pounded in the hall, then a boy's voice broadcast into the room. "Guess who gets to go to college after all!" A red-faced freshman—a guess, but he had that look about him—waved a sheet of paper. "Someone finally wants Carter." The kid pivoted one way and another, like six-four Anson might materialize from nowhere.

He spotted David through the office doorway and lowered the paper, his shoulders dropping. "My brother got a scholarship. It's a good one at a school with the major he wants too."

"Sounds like the kind of thing he'd want to announce himself."

"He's off at a basketball tournament with his club." The kid shrugged. "You snooze, you lose."

David snorted. The kid had spunk. "I don't know where Anson went."

The boy slid the paper onto the table Anson had just assembled. Then he crossed the room and sat near the bookshelf directions. After cocking his head at them for a moment, he grabbed a handful of parts. "I'm Dylan. Who're you?"

"What do you think you're doing?" No way he trusted this punk with a screwdriver any more than he trusted Marissa.

The kid turned his head to an impossible angle, focused on a sideways label on one of the parts. "Helping."

"What if I don't want help?"

Dylan righted his head and grinned. "Needing help isn't bad. That's what my family's counselor says."

"Your family has a counselor?" And the kid wasn't embarrassed enough to keep the fact to himself?

"Yeah. I mean, mostly, she's for my parents, but they dragged us—me and my brother—along a couple of times." He lined up a shelf and a sidewall and wiggled his fingers as he scanned the screws. "She's all right. I mean, things are a lot better now. You ever see a counselor?" He shot a self-conscious glance at David.

He didn't believe in lying, so he said, "A couple times." He also didn't believe in baring his soul, but this kid seemed more interested in unloading than in learning anyone's secrets.

He watched Dylan work for a minute. He was better at following the directions than Marissa. David ventured out for the drill Anson had abandoned. With the power tool, he finished Marissa's bookshelf in no time and stepped over

Bonus Epilogue

where Dylan worked on the second shelf to begin assembling the last one.

"This place is pretty nice, right?" The kid blindly pulled screws out of a bag as he looked into the classroom.

The entire place smelled like a kindergarten craft supply cabinet. Stains blotched the ceiling tiles, moisture clung between the panes of the windows, and the floor should've been replaced a decade ago. But Sterling said the former preschool was only a temporary home for the church, until they rebuilt.

"Beats the burned one."

"Yeah." Dylan's head bobbed. "That was an accident. I was just ... you know how some people light candles when they pray for people? It seemed like if there was something I could see, my prayers would mean more. I guess it wasn't a good idea, though."

David's shock came out in a loud laugh before he checked it. "You're *that* kid?"

The boy's eyes bugged. "You didn't know?"

"I'm just here because a friend asked. *You* burned the old place down?"

"Not on purpose."

"Right." David directed his focus to his work. He probably shouldn't find it so entertaining that this goofball set the church on fire. "How many candles did you light?"

"Just one ... at first. Some wax got on a railing, and I was going to clean it off, but then I realized I could stick the candle bottom to the puddle and the candle would stand up. Then I didn't have to hold it anymore, so I started setting up other candles. I just didn't realize how close some of them were to the flowers and how close the flowers were to the banner thing and ...."

Bonus Epilogue

"Went up quick, huh?"

The boy threw his hands up. "So quick. And do you know how hard it is to get a fire extinguisher to work? Like, shouldn't they be easy?"

"You'd think." David had never had occasion to use one.

"Anyway, everything got really bad really fast."

"That's how it goes."

"Huh?"

David sank another screw. "In my experience, bad things are bound to happen."

"Good things are too, though, right? I mean, I was praying about my parents when I lit the candles, and they're doing a lot better now. And the church has this building. Plus, I'm not in jail." The kid lifted his hands, as though to say *ta-da*.

David chuckled. "Living the dream."

"Are you being sarcastic?"

"Nope." But he couldn't keep from grinning. "I'm glad you're not in jail. Try and keep it that way."

"Yeah." Dylan nodded earnestly and picked up another shelf. "That's definitely the plan."

This kid was a riot.

Sydney leaned into the office. "If you guys are all set with your stay-out-of-jail plans, there's pizza in the sanctuary."

Dylan jumped to his feet and ran.

"Coming?" Sydney lifted an eyebrow.

"I'm not leaving this half-done." He zipped another screw into place.

She settled against the doorframe. "You know we could use you in the mentoring program at the community center."

"Never been a fan of being used."

Bonus Epilogue

"How about this? *You* could use your talents to help kids at the community center."

"Which talents?"

"I heard you with Dylan. You didn't freak out or judge him. Some kids really need a listening ear. And hey, the more of them who don't end up in jail, the better."

He scoffed. "Avoiding jail isn't much of a life goal."

"You could help them aim higher."

"Yeah. Gather 'round, kids." He motioned with the drill. "Let me tell you all about how to avoid jail and become"—he paused for effect—"a waiter."

"This is a small town, David Hunter." Her tone reminded him of his senior-year English teacher. "I know you, and you can't pass yourself off as a waiter to me. You're a hero."

She knew about the medals then.

He glared at her from his spot on the floor. He didn't have the height advantage or a clear path to the exit, but he refused to let being cornered defeat him into surrender. There was a lot more to a person than their name or their medals. If she thought he was a good role model for kids, she didn't know him at all.

Sydney pushed away from the wall. "See you around."

Not if he could help it. Eventually, her rose-colored glasses would break and she'd see the truth. David Hunter was nobody's hero.

A sweet small-town romance exclusively for Emily's email subscribers.

Food trailer owner Asher has seen too many tears he couldn't dry. Determined to be part of the solution, he avoids romance and all the heartbreaking drama that comes along with it.

At least, that's the plan until his heart decides it has a mind of its own. If he can't rein it in, he's destined to break not one, but two women's hearts.

Sign up for email newsletters at emilyconradauthor.com and receive *Between The Two of Us* as a welcome gift.

ALSO BY EMILY CONRAD

The Rhythms of Redemption Romances

  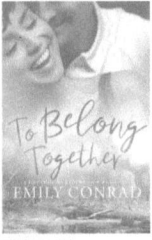

To Bring You Back

An Awestruck Christmas Medley

To Belong Together

To Begin Again

To Believe in You

The Many Oaks Romances

Now or Never

A Surefire Love

Christmas In Redemption Ridge

Bidding on a Second Chance

DID YOU ENJOY THIS BOOK?

Help others discover it by leaving a review on Goodreads and the site you purchased from!

DISCUSSION GUIDE

Blaze credits her baking ability to finding great recipes online. Have you found one that way that's especially good? Before you meet up for a discussion, consider printing off a couple of copies or sharing the link with your book club!

1. Do you have a favorite line or scene?
2. Did you learn anything new about ADHD? Or do you have something to add?
3. What are some of the preconceived ideas Blaze and Anson each have? Do any of them turn out to be right?
4. Anson describes God as a coach, and Mercy pictures him as a father. How do you tend to think of God?
5. Blaze and Anson must decide how much of their stories to tell and when. What advice would you give them as they're making those decisions?

Discussion Guide

6. Was there a time in your life when obeying the Lord didn't turn out the way you expected? What hope or comfort did you find during that time?
7. Before Carter called Anson at the end of the story, who did you think had been breaking into the church? Who did you suspect had started the fire?
8. Did an aspect of the story encourage or challenge you in your faith? How so?
9. Which of the secondary characters would you like to see a story for in the future?

ACKNOWLEDGMENTS

I had no idea how impactful ADHD could be until I began to research this story. Thank you, Sarah Strong and Liz Jacobson, for taking the time to answer so many questions, share your experiences, and provide feedback on that aspect of the story. Any mistakes or misrepresentations are on me.

While writing this story, I discovered I was low on vitamin D. Not operating at my best for a few months gave me a glimpse into what it's like to have something hindering me in my daily tasks. Finding answers and effective treatment to the things that hold us back truly is life-changing. If something seems to you like it might be off, I hope you'll pursue help and healing and pray the Lord would lead you to the right resources.

Thank you, too, to my critique partners, beta readers, and volunteer proofreaders: Jessica Johnson, Katie Powner, Janet Ferguson, Jessica Bradley, Danielle Schroeder, Teresa Fritschle, Jane Bradley, and Maria Thouron.

Thank you, Lord, for being our Healer. It is because of you that we can be whole, not broken, and free from curses.

ABOUT THE AUTHOR

Emily Conrad writes contemporary Christian romance that explores life's relevant questions. Though she likes to think some of her characters are pretty great, the ultimate hero of her stories (including the one she's living) is Jesus. She lives in Wisconsin with her husband, an energetic coonhound rescue, and two lop-ear bunnies. Learn more about her and her books at emilyconradauthor.com.

 facebook.com/emilyconradauthor
 instagram.com/emilyrconrad

www.ingramcontent.com/pod-product-compliance
Lightning Source LLC
LaVergne TN
LVHW040039080526
838202LV00045B/3397